Emily
AND the Strangers

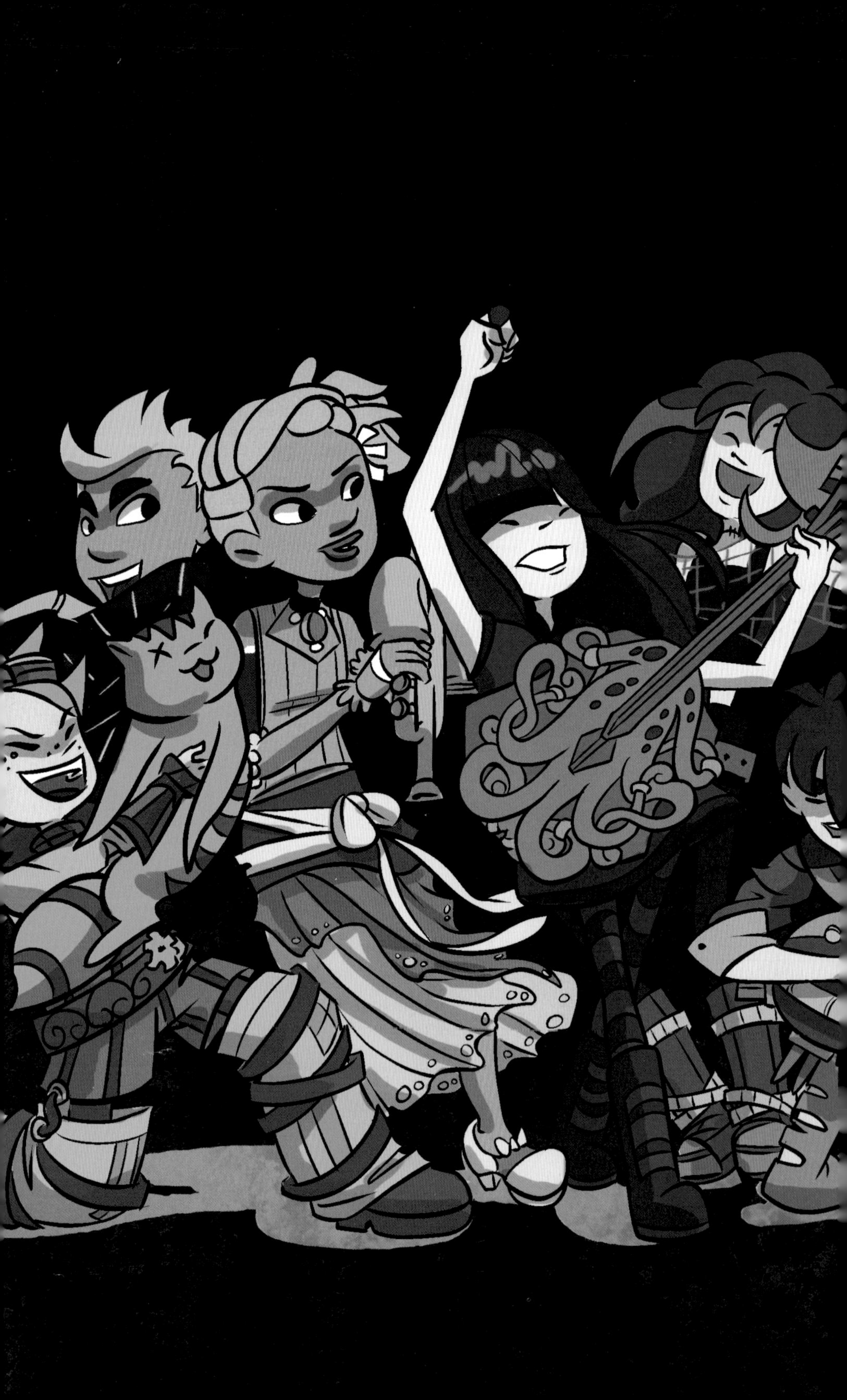

Emily AND the Strangers

Volume 2
BREAKING THE RECORD

Created by
ROB REGER

Written by
MARIAH HUEHNER
and **ROB REGER**

Art by
CAT FARRIS

Lettering by
NATE PIEKOS of **BLAMBOT®**

Cover and chapter break art by
CAT FARRIS and **BUZZ PARKER**

Endpaper art by
EMILY IVIE

DARK HORSE BOOKS

Publisher

Mike Richardson

Editor

Jim Gibbons

Digital Production

Jason Rickerd

Collection Designer

Tina Alessi

Published by Dark Horse Books
A division of Dark Horse Comics, Inc.
10956 SE Main Street
Milwaukie, OR 97222

First edition: March 2015
ISBN 978-1-61655-598-6

1 3 5 7 9 10 8 6 4 2
Printed in China

International Licensing: (503) 905-2377
Comic Shop Locator Service: (888) 266-4226

EMILY AND THE STRANGERS VOLUME 2: BREAKING THE RECORD

This volume collects Emily and the Strangers: Breaking the Record #1–#3, from Dark Horse Comics, and "The Idea Factory," originally published in The CBLDF Presents Liberty Annual 2014.

MIKE RICHARDSON, President and Publisher / NEIL HANKERSON, Executive Vice President / TOM WEDDLE, Chief Financial Officer / RANDY STRADLEY, Vice President of Publishing / MICHAEL MARTENS, Vice President of Book Trade Sales / SCOTT ALLIE, Editor in Chief / MATT PARKINSON, Vice President of Marketing / DAVID SCROGGY, Vice President of Product Development / DALE LaFOUNTAIN, Vice President of Information Technology / DARLENE VOGEL, Senior Director of Print, Design, and Production / KEN LIZZI, General Counsel / DAVEY ESTRADA, Editorial Director / CHRIS WARNER, Senior Books Editor / DIANA SCHUTZ, Executive Editor / CARY GRAZZINI, Director of Print and Development / LIA RIBACCHI, Art Director / CARA NIECE, Director of Scheduling / MARK BERNARDI, Director of Digital Publishing

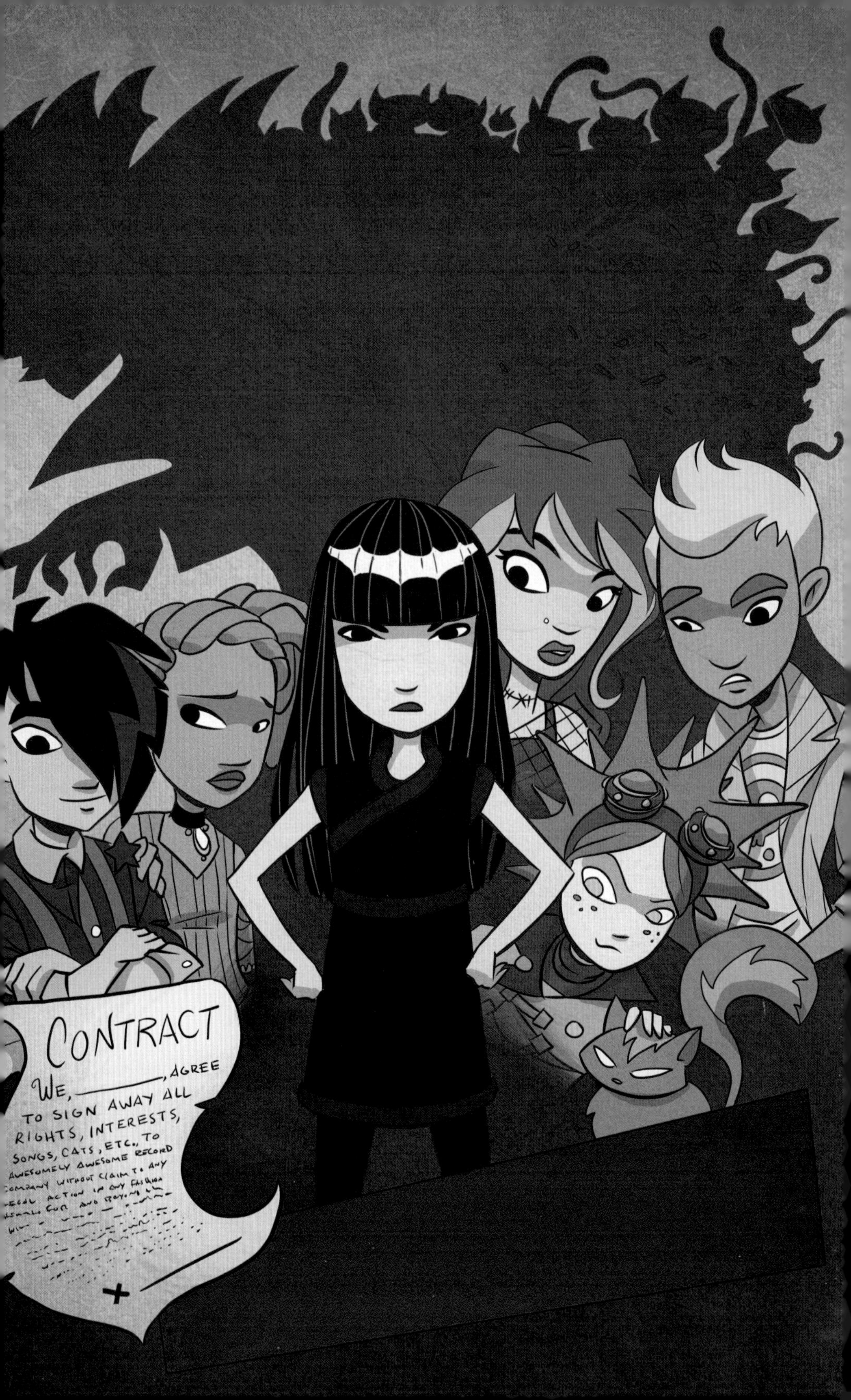
CONTRACT
WE, ________, AGREE
TO SIGN AWAY ALL
RIGHTS, INTERESTS,
SONGS, CATS, ETC., TO
AWESOMELY AWESOME RECORD
COMPANY WITHOUT CLAIM TO ANY
ACTION IN ANY FASHION

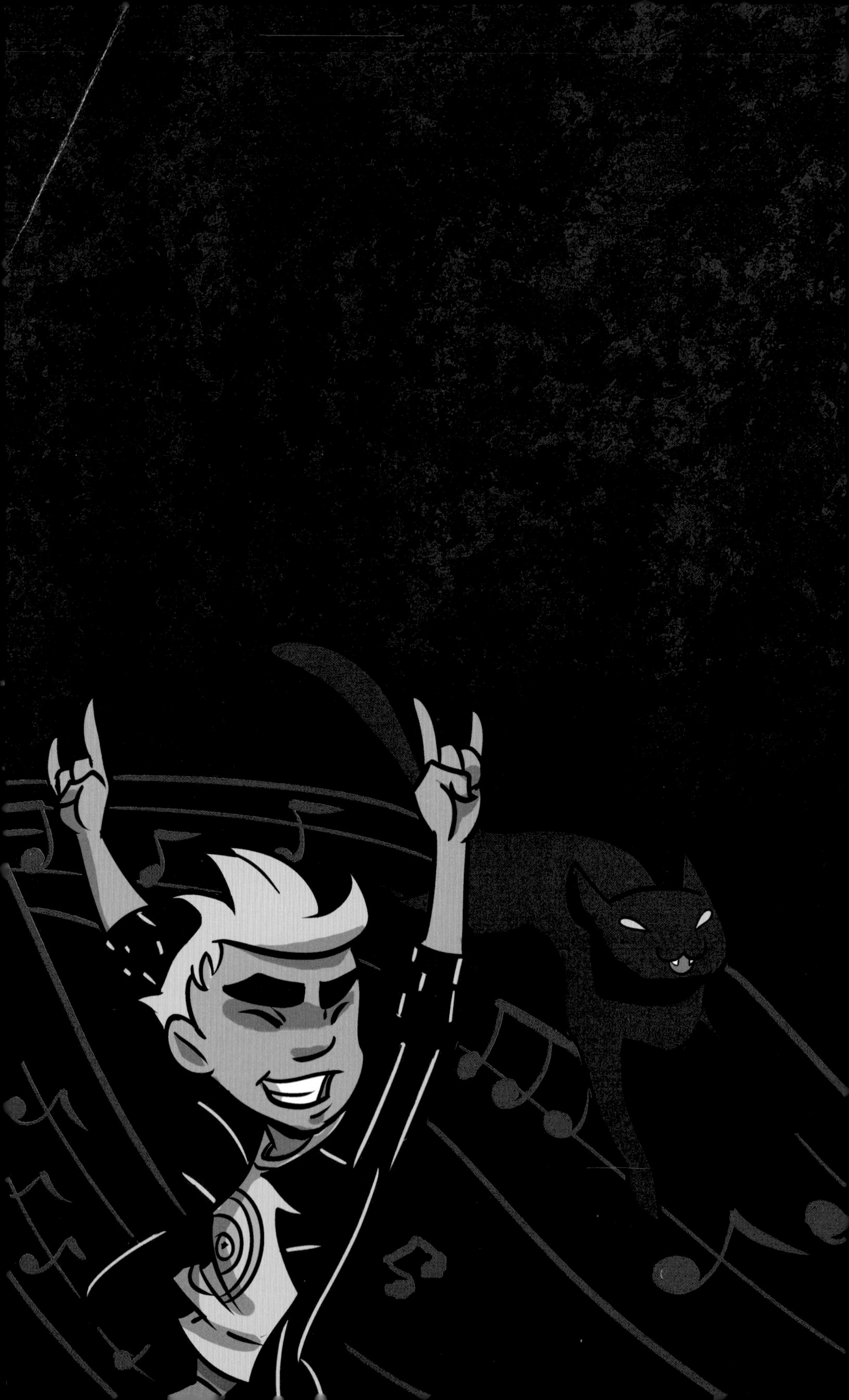

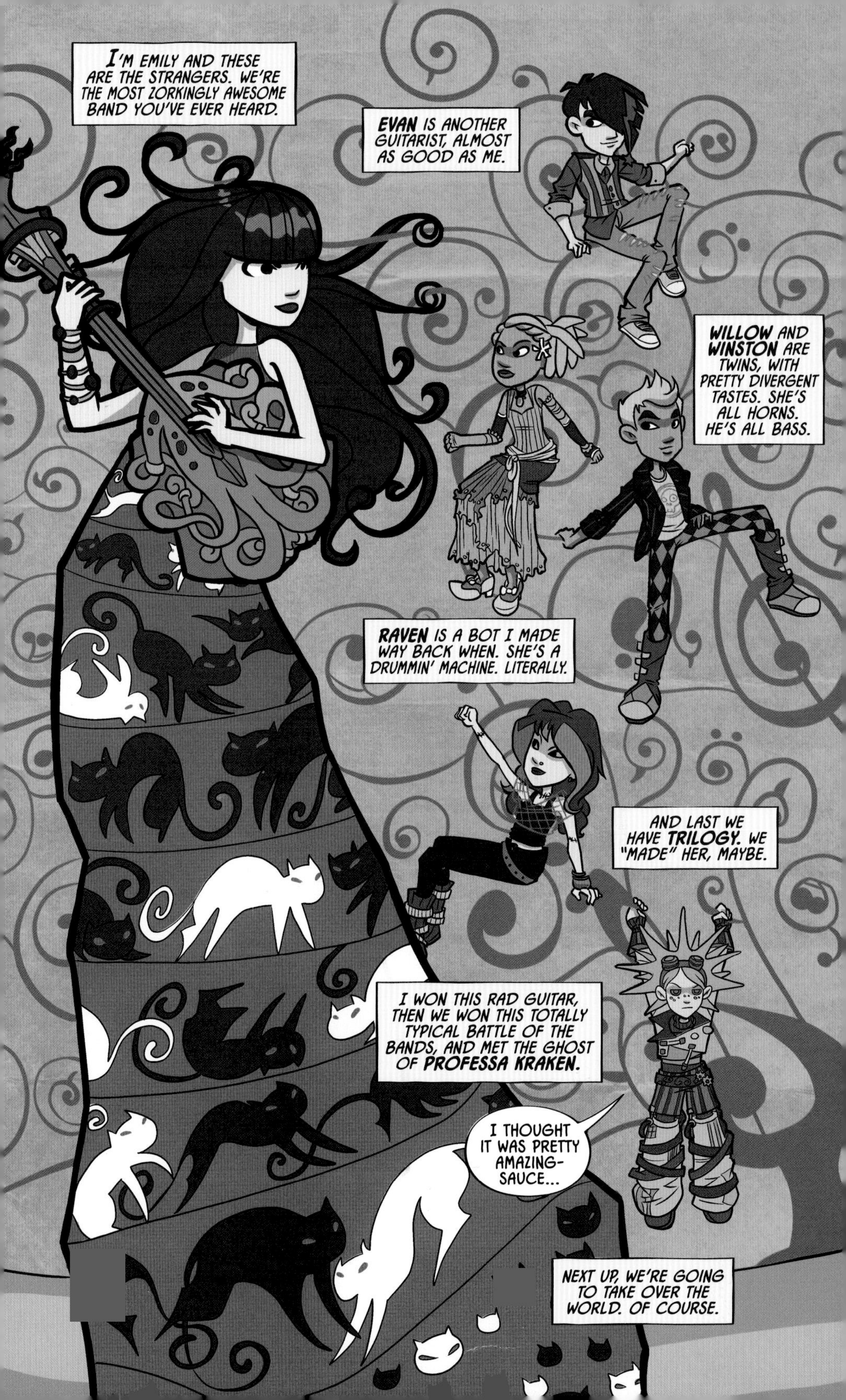
I'M EMILY AND THESE ARE THE STRANGERS. WE'RE THE MOST ZORKINGLY AWESOME BAND YOU'VE EVER HEARD.
EVAN IS ANOTHER GUITARIST, ALMOST AS GOOD AS ME.
WILLOW AND WINSTON ARE TWINS, WITH PRETTY DIVERGENT TASTES. SHE'S ALL HORNS. HE'S ALL BASS.
RAVEN IS A BOT I MADE WAY BACK WHEN. SHE'S A DRUMMIN' MACHINE. LITERALLY.
AND LAST WE HAVE TRILOGY. WE "MADE" HER, MAYBE.
I WON THIS RAD GUITAR, THEN WE WON THIS TOTALLY TYPICAL BATTLE OF THE BANDS, AND MET THE GHOST OF PROFESSA KRAKEN.
I THOUGHT IT WAS PRETTY AMAZING-SAUCE...
NEXT UP, WE'RE GOING TO TAKE OVER THE WORLD. OF COURSE.

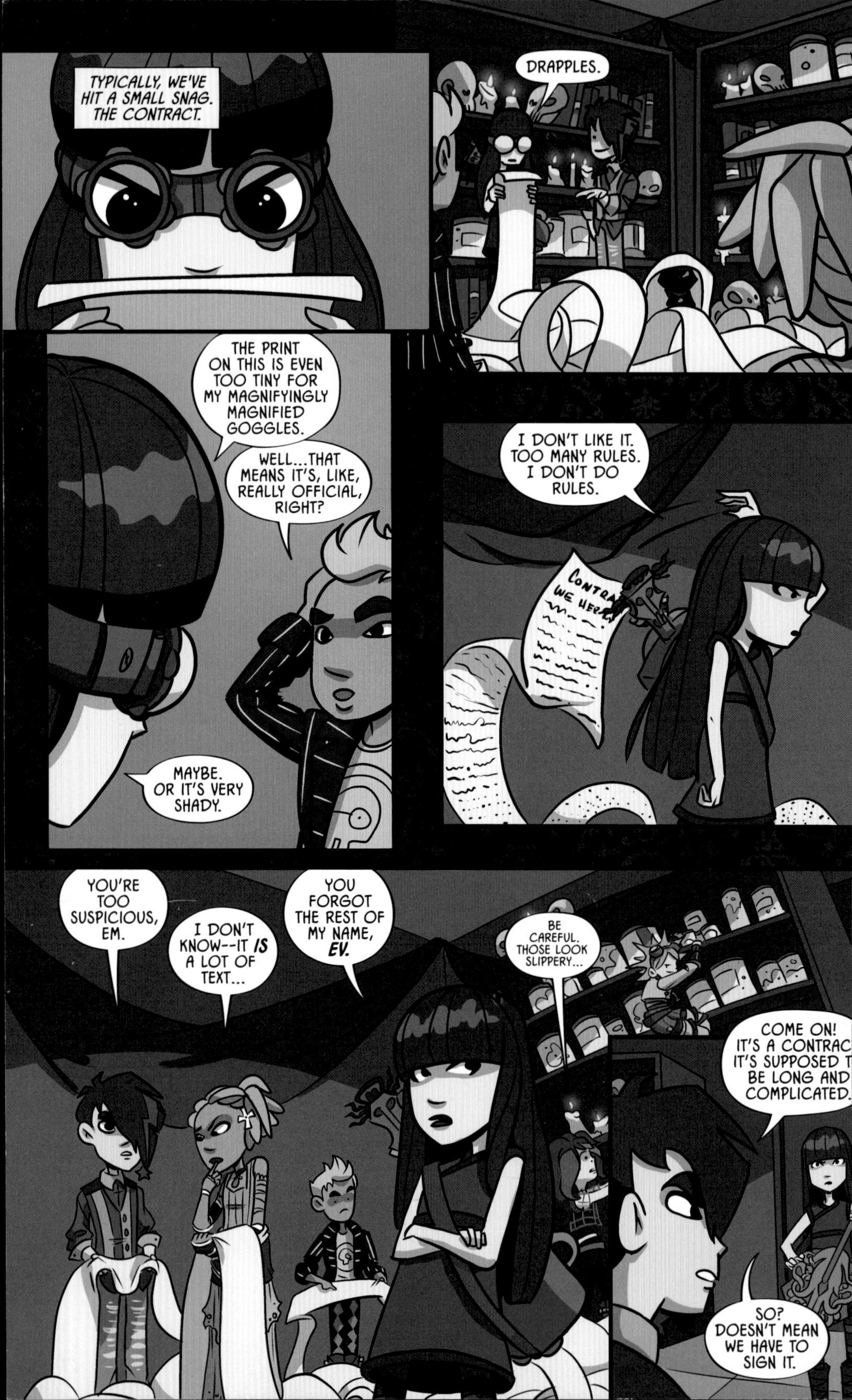
TYPICALLY, WE'VE HIT A SMALL SNAG. THE CONTRACT.
DRAPPLES.
THE PRINT ON THIS IS EVEN TOO TINY FOR MY MAGNIFYINGLY MAGNIFIED GOGGLES.
WELL...THAT MEANS IT'S, LIKE, REALLY OFFICIAL, RIGHT?
MAYBE. OR IT'S VERY SHADY.
I DON'T LIKE IT. TOO MANY RULES. I DON'T DO RULES.
YOU'RE TOO SUSPICIOUS, EM.
I DON'T KNOW--IT *IS* A LOT OF TEXT...
YOU FORGOT THE REST OF MY NAME, ***EV.***
BE CAREFUL. THOSE LOOK SLIPPERY...
COME ON! IT'S A CONTRAC IT'S SUPPOSED T BE LONG AND COMPLICATED.
SO? DOESN'T MEAN WE HAVE TO SIGN IT.

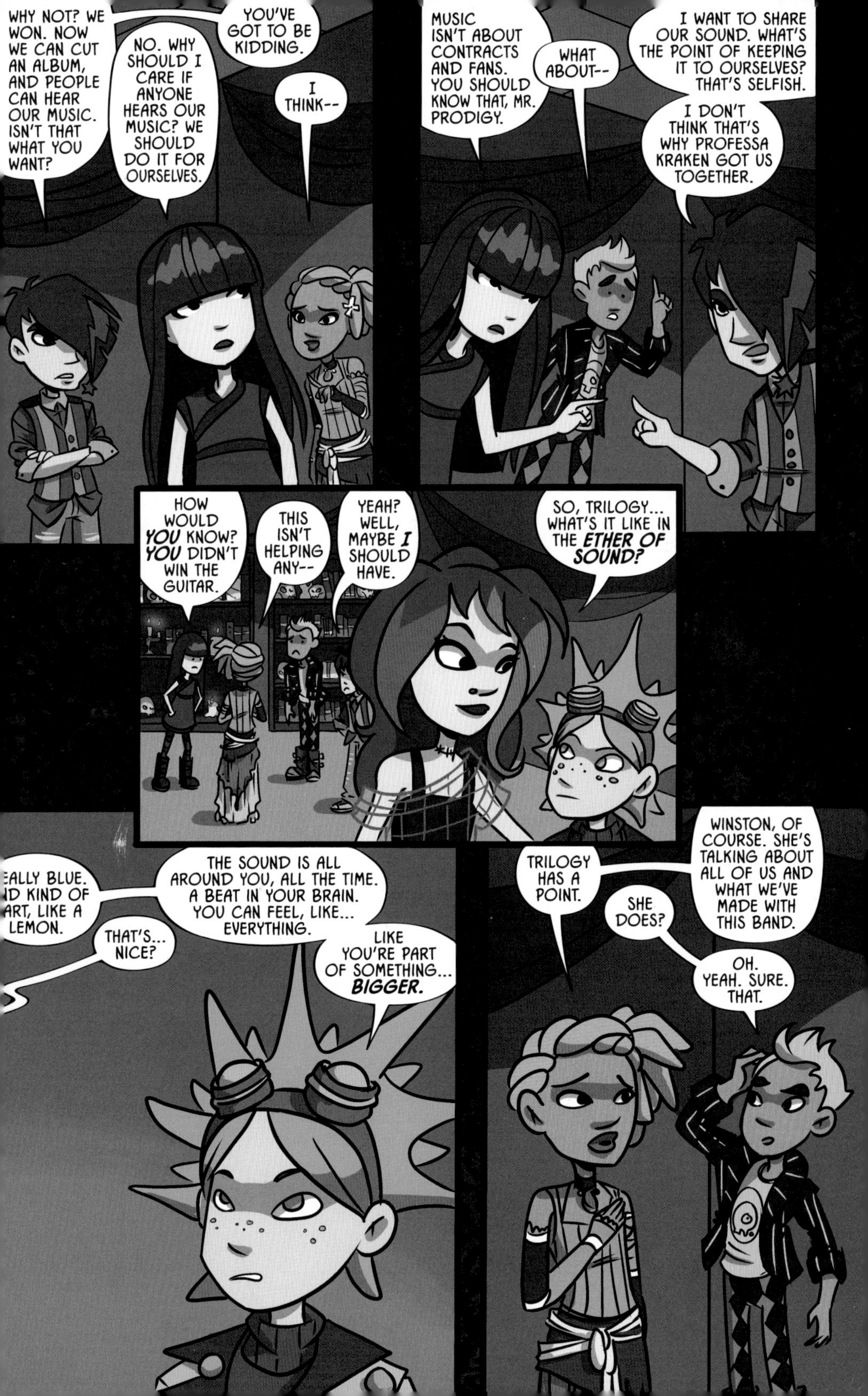

WHY NOT? WE WON. NOW WE CAN CUT AN ALBUM, AND PEOPLE CAN HEAR OUR MUSIC. ISN'T THAT WHAT YOU WANT?
YOU'VE GOT TO BE KIDDING.
NO. WHY SHOULD I CARE IF ANYONE HEARS OUR MUSIC? WE SHOULD DO IT FOR OURSELVES.
I THINK--
MUSIC ISN'T ABOUT CONTRACTS AND FANS. YOU SHOULD KNOW THAT, MR. PRODIGY.
WHAT ABOUT--
I WANT TO SHARE OUR SOUND. WHAT'S THE POINT OF KEEPING IT TO OURSELVES? THAT'S SELFISH.
I DON'T THINK THAT'S WHY PROFESSA KRAKEN GOT US TOGETHER.
HOW WOULD YOU KNOW? YOU DIDN'T WIN THE GUITAR.
THIS ISN'T HELPING ANY--
YEAH? WELL, MAYBE I SHOULD HAVE.
SO, TRILOGY... WHAT'S IT LIKE IN THE ETHER OF SOUND?
EALLY BLUE. ND KIND OF ART, LIKE A LEMON.
THE SOUND IS ALL AROUND YOU, ALL THE TIME. A BEAT IN YOUR BRAIN. YOU CAN FEEL, LIKE... EVERYTHING.
THAT'S... NICE?
LIKE YOU'RE PART OF SOMETHING... BIGGER.
TRILOGY HAS A POINT.
WINSTON, OF COURSE. SHE'S TALKING ABOUT ALL OF US AND WHAT WE'VE MADE WITH THIS BAND.
SHE DOES?
OH. YEAH. SURE. THAT.

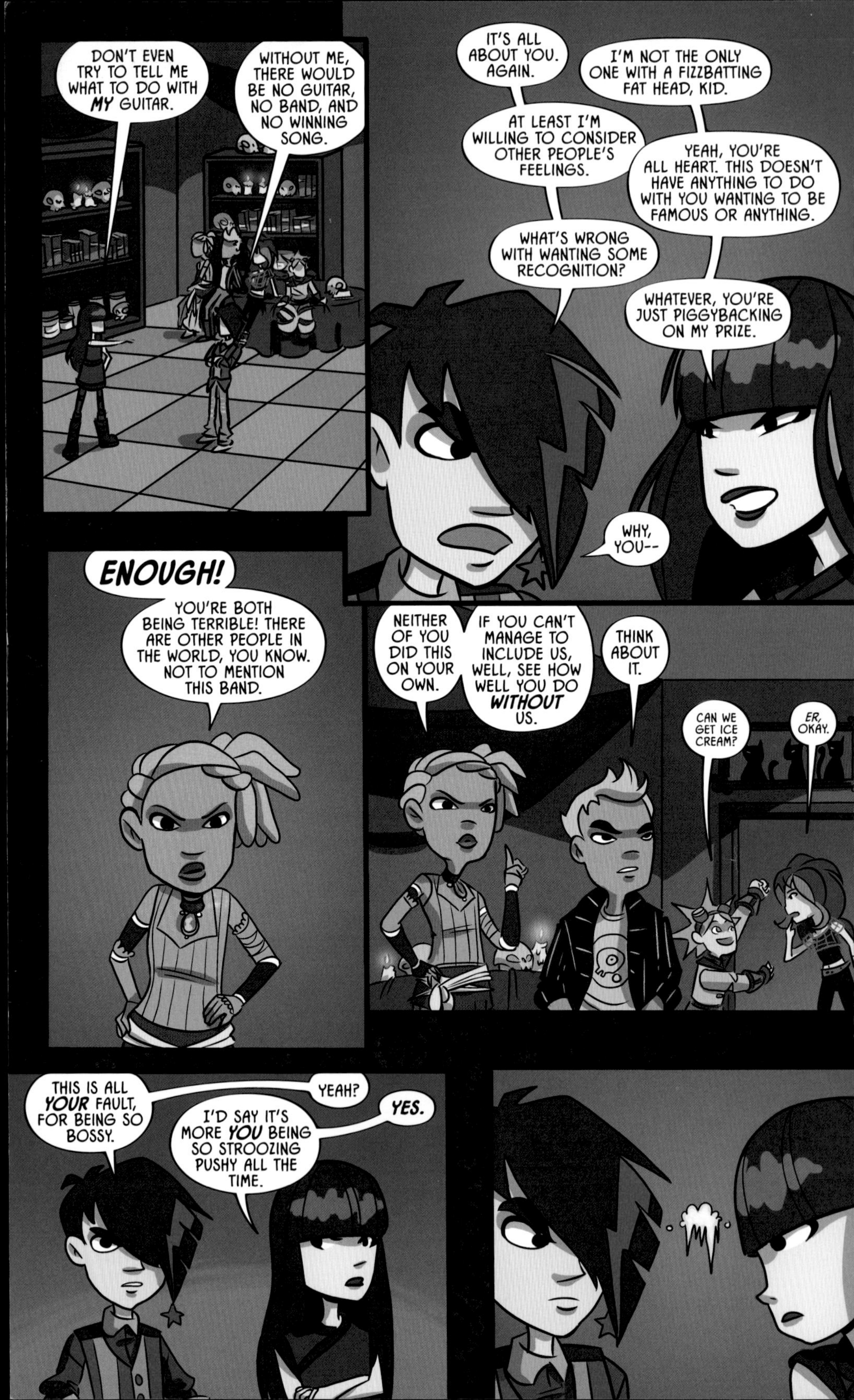
DON'T EVEN TRY TO TELL ME WHAT TO DO WITH MY GUITAR.
WITHOUT ME, THERE WOULD BE NO GUITAR, NO BAND, AND NO WINNING SONG.
IT'S ALL ABOUT YOU. AGAIN.
I'M NOT THE ONLY ONE WITH A FIZZBATTING FAT HEAD, KID.
AT LEAST I'M WILLING TO CONSIDER OTHER PEOPLE'S FEELINGS.
YEAH, YOU'RE ALL HEART. THIS DOESN'T HAVE ANYTHING TO DO WITH YOU WANTING TO BE FAMOUS OR ANYTHING.
WHAT'S WRONG WITH WANTING SOME RECOGNITION?
WHATEVER, YOU'RE JUST PIGGYBACKING ON MY PRIZE.
WHY, YOU--
ENOUGH!
YOU'RE BOTH BEING TERRIBLE! THERE ARE OTHER PEOPLE IN THE WORLD, YOU KNOW. NOT TO MENTION THIS BAND.
NEITHER OF YOU DID THIS ON YOUR OWN.
IF YOU CAN'T MANAGE TO INCLUDE US, WELL, SEE HOW WELL YOU DO WITHOUT US.
THINK ABOUT IT.
CAN WE GET ICE CREAM?
ER, OKAY.
THIS IS ALL YOUR FAULT, FOR BEING SO BOSSY.
YEAH?
I'D SAY IT'S MORE YOU BEING SO STROOZING PUSHY ALL THE TIME.
YES.

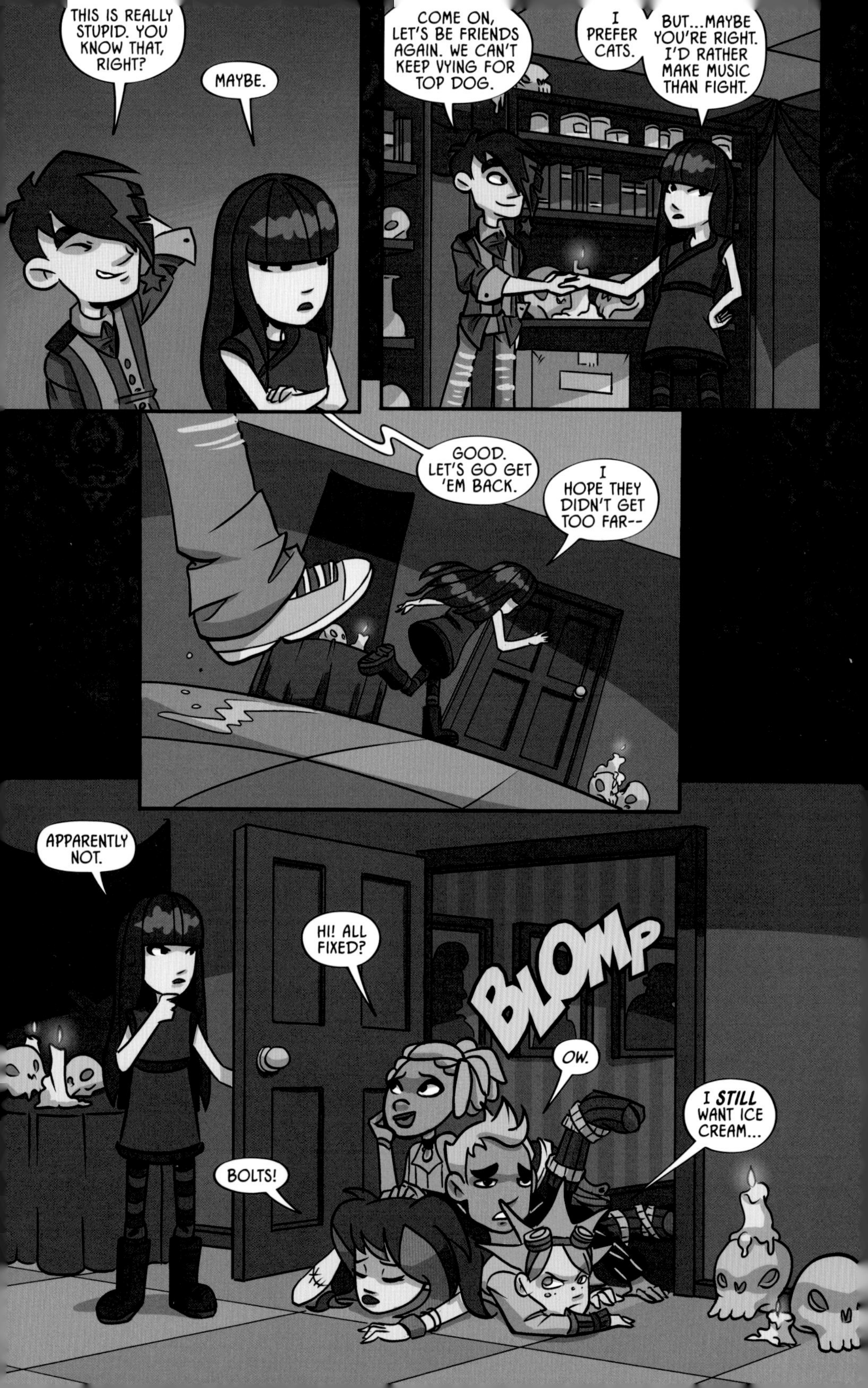
THIS IS REALLY STUPID. YOU KNOW THAT, RIGHT?
MAYBE.
COME ON, LET'S BE FRIENDS AGAIN. WE CAN'T KEEP VYING FOR TOP DOG.
I PREFER CATS.
BUT...MAYBE YOU'RE RIGHT. I'D RATHER MAKE MUSIC THAN FIGHT.
GOOD. LET'S GO GET 'EM BACK.
I HOPE THEY DIDN'T GET TOO FAR--
APPARENTLY NOT.
HI! ALL FIXED?
BLOMP
OW.
I *STILL* WANT ICE CREAM...
BOLTS!

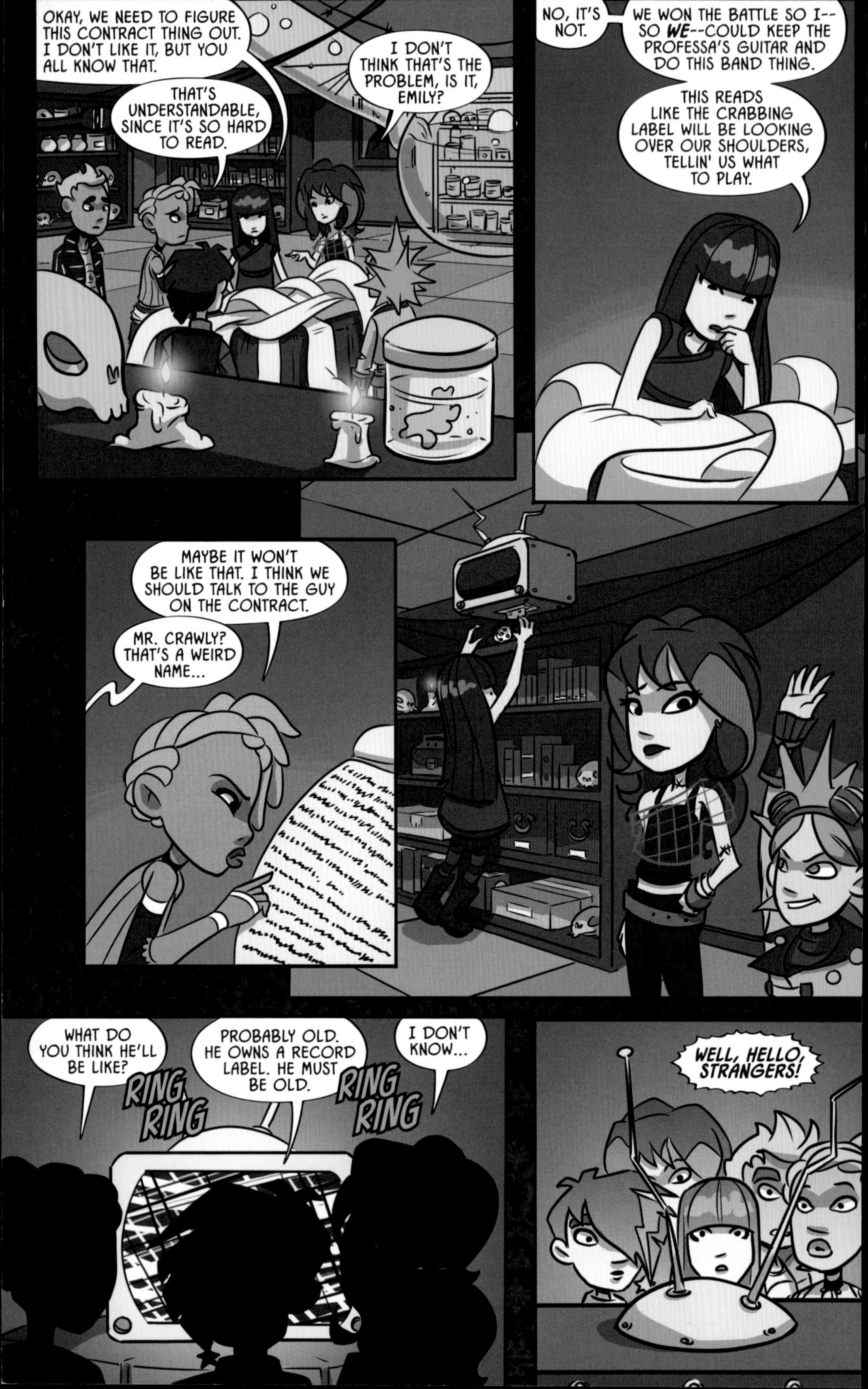

OKAY, WE NEED TO FIGURE THIS CONTRACT THING OUT. I DON'T LIKE IT, BUT YOU ALL KNOW THAT.
THAT'S UNDERSTANDABLE, SINCE IT'S SO HARD TO READ.
I DON'T THINK THAT'S THE PROBLEM, IS IT, EMILY?
NO, IT'S NOT.
WE WON THE BATTLE SO I--SO WE--COULD KEEP THE PROFESSA'S GUITAR AND DO THIS BAND THING.
THIS READS LIKE THE CRABBING LABEL WILL BE LOOKING OVER OUR SHOULDERS, TELLIN' US WHAT TO PLAY.
MAYBE IT WON'T BE LIKE THAT. I THINK WE SHOULD TALK TO THE GUY ON THE CONTRACT.
MR. CRAWLY? THAT'S A WEIRD NAME...
WHAT DO YOU THINK HE'LL BE LIKE?
RING RING
PROBABLY OLD. HE OWNS A RECORD LABEL. HE MUST BE OLD.
RING RING
I DON'T KNOW...
WELL, HELLO, STRANGERS!

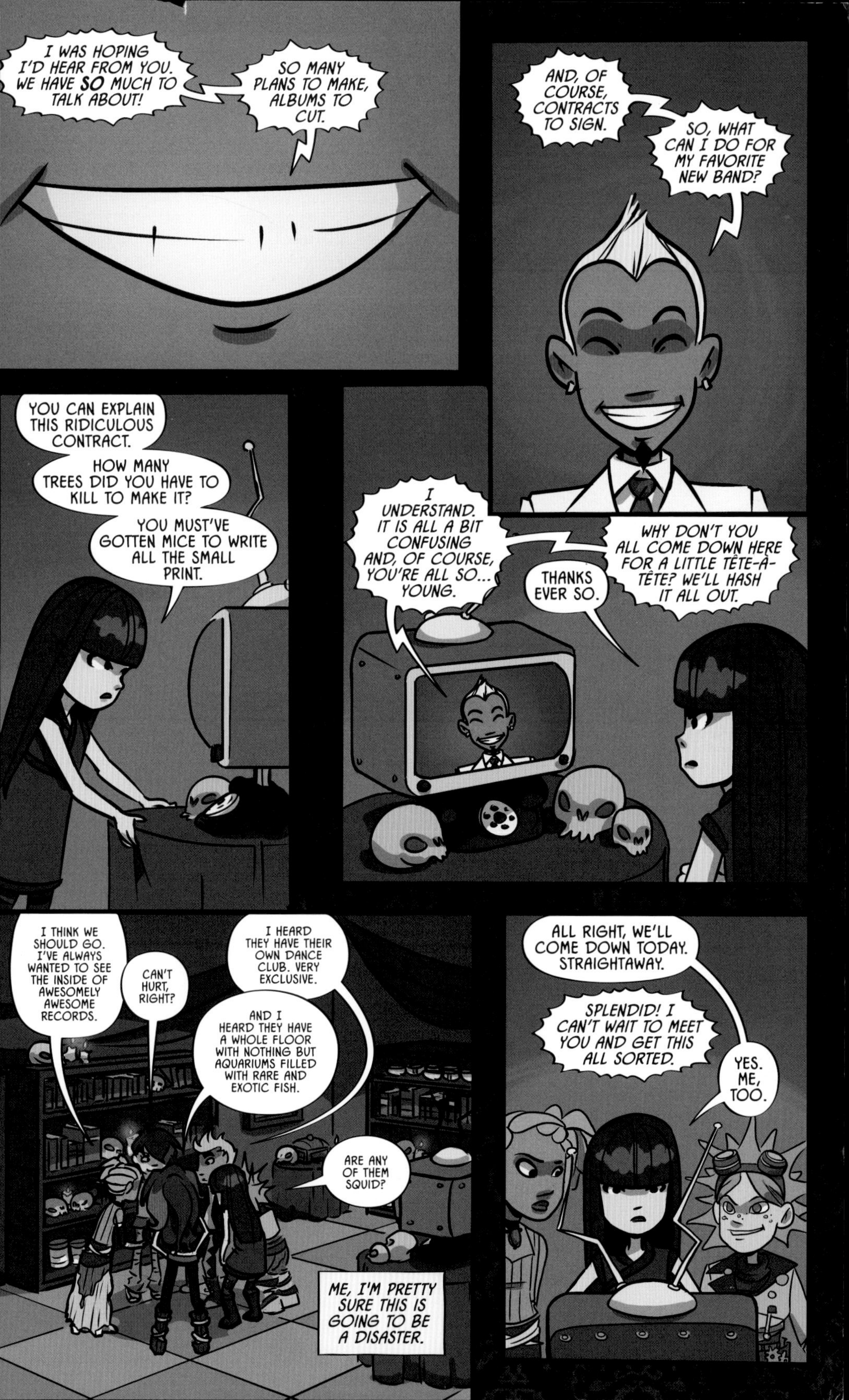
I WAS HOPING I'D HEAR FROM YOU. WE HAVE **SO** MUCH TO TALK ABOUT!
SO MANY PLANS TO MAKE, ALBUMS TO CUT.
AND, OF COURSE, CONTRACTS TO SIGN.
SO, WHAT CAN I DO FOR MY FAVORITE NEW BAND?
YOU CAN EXPLAIN THIS RIDICULOUS CONTRACT.
HOW MANY TREES DID YOU HAVE TO KILL TO MAKE IT?
YOU MUST'VE GOTTEN MICE TO WRITE ALL THE SMALL PRINT.
I UNDERSTAND. IT IS ALL A BIT CONFUSING AND, OF COURSE, YOU'RE ALL SO... YOUNG.
THANKS EVER SO.
WHY DON'T YOU ALL COME DOWN HERE FOR A LITTLE TÊTE-À-TÊTE? WE'LL HASH IT ALL OUT.
I THINK WE SHOULD GO. I'VE ALWAYS WANTED TO SEE THE INSIDE OF AWESOMELY AWESOME RECORDS.
CAN'T HURT, RIGHT?
I HEARD THEY HAVE THEIR OWN DANCE CLUB. VERY EXCLUSIVE.
AND I HEARD THEY HAVE A WHOLE FLOOR WITH NOTHING BUT AQUARIUMS FILLED WITH RARE AND EXOTIC FISH.
ARE ANY OF THEM SQUID?
ME, I'M PRETTY SURE THIS IS GOING TO BE A DISASTER.
ALL RIGHT, WE'LL COME DOWN TODAY. STRAIGHTAWAY.
SPLENDID! I CAN'T WAIT TO MEET YOU AND GET THIS ALL SORTED.
YES. ME, TOO.

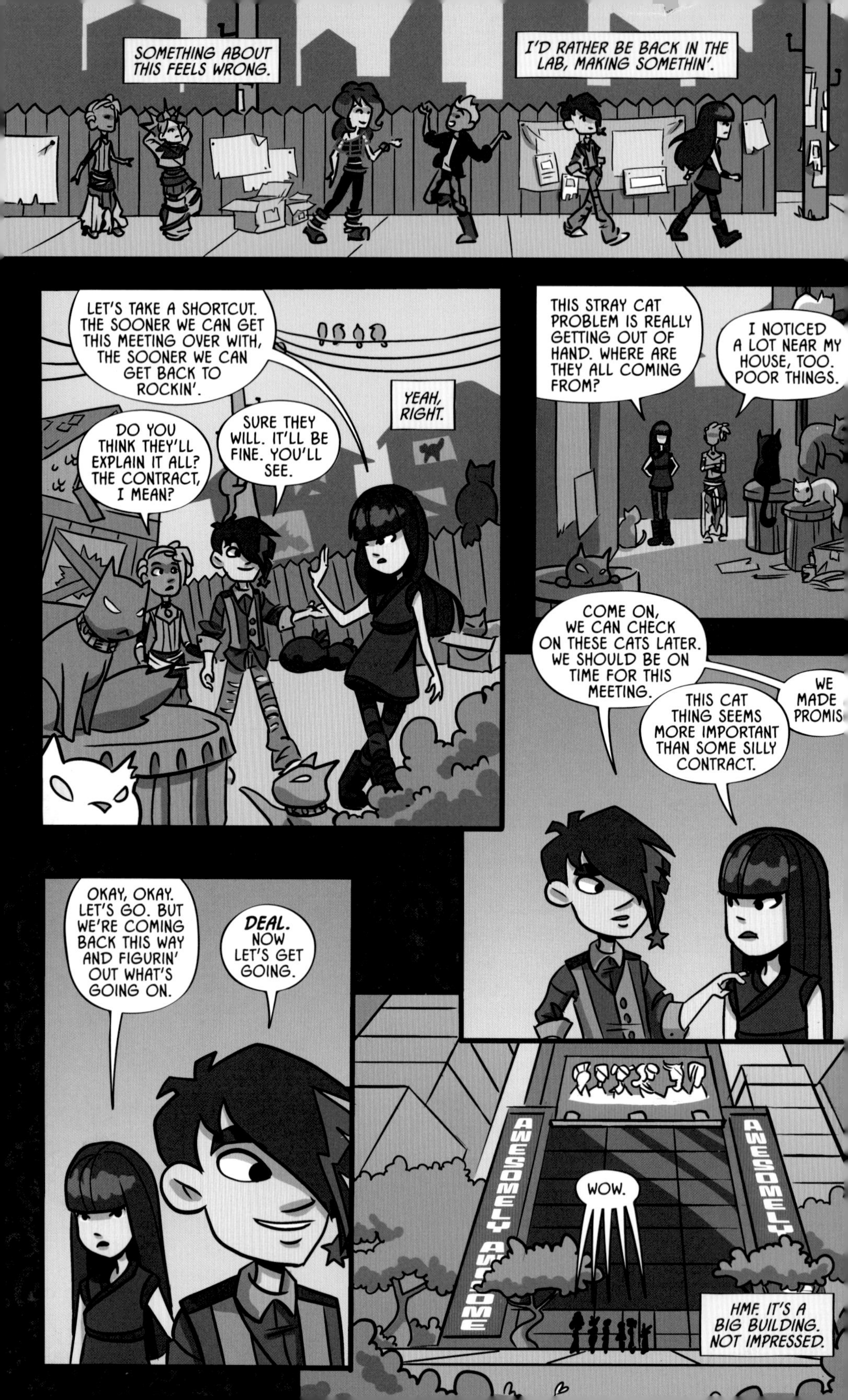

SOMETHING ABOUT THIS FEELS WRONG.
I'D RATHER BE BACK IN THE LAB, MAKING SOMETHIN'.
LET'S TAKE A SHORTCUT. THE SOONER WE CAN GET THIS MEETING OVER WITH, THE SOONER WE CAN GET BACK TO ROCKIN'.
YEAH, RIGHT.
DO YOU THINK THEY'LL EXPLAIN IT ALL? THE CONTRACT, I MEAN?
SURE THEY WILL. IT'LL BE FINE. YOU'LL SEE.
THIS STRAY CAT PROBLEM IS REALLY GETTING OUT OF HAND. WHERE ARE THEY ALL COMING FROM?
I NOTICED A LOT NEAR MY HOUSE, TOO. POOR THINGS.
COME ON, WE CAN CHECK ON THESE CATS LATER. WE SHOULD BE ON TIME FOR THIS MEETING.
WE MADE PROMIS
THIS CAT THING SEEMS MORE IMPORTANT THAN SOME SILLY CONTRACT.
OKAY, OKAY. LET'S GO. BUT WE'RE COMING BACK THIS WAY AND FIGURIN' OUT WHAT'S GOING ON.
DEAL. NOW LET'S GET GOING.
AWESOMELY
AWESOMELY
WOW.
HMF. IT'S A BIG BUILDING. NOT IMPRESSED.

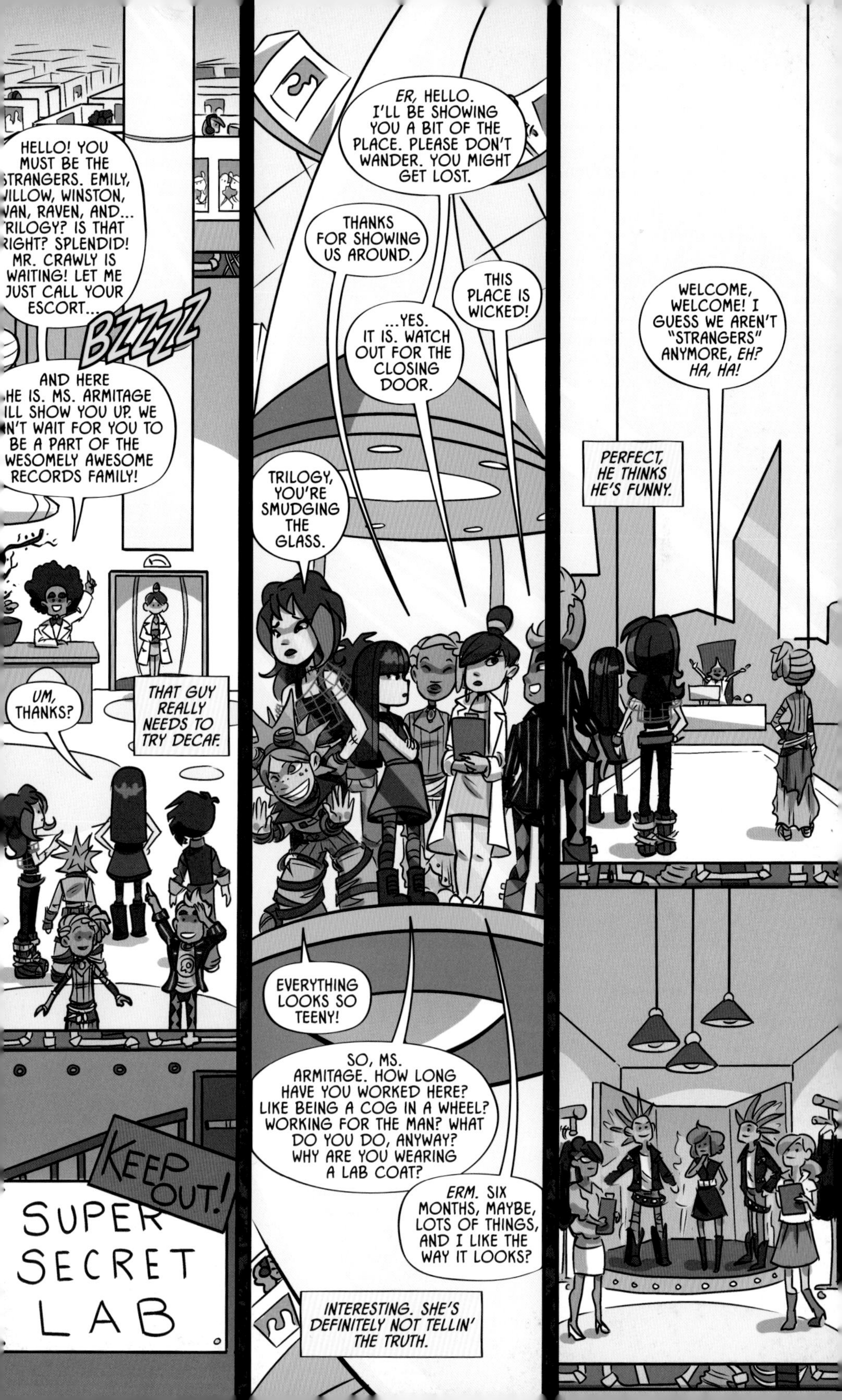
HELLO! YOU MUST BE THE STRANGERS. EMILY, WILLOW, WINSTON, IVAN, RAVEN, AND... TRILOGY? IS THAT RIGHT? SPLENDID! MR. CRAWLY IS WAITING! LET ME JUST CALL YOUR ESCORT...
BZZZZ
AND HERE SHE IS. MS. ARMITAGE WILL SHOW YOU UP. WE CAN'T WAIT FOR YOU TO BE A PART OF THE AWESOMELY AWESOME RECORDS FAMILY!
UM, THANKS?
THAT GUY REALLY NEEDS TO TRY DECAF.
KEEP OUT!
SUPER SECRET LAB
ER, HELLO. I'LL BE SHOWING YOU A BIT OF THE PLACE. PLEASE DON'T WANDER. YOU MIGHT GET LOST.
THANKS FOR SHOWING US AROUND.
THIS PLACE IS WICKED!
...YES. IT IS. WATCH OUT FOR THE CLOSING DOOR.
TRILOGY, YOU'RE SMUDGING THE GLASS.
EVERYTHING LOOKS SO TEENY!
SO, MS. ARMITAGE. HOW LONG HAVE YOU WORKED HERE? LIKE BEING A COG IN A WHEEL? WORKING FOR THE MAN? WHAT DO YOU DO, ANYWAY? WHY ARE YOU WEARING A LAB COAT?
ERM. SIX MONTHS, MAYBE, LOTS OF THINGS, AND I LIKE THE WAY IT LOOKS?
INTERESTING. SHE'S DEFINITELY NOT TELLIN' THE TRUTH.
WELCOME, WELCOME! I GUESS WE AREN'T "STRANGERS" ANYMORE, EH? HA, HA!
PERFECT, HE THINKS HE'S FUNNY.

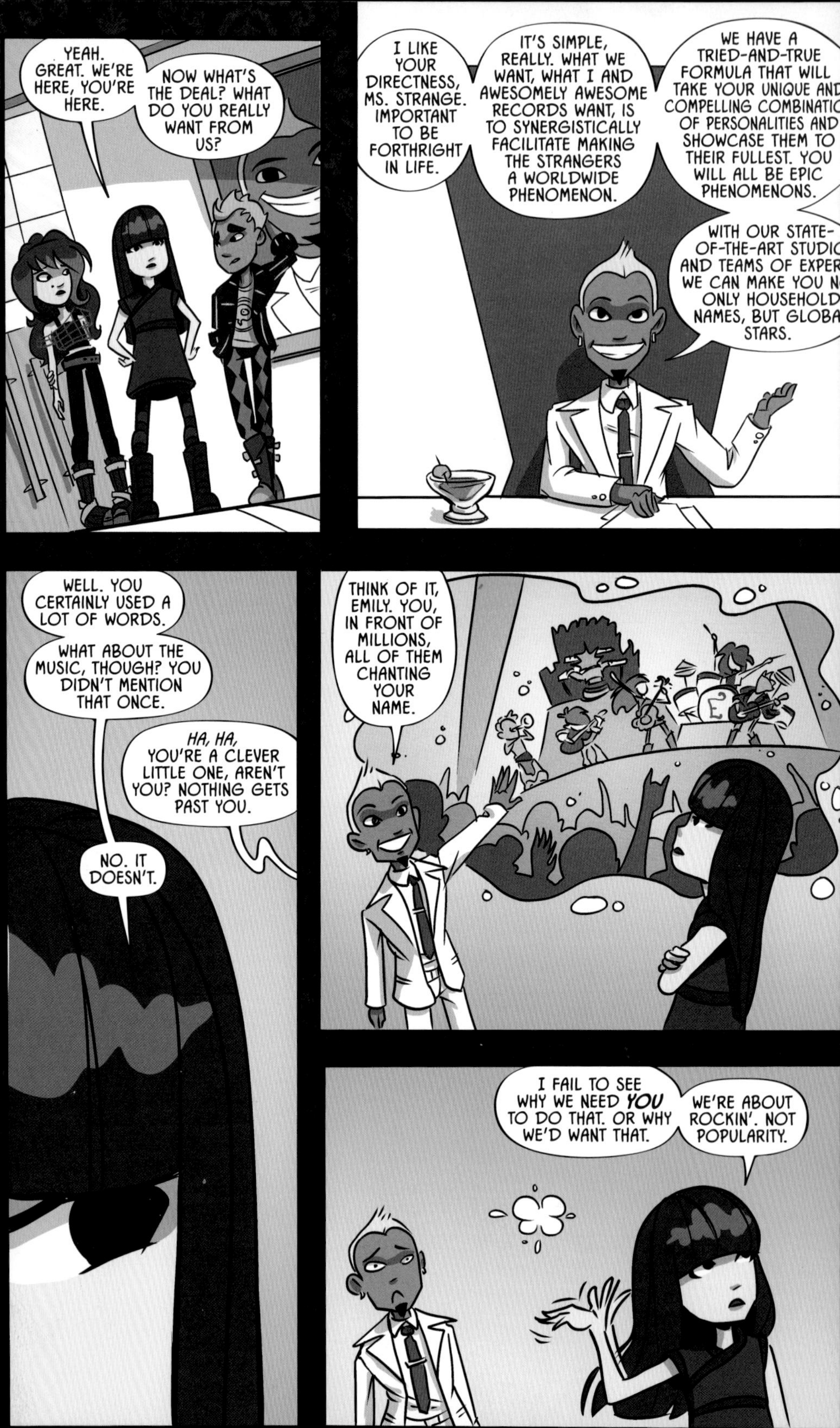
YEAH. GREAT. WE'RE HERE, YOU'RE HERE.
NOW WHAT'S THE DEAL? WHAT DO YOU REALLY WANT FROM US?
I LIKE YOUR DIRECTNESS, MS. STRANGE. IMPORTANT TO BE FORTHRIGHT IN LIFE.
IT'S SIMPLE, REALLY. WHAT WE WANT, WHAT I AND AWESOMELY AWESOME RECORDS WANT, IS TO SYNERGISTICALLY FACILITATE MAKING THE STRANGERS A WORLDWIDE PHENOMENON.
WE HAVE A TRIED-AND-TRUE FORMULA THAT WILL TAKE YOUR UNIQUE AND COMPELLING COMBINATIO OF PERSONALITIES AND SHOWCASE THEM TO THEIR FULLEST. YOU WILL ALL BE EPIC PHENOMENONS.
WITH OUR STATE-OF-THE-ART STUDIO AND TEAMS OF EXPER WE CAN MAKE YOU N ONLY HOUSEHOLD NAMES, BUT GLOBA STARS.
WELL. YOU CERTAINLY USED A LOT OF WORDS.
WHAT ABOUT THE MUSIC, THOUGH? YOU DIDN'T MENTION THAT ONCE.
HA, HA, YOU'RE A CLEVER LITTLE ONE, AREN'T YOU? NOTHING GETS PAST YOU.
NO. IT DOESN'T.
THINK OF IT, EMILY. YOU, IN FRONT OF MILLIONS, ALL OF THEM CHANTING YOUR NAME.
E
I FAIL TO SEE WHY WE NEED ***YOU*** TO DO THAT. OR WHY WE'D WANT THAT.
WE'RE ABOUT ROCKIN'. NOT POPULARITY.

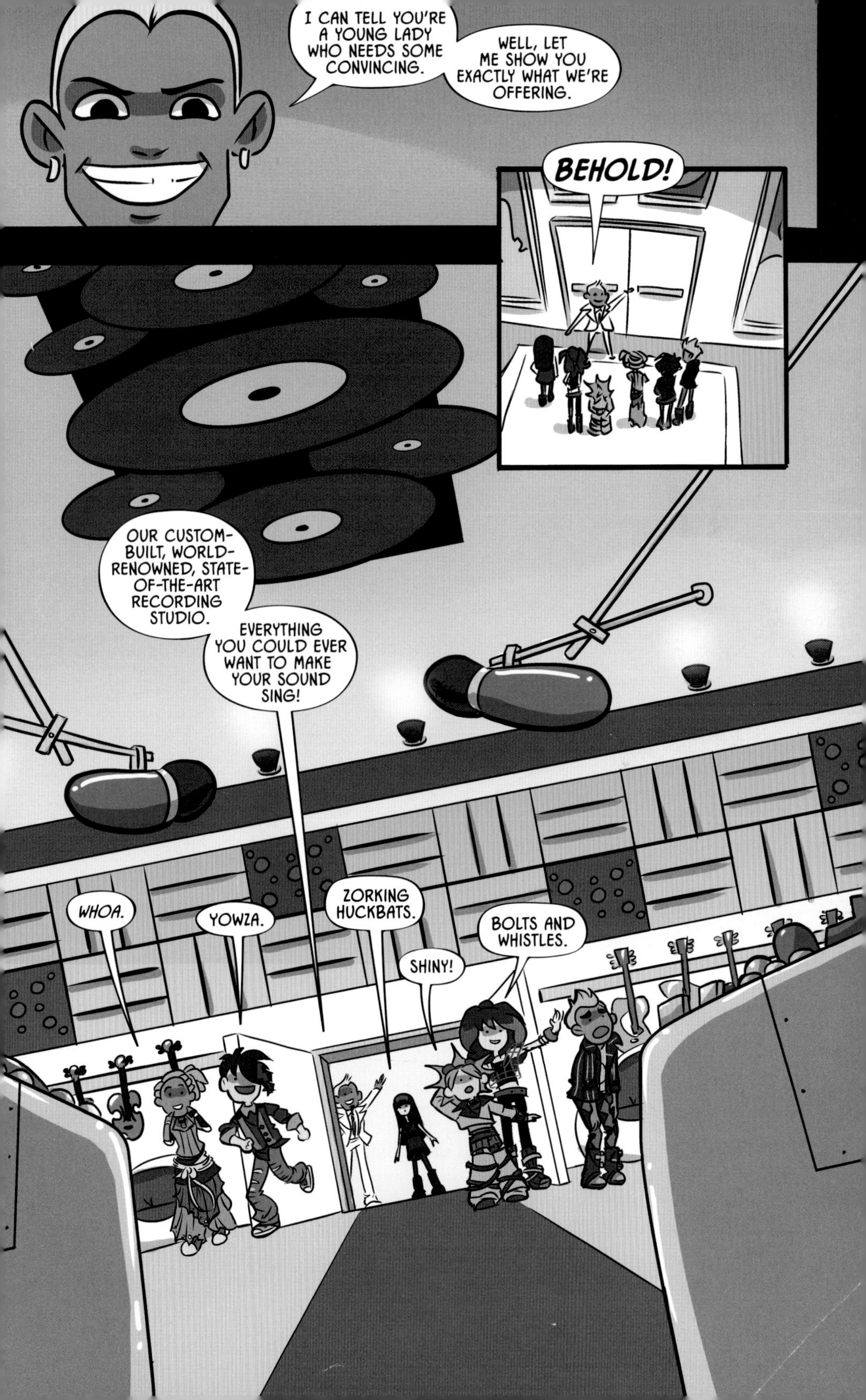
I CAN TELL YOU'RE A YOUNG LADY WHO NEEDS SOME CONVINCING.
WELL, LET ME SHOW YOU EXACTLY WHAT WE'RE OFFERING.
BEHOLD!
OUR CUSTOM-BUILT, WORLD-RENOWNED, STATE-OF-THE-ART RECORDING STUDIO.
EVERYTHING YOU COULD EVER WANT TO MAKE YOUR SOUND SING!
WHOA.
YOWZA.
ZORKING HUCKBATS.
SHINY!
BOLTS AND WHISTLES.

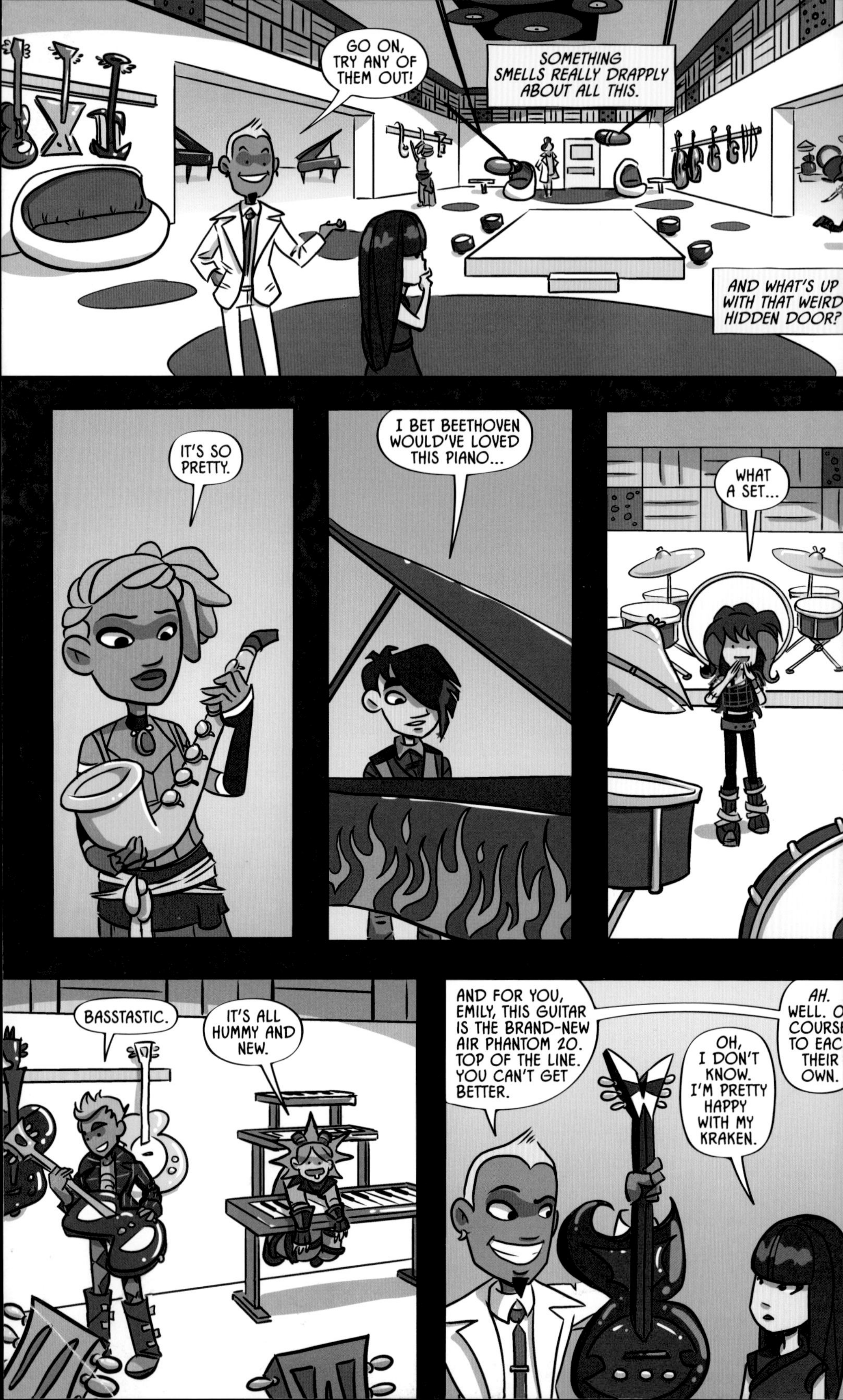
GO ON, TRY ANY OF THEM OUT!
SOMETHING SMELLS REALLY DRAPPLY ABOUT ALL THIS.
AND WHAT'S UP WITH THAT WEIRD HIDDEN DOOR?
IT'S SO PRETTY.
I BET BEETHOVEN WOULD'VE LOVED THIS PIANO...
WHAT A SET...
BASSTASTIC.
IT'S ALL HUMMY AND NEW.
AND FOR YOU, EMILY, THIS GUITAR IS THE BRAND-NEW AIR PHANTOM 20. TOP OF THE LINE. YOU CAN'T GET BETTER.
OH, I DON'T KNOW. I'M PRETTY HAPPY WITH MY KRAKEN.

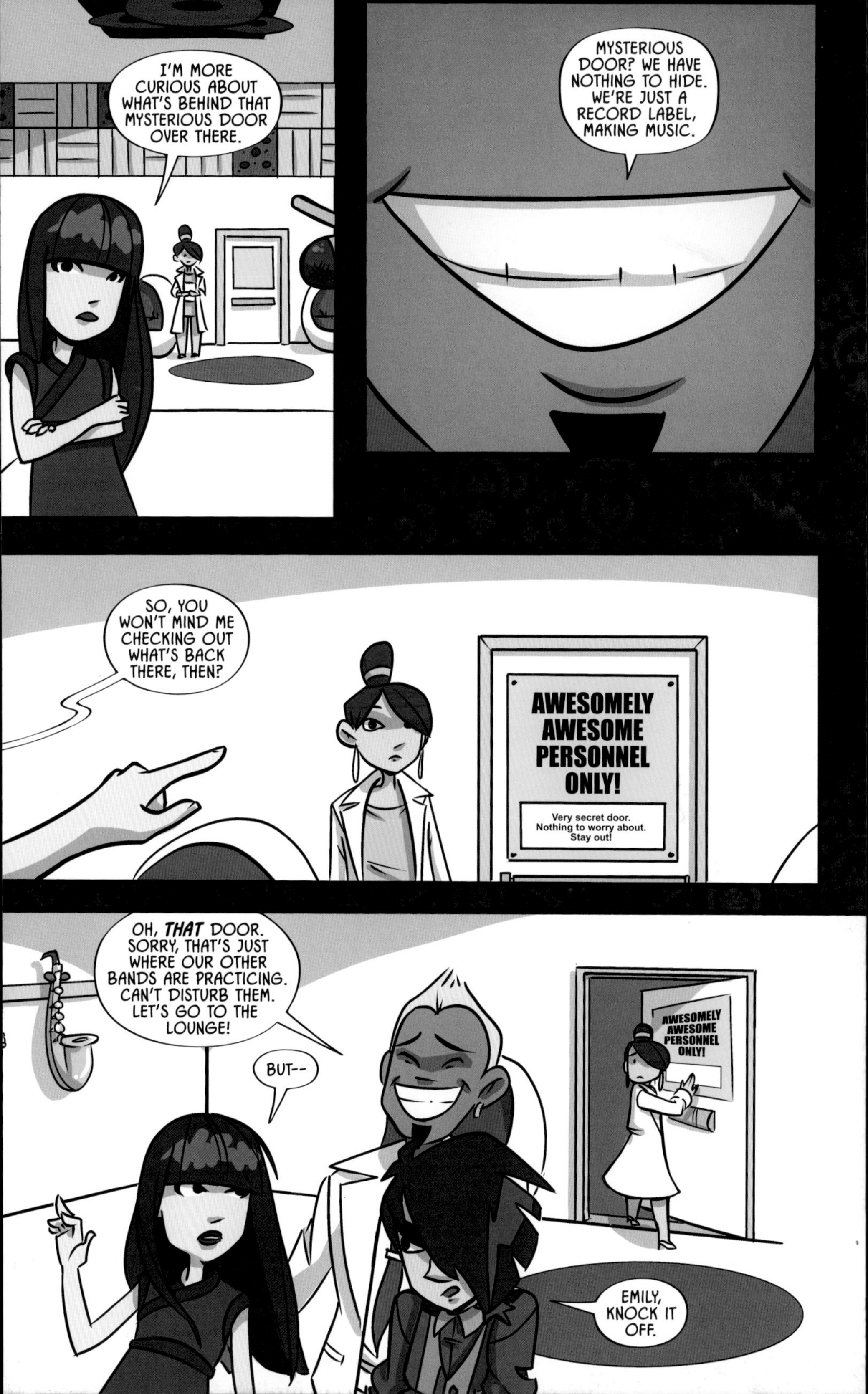
I'M MORE CURIOUS ABOUT WHAT'S BEHIND THAT MYSTERIOUS DOOR OVER THERE.
MYSTERIOUS DOOR? WE HAVE NOTHING TO HIDE. WE'RE JUST A RECORD LABEL, MAKING MUSIC.
SO, YOU WON'T MIND ME CHECKING OUT WHAT'S BACK THERE, THEN?
AWESOMELY AWESOME PERSONNEL ONLY!
Very secret door. Nothing to worry about. Stay out!
OH, *THAT* DOOR. SORRY, THAT'S JUST WHERE OUR OTHER BANDS ARE PRACTICING. CAN'T DISTURB THEM. LET'S GO TO THE LOUNGE!
BUT--
AWESOMELY AWESOME PERSONNEL ONLY!
EMILY, KNOCK IT OFF.

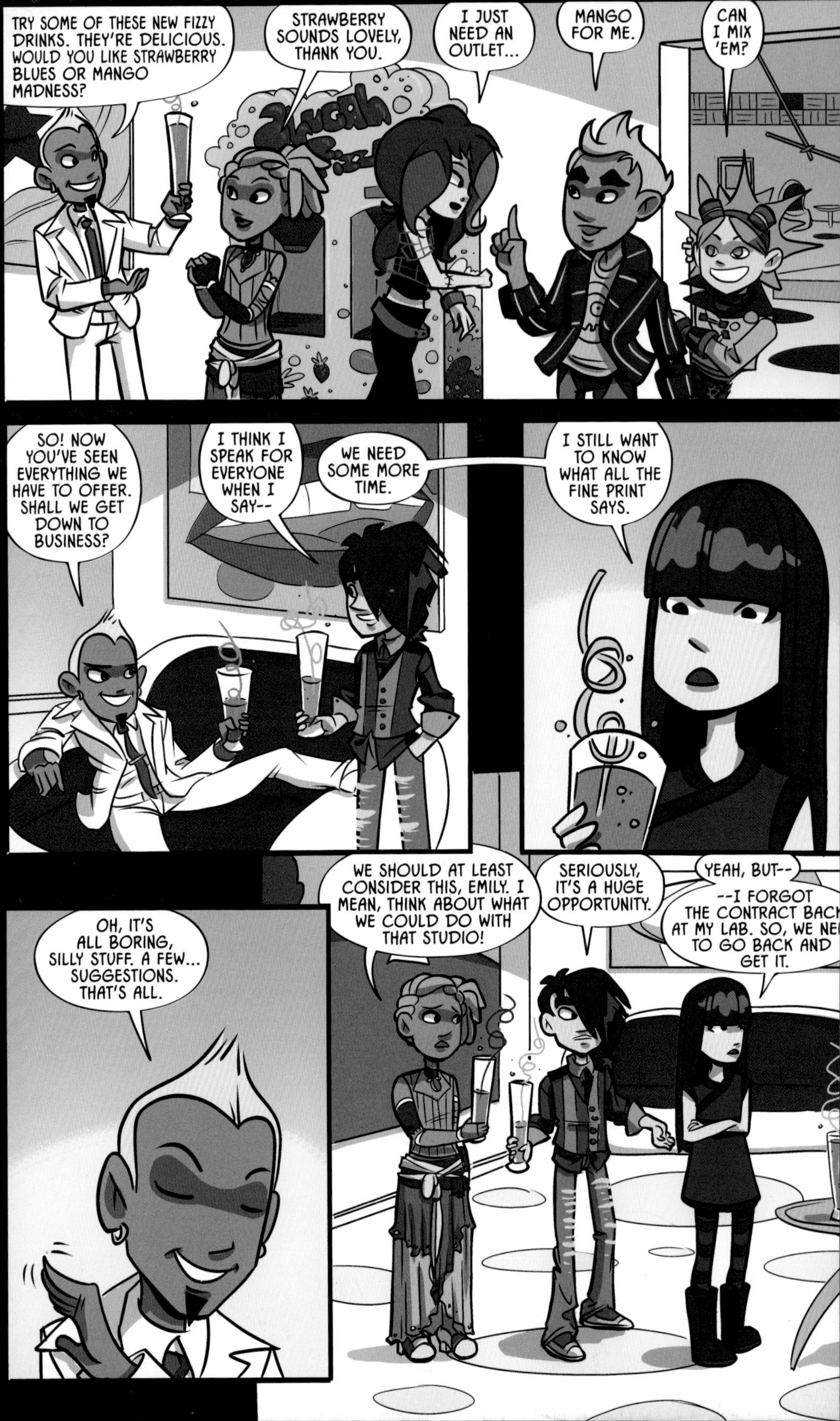
TRY SOME OF THESE NEW FIZZY DRINKS. THEY'RE DELICIOUS. WOULD YOU LIKE STRAWBERRY BLUES OR MANGO MADNESS?
STRAWBERRY SOUNDS LOVELY, THANK YOU.
I JUST NEED AN OUTLET...
MANGO FOR ME.
CAN I MIX 'EM?
SO! NOW YOU'VE SEEN EVERYTHING WE HAVE TO OFFER. SHALL WE GET DOWN TO BUSINESS?
I THINK I SPEAK FOR EVERYONE WHEN I SAY--
WE NEED SOME MORE TIME.
I STILL WANT TO KNOW WHAT ALL THE FINE PRINT SAYS.
OH, IT'S ALL BORING, SILLY STUFF. A FEW... SUGGESTIONS. THAT'S ALL.
WE SHOULD AT LEAST CONSIDER THIS, EMILY. I MEAN, THINK ABOUT WHAT WE COULD DO WITH THAT STUDIO!
SERIOUSLY, IT'S A HUGE OPPORTUNITY.
YEAH, BUT--
--I FORGOT THE CONTRACT BACK AT MY LAB. SO, WE NEED TO GO BACK AND GET IT.

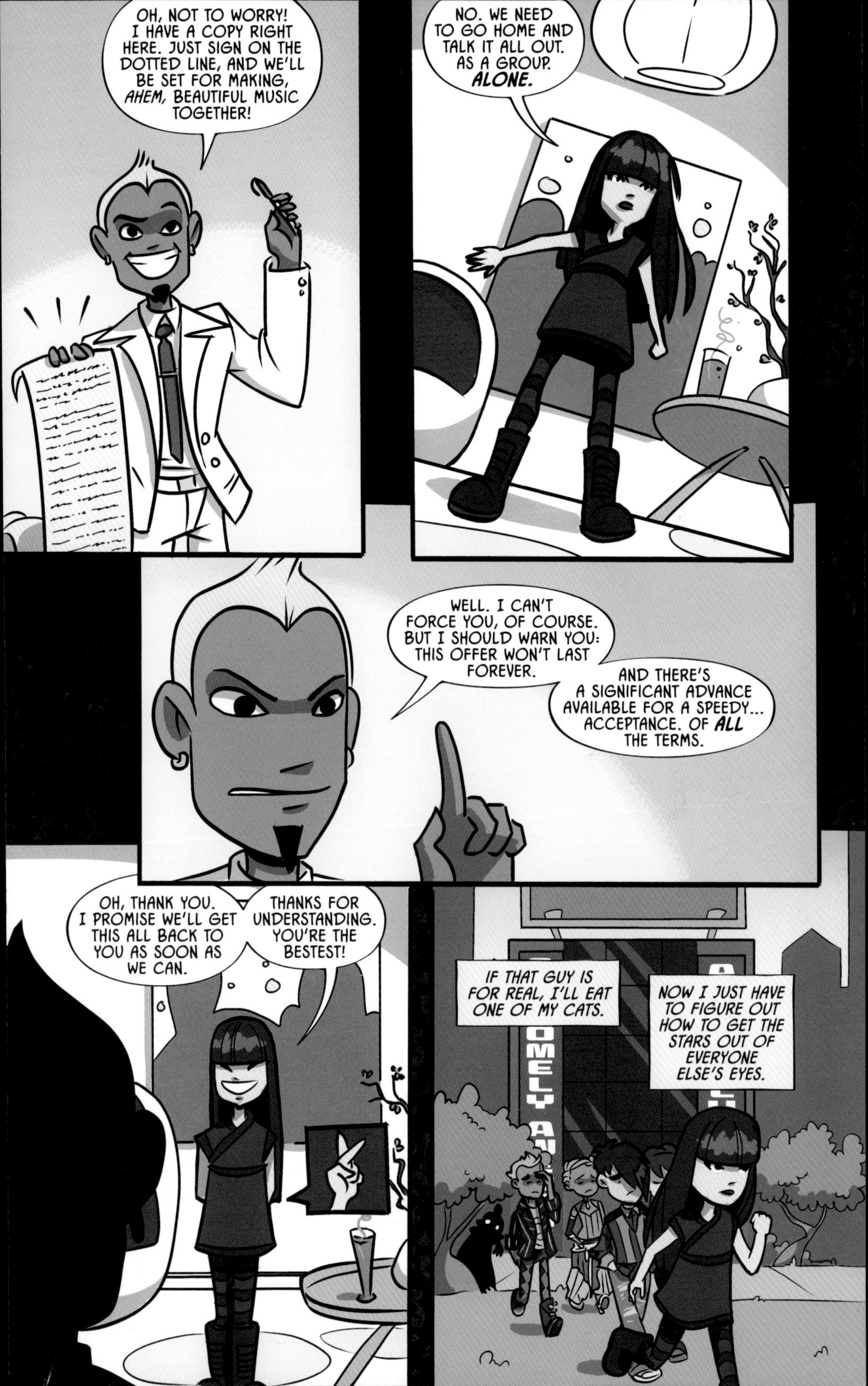
OH, NOT TO WORRY! I HAVE A COPY RIGHT HERE. JUST SIGN ON THE DOTTED LINE, AND WE'LL BE SET FOR MAKING, AHEM, BEAUTIFUL MUSIC TOGETHER!
NO. WE NEED TO GO HOME AND TALK IT ALL OUT. AS A GROUP. ALONE.
WELL. I CAN'T FORCE YOU, OF COURSE. BUT I SHOULD WARN YOU: THIS OFFER WON'T LAST FOREVER.
AND THERE'S A SIGNIFICANT ADVANCE AVAILABLE FOR A SPEEDY... ACCEPTANCE. OF ALL THE TERMS.
OH, THANK YOU. I PROMISE WE'LL GET THIS ALL BACK TO YOU AS SOON AS WE CAN.
THANKS FOR UNDERSTANDING. YOU'RE THE BESTEST!
IF THAT GUY IS FOR REAL, I'LL EAT ONE OF MY CATS.
NOW I JUST HAVE TO FIGURE OUT HOW TO GET THE STARS OUT OF EVERYONE ELSE'S EYES.

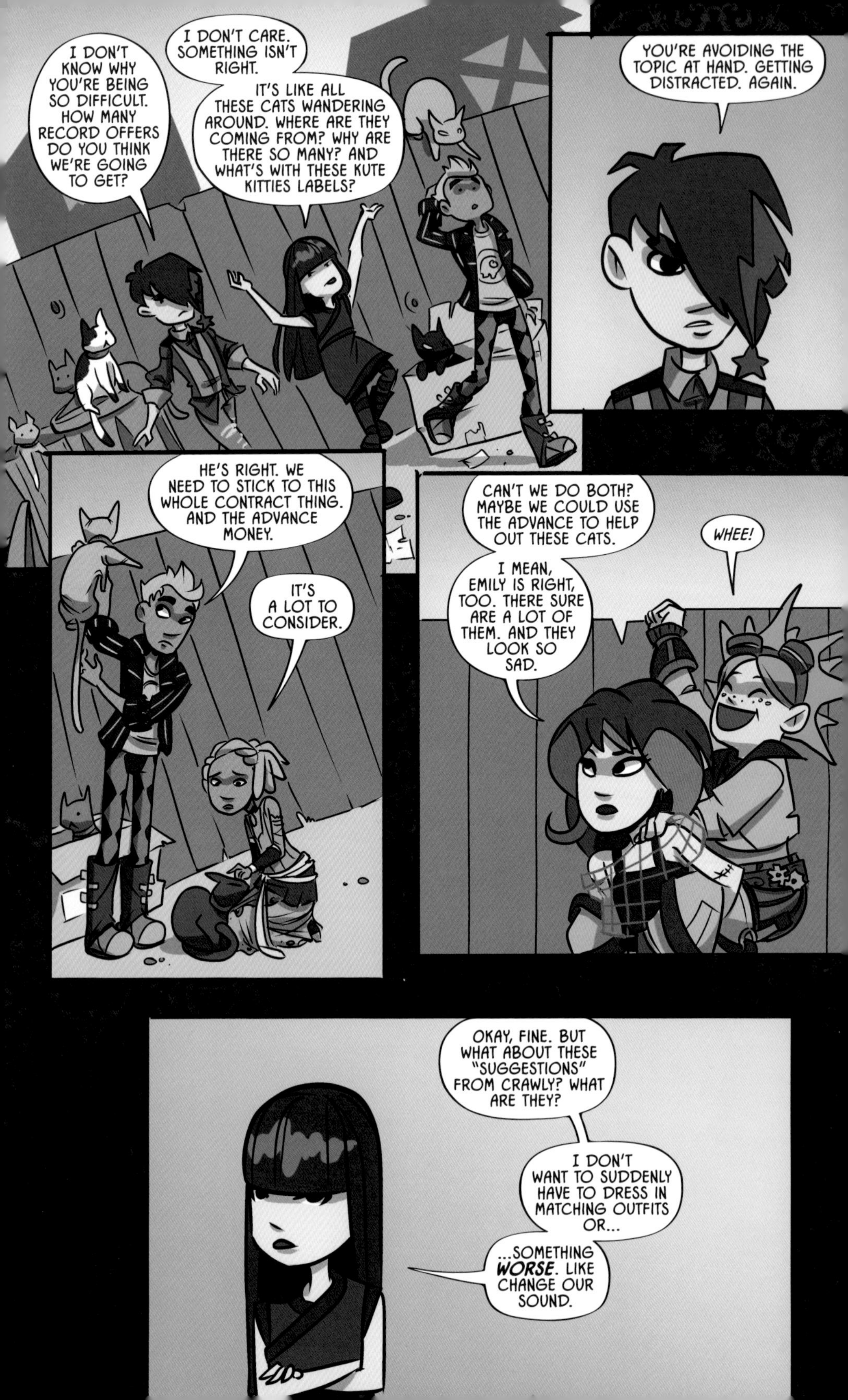
I DON'T KNOW WHY YOU'RE BEING SO DIFFICULT. HOW MANY RECORD OFFERS DO YOU THINK WE'RE GOING TO GET?
I DON'T CARE. SOMETHING ISN'T RIGHT.
IT'S LIKE ALL THESE CATS WANDERING AROUND. WHERE ARE THEY COMING FROM? WHY ARE THERE SO MANY? AND WHAT'S WITH THESE KUTE KITTIES LABELS?
YOU'RE AVOIDING THE TOPIC AT HAND. GETTING DISTRACTED. AGAIN.
HE'S RIGHT. WE NEED TO STICK TO THIS WHOLE CONTRACT THING. AND THE ADVANCE MONEY.
IT'S A LOT TO CONSIDER.
CAN'T WE DO BOTH? MAYBE WE COULD USE THE ADVANCE TO HELP OUT THESE CATS.
I MEAN, EMILY IS RIGHT, TOO. THERE SURE ARE A LOT OF THEM. AND THEY LOOK SO SAD.
WHEE!
OKAY, FINE. BUT WHAT ABOUT THESE "SUGGESTIONS" FROM CRAWLY? WHAT ARE THEY?
I DON'T WANT TO SUDDENLY HAVE TO DRESS IN MATCHING OUTFITS OR...
...SOMETHING WORSE. LIKE CHANGE OUR SOUND.

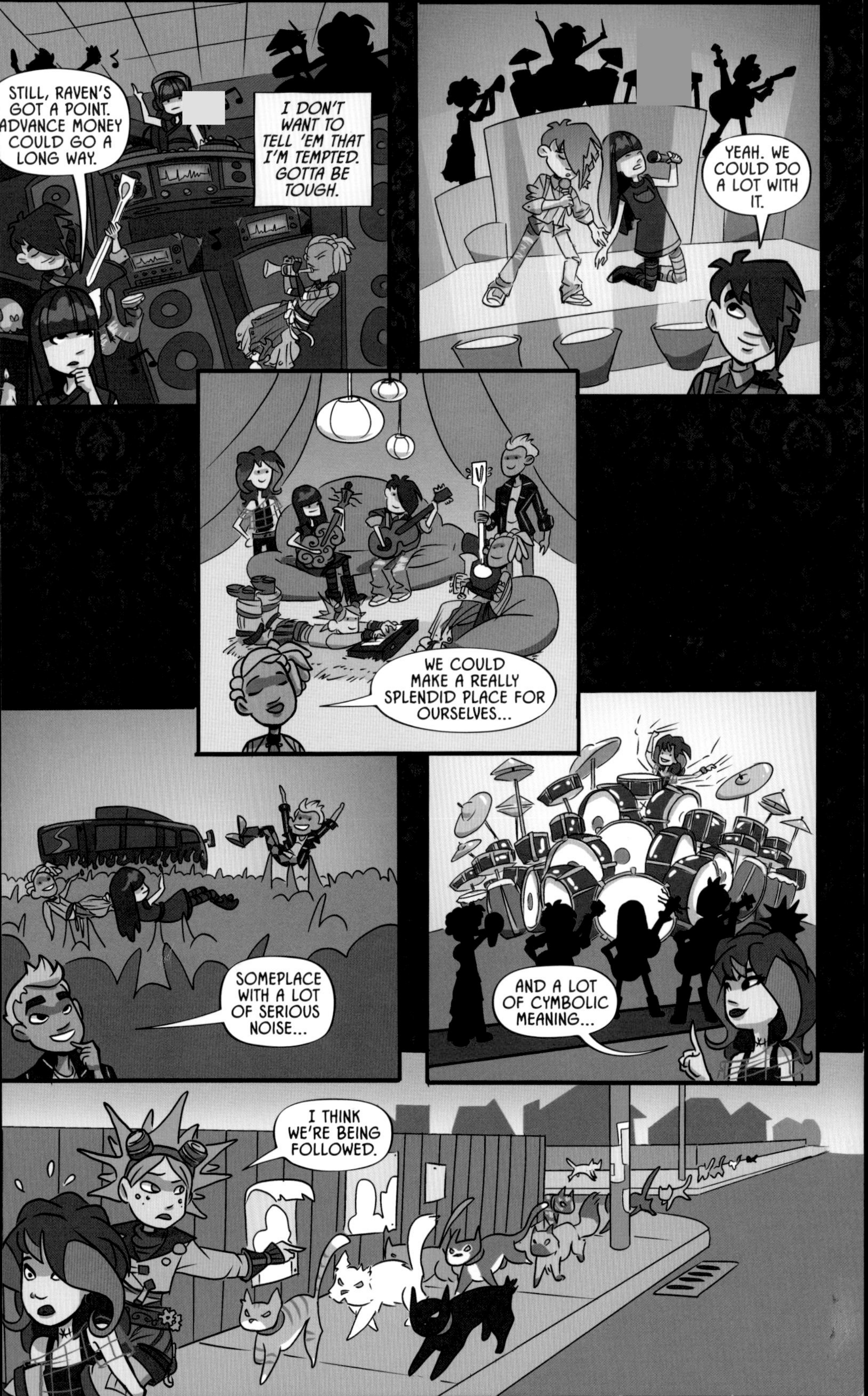
STILL, RAVEN'S GOT A POINT. ADVANCE MONEY COULD GO A LONG WAY.
I DON'T WANT TO TELL 'EM THAT I'M TEMPTED. GOTTA BE TOUGH.
YEAH. WE COULD DO A LOT WITH IT.
WE COULD MAKE A REALLY SPLENDID PLACE FOR OURSELVES...
SOMEPLACE WITH A LOT OF SERIOUS NOISE...
AND A LOT OF CYMBOLIC MEANING...
I THINK WE'RE BEING FOLLOWED.

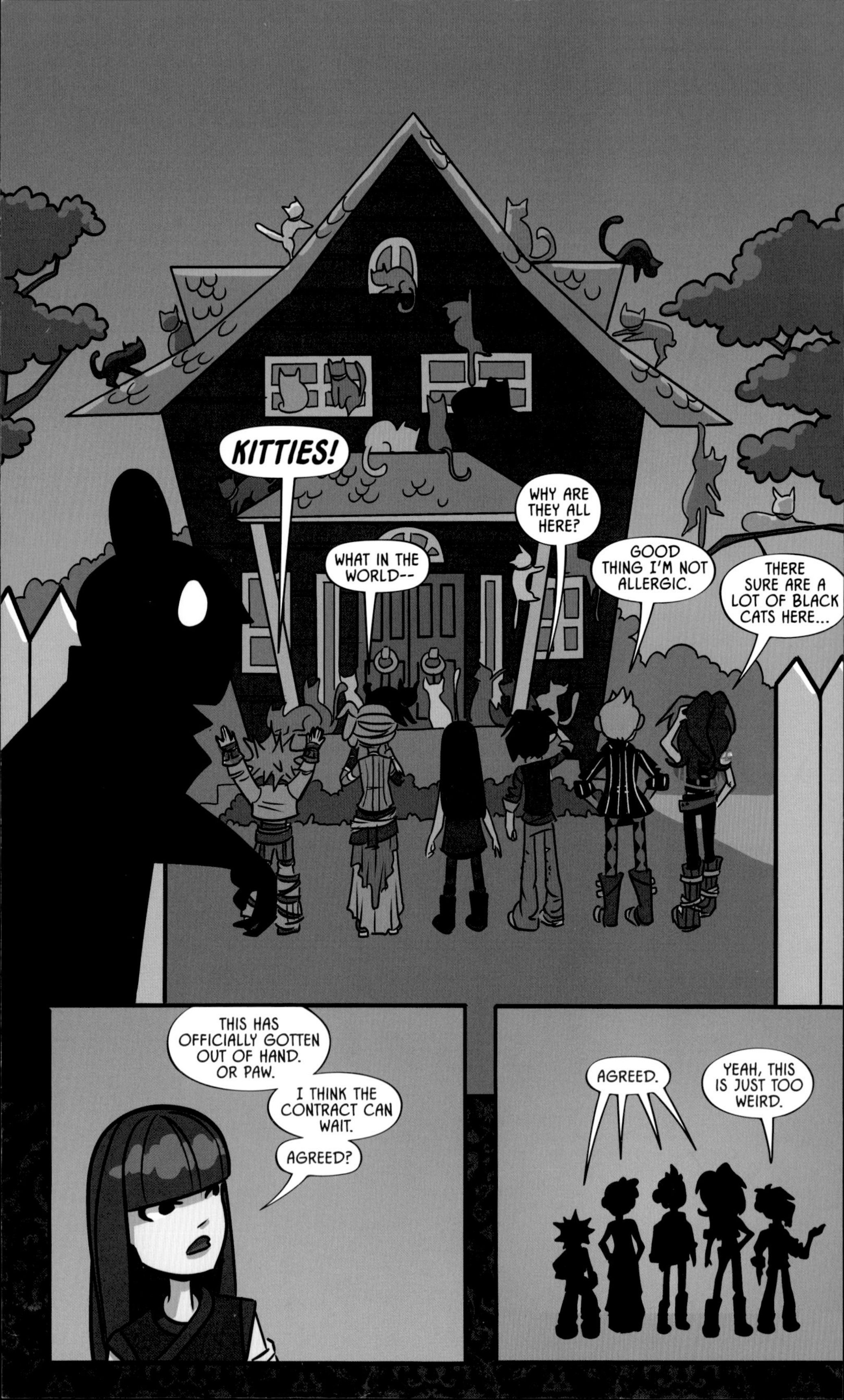
KITTIES!
WHAT IN THE WORLD--
WHY ARE THEY ALL HERE?
GOOD THING I'M NOT ALLERGIC.
THERE SURE ARE A LOT OF BLACK CATS HERE...
THIS HAS OFFICIALLY GOTTEN OUT OF HAND. OR PAW.
I THINK THE CONTRACT CAN WAIT.
AGREED?
AGREED.
YEAH, THIS IS JUST TOO WEIRD.

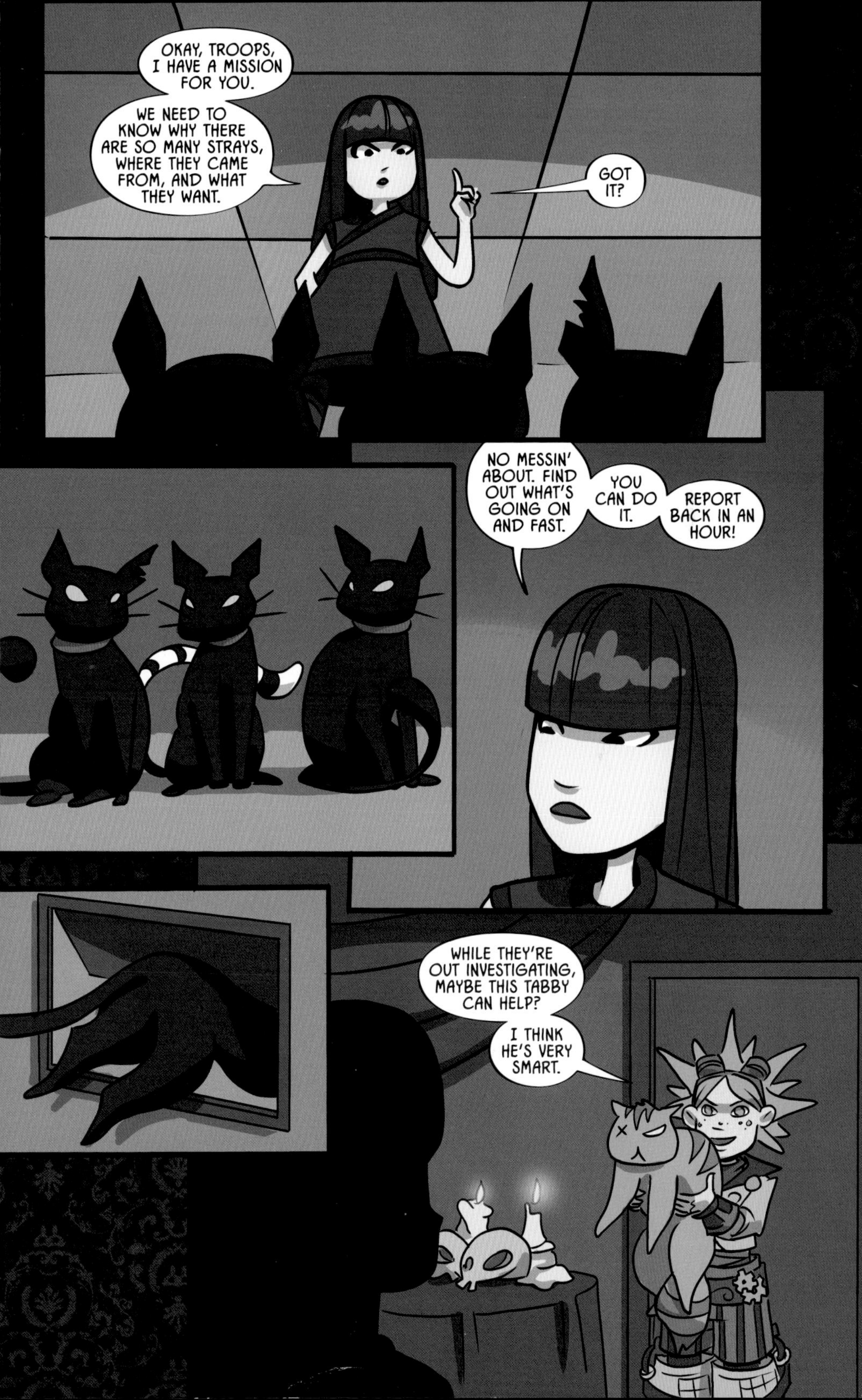
OKAY, TROOPS, I HAVE A MISSION FOR YOU.
WE NEED TO KNOW WHY THERE ARE SO MANY STRAYS, WHERE THEY CAME FROM, AND WHAT THEY WANT.
GOT IT?
NO MESSIN' ABOUT. FIND OUT WHAT'S GOING ON AND FAST.
YOU CAN DO IT.
REPORT BACK IN AN HOUR!
WHILE THEY'RE OUT INVESTIGATING, MAYBE THIS TABBY CAN HELP?
I THINK HE'S VERY SMART.

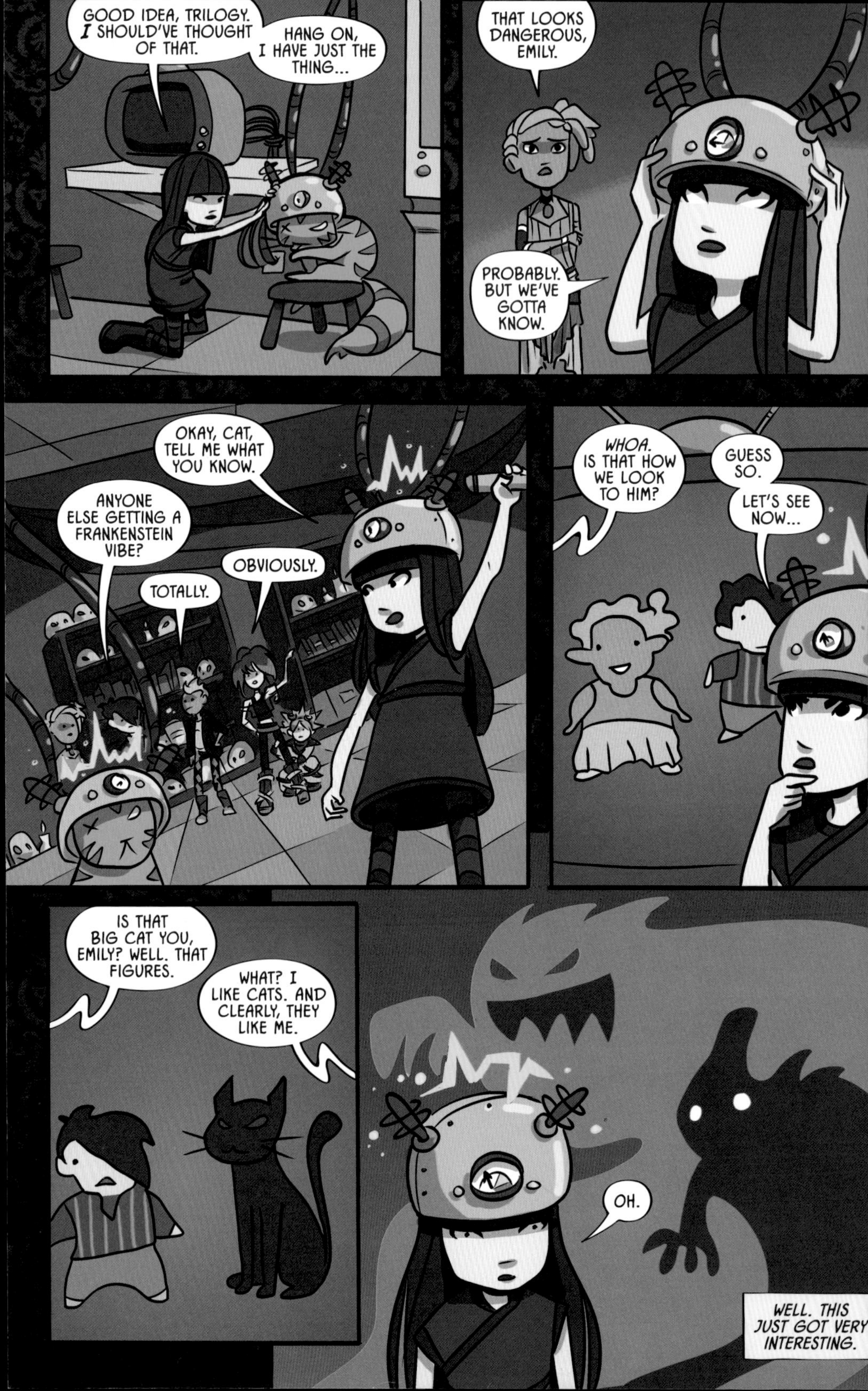
GOOD IDEA, TRILOGY. *I* SHOULD'VE THOUGHT OF THAT.
HANG ON, I HAVE JUST THE THING...
THAT LOOKS DANGEROUS, EMILY.
PROBABLY. BUT WE'VE GOTTA KNOW.
OKAY, CAT, TELL ME WHAT YOU KNOW.
ANYONE ELSE GETTING A FRANKENSTEIN VIBE?
TOTALLY.
OBVIOUSLY.
WHOA. IS THAT HOW WE LOOK TO HIM?
GUESS SO.
LET'S SEE NOW...
IS THAT BIG CAT YOU, EMILY? WELL. THAT FIGURES.
WHAT? I LIKE CATS. AND CLEARLY, THEY LIKE ME.
OH.
WELL. THIS JUST GOT VERY INTERESTING.

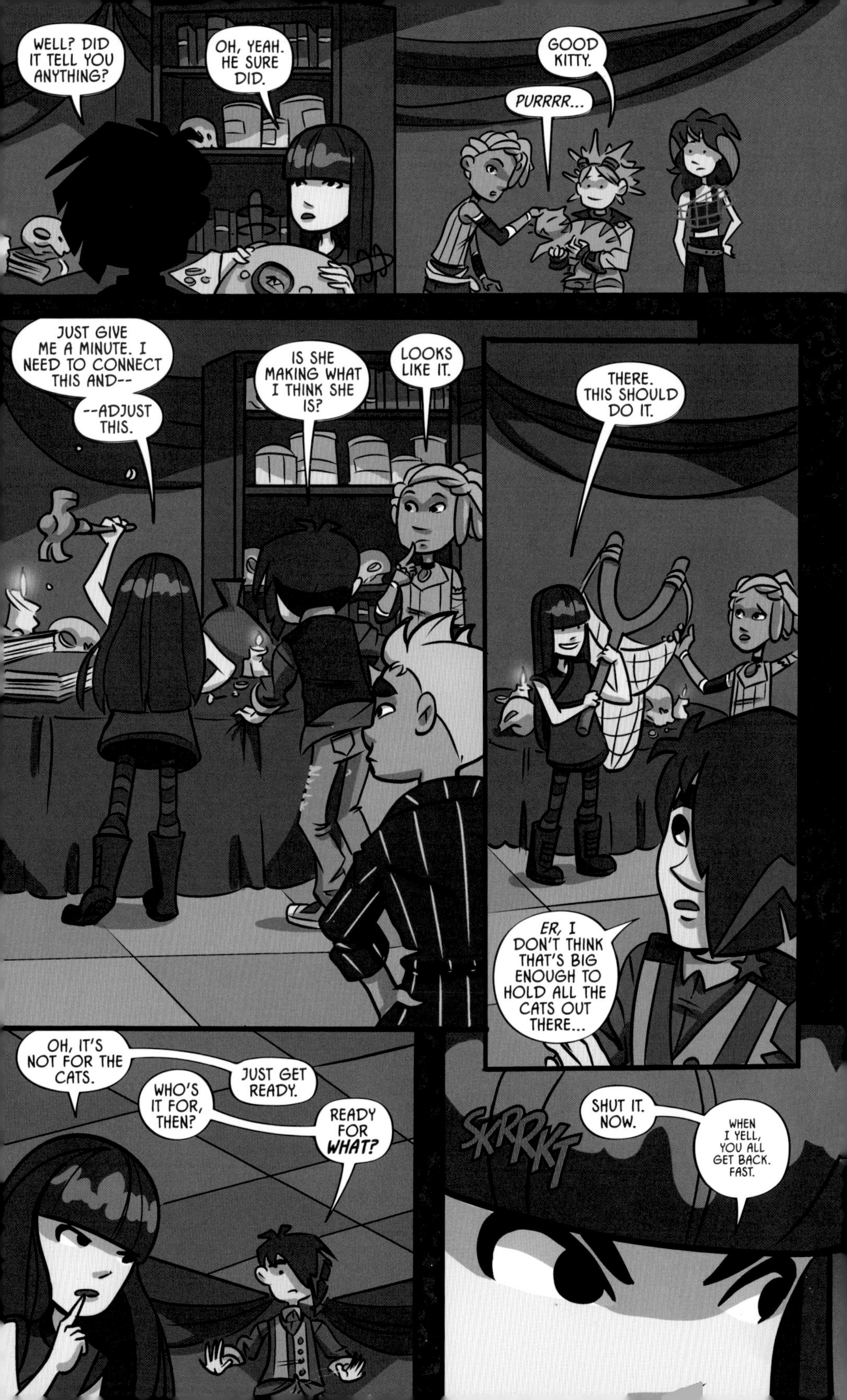
WELL? DID IT TELL YOU ANYTHING?
OH, YEAH. HE SURE DID.
GOOD KITTY.
PURRRR...
JUST GIVE ME A MINUTE. I NEED TO CONNECT THIS AND--
--ADJUST THIS.
IS SHE MAKING WHAT I THINK SHE IS?
LOOKS LIKE IT.
THERE. THIS SHOULD DO IT.
ER, I DON'T THINK THAT'S BIG ENOUGH TO HOLD ALL THE CATS OUT THERE...
OH, IT'S NOT FOR THE CATS.
WHO'S IT FOR, THEN?
JUST GET READY.
READY FOR WHAT?
SKRRKT
SHUT IT. NOW.
WHEN I YELL, YOU ALL GET BACK. FAST.

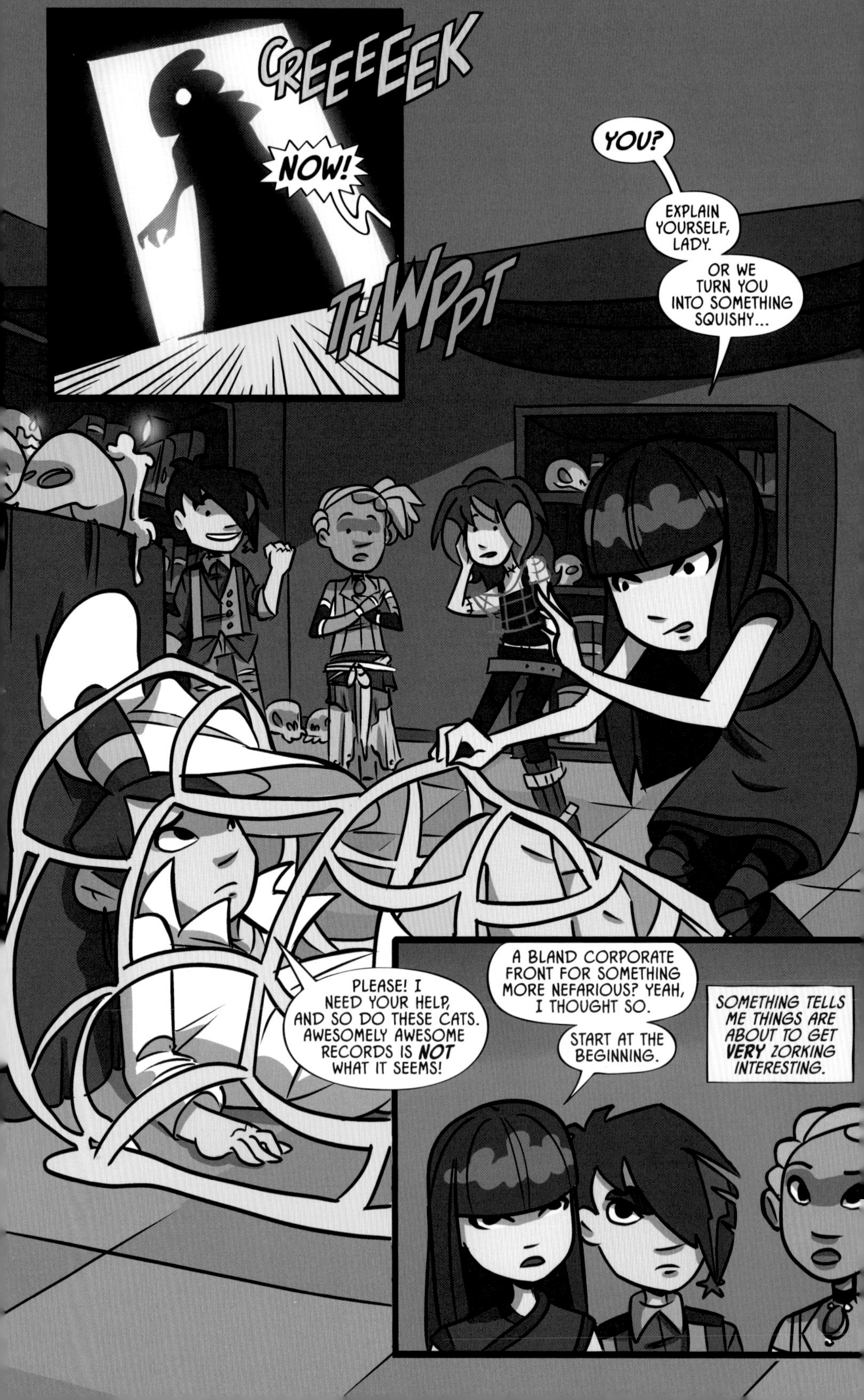
CREEEEEK
NOW!
THWPPT
YOU?
EXPLAIN YOURSELF, LADY.
OR WE TURN YOU INTO SOMETHING SQUISHY...
PLEASE! I NEED YOUR HELP, AND SO DO THESE CATS. AWESOMELY AWESOME RECORDS IS NOT WHAT IT SEEMS!
A BLAND CORPORATE FRONT FOR SOMETHING MORE NEFARIOUS? YEAH, I THOUGHT SO.
START AT THE BEGINNING.
SOMETHING TELLS ME THINGS ARE ABOUT TO GET VERY ZORKING INTERESTING.

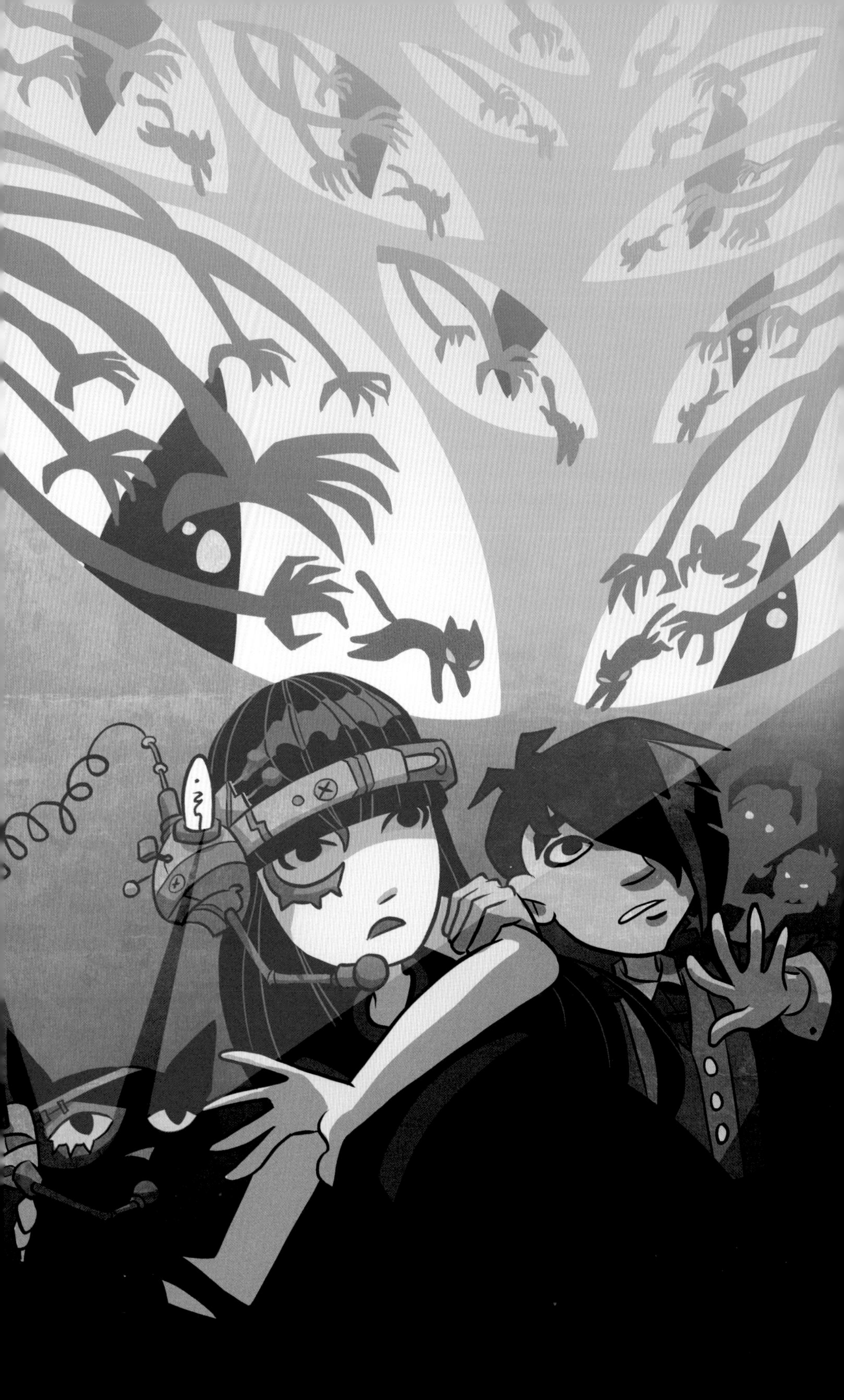

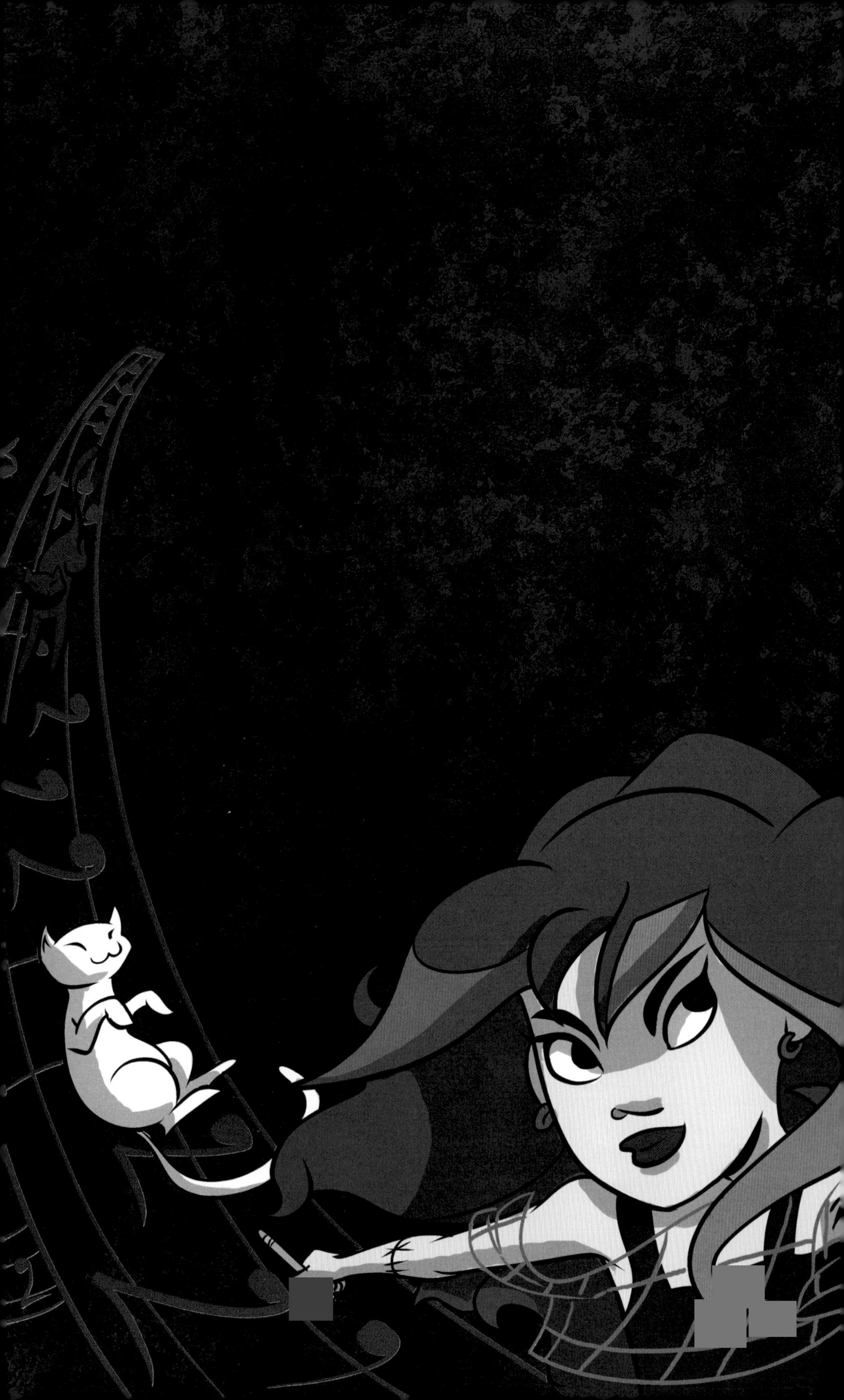

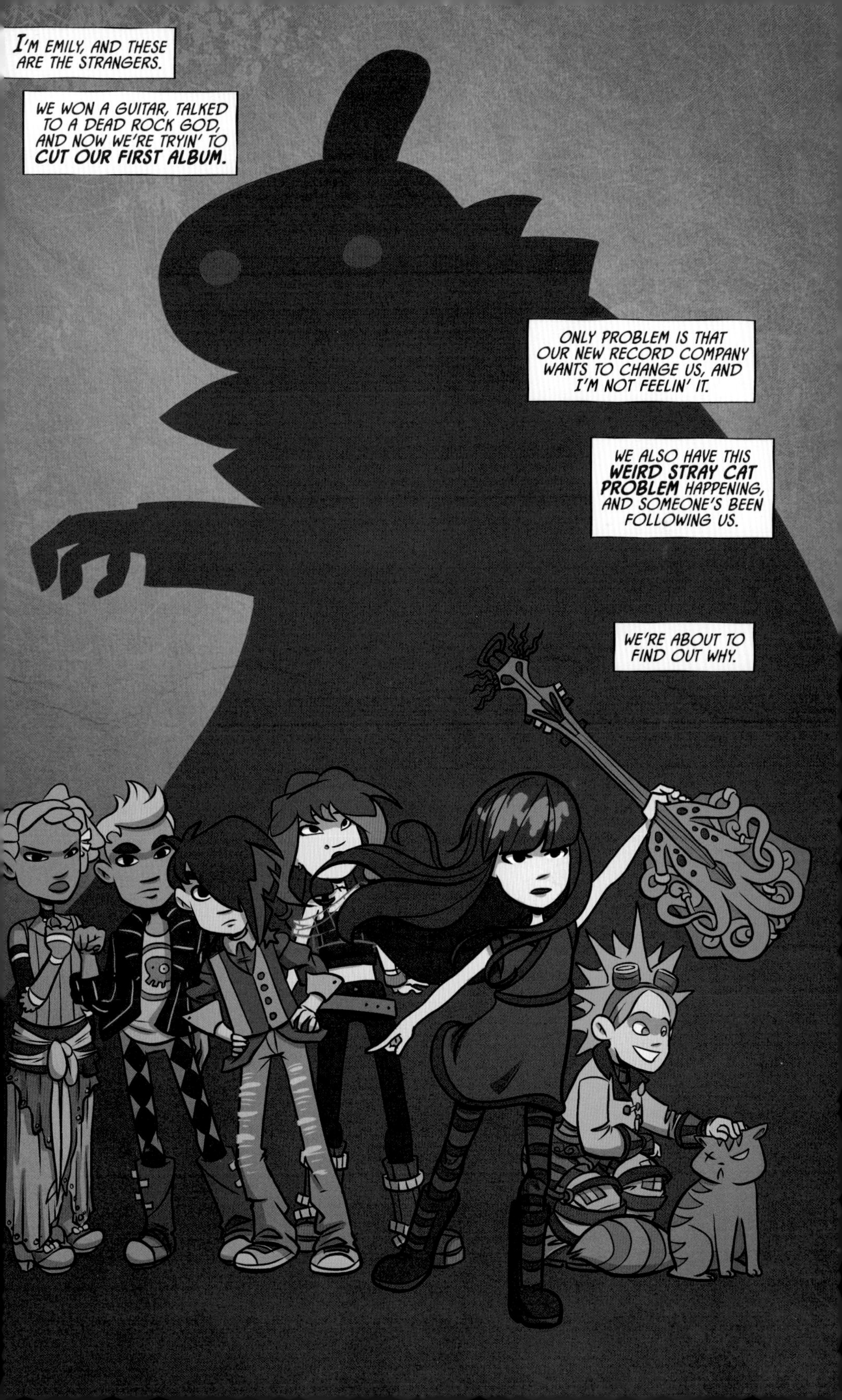

I'M EMILY, AND THESE ARE THE STRANGERS.
WE WON A GUITAR, TALKED TO A DEAD ROCK GOD, AND NOW WE'RE TRYIN' TO CUT OUR FIRST ALBUM.
ONLY PROBLEM IS THAT OUR NEW RECORD COMPANY WANTS TO CHANGE US, AND I'M NOT FEELIN' IT.
WE ALSO HAVE THIS WEIRD STRAY CAT PROBLEM HAPPENING, AND SOMEONE'S BEEN FOLLOWING US.
WE'RE ABOUT TO FIND OUT WHY.

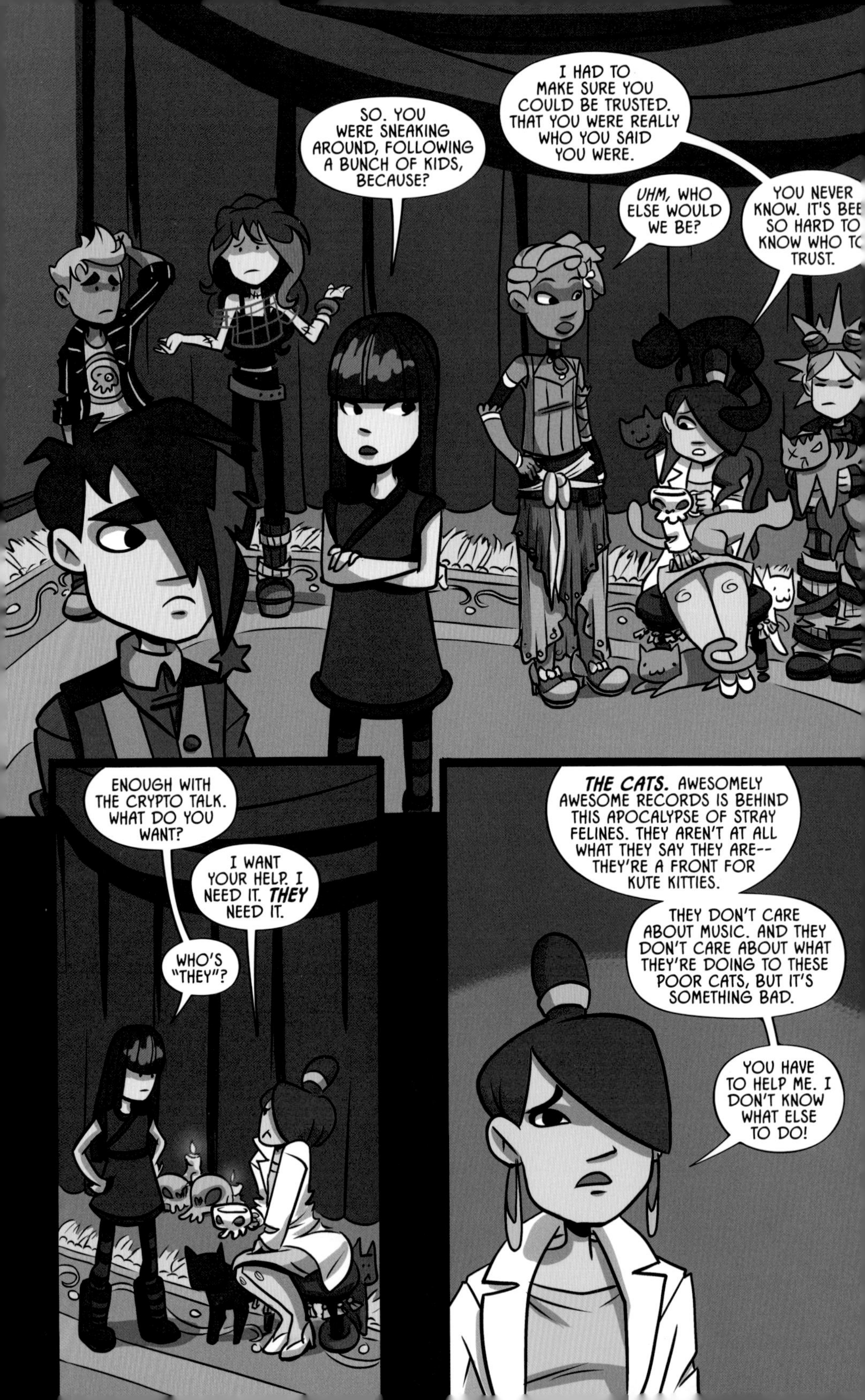
SO. YOU WERE SNEAKING AROUND, FOLLOWING A BUNCH OF KIDS, BECAUSE?
I HAD TO MAKE SURE YOU COULD BE TRUSTED. THAT YOU WERE REALLY WHO YOU SAID YOU WERE.
UHM, WHO ELSE WOULD WE BE?
YOU NEVER KNOW. IT'S BEE SO HARD TO KNOW WHO TO TRUST.
ENOUGH WITH THE CRYPTO TALK. WHAT DO YOU WANT?
I WANT YOUR HELP. I NEED IT. THEY NEED IT.
WHO'S "THEY"?
THE CATS. AWESOMELY AWESOME RECORDS IS BEHIND THIS APOCALYPSE OF STRAY FELINES. THEY AREN'T AT ALL WHAT THEY SAY THEY ARE-- THEY'RE A FRONT FOR KUTE KITTIES.
THEY DON'T CARE ABOUT MUSIC. AND THEY DON'T CARE ABOUT WHAT THEY'RE DOING TO THESE POOR CATS, BUT IT'S SOMETHING BAD.
YOU HAVE TO HELP ME. I DON'T KNOW WHAT ELSE TO DO!

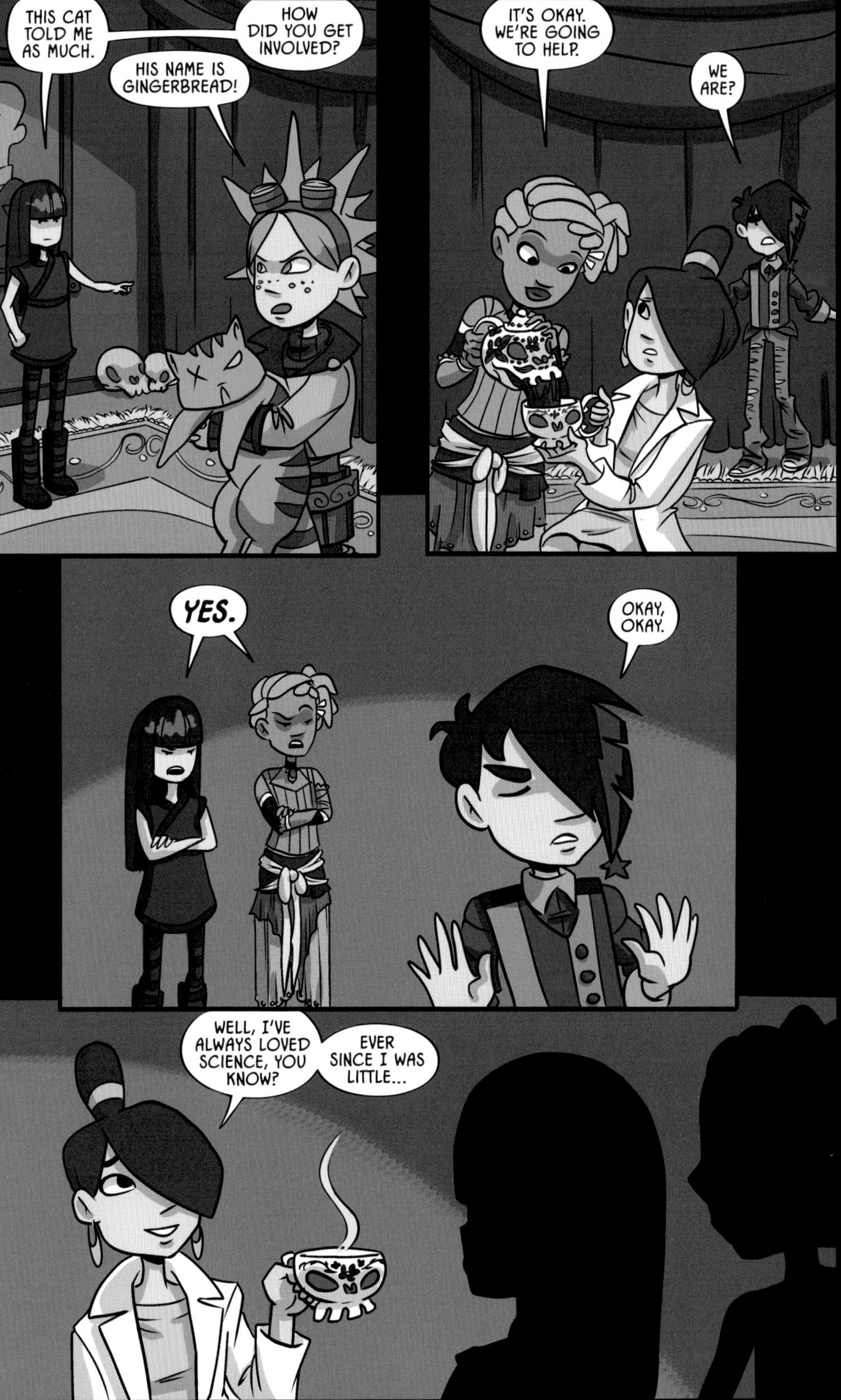
THIS CAT TOLD ME AS MUCH.
HOW DID YOU GET INVOLVED?
HIS NAME IS GINGERBREAD!
IT'S OKAY. WE'RE GOING TO HELP.
WE ARE?
YES.
OKAY, OKAY.
WELL, I'VE ALWAYS LOVED SCIENCE, YOU KNOW?
EVER SINCE I WAS LITTLE...

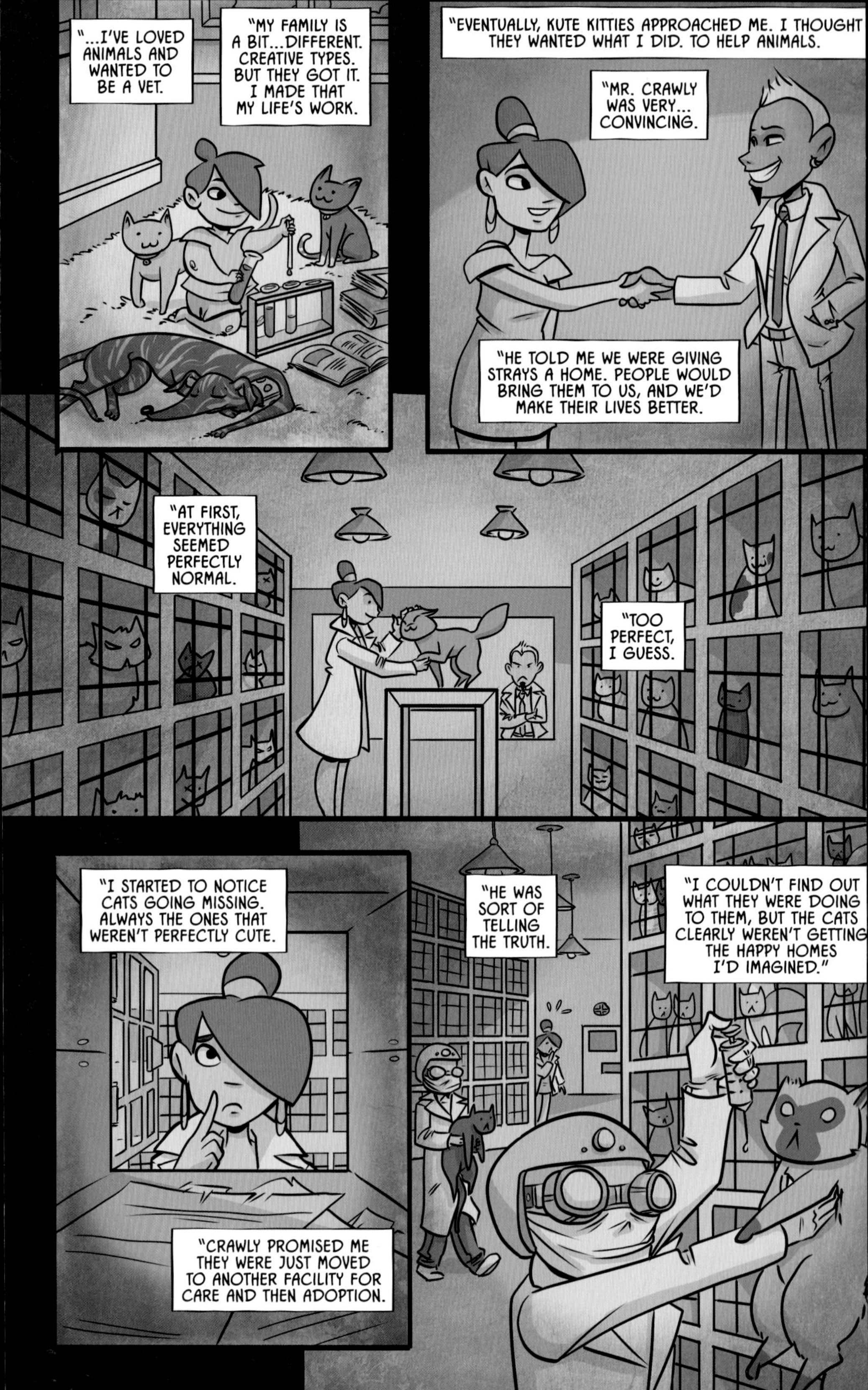
"...I'VE LOVED ANIMALS AND WANTED TO BE A VET.
"MY FAMILY IS A BIT...DIFFERENT. CREATIVE TYPES. BUT THEY GOT IT. I MADE THAT MY LIFE'S WORK.
"EVENTUALLY, KUTE KITTIES APPROACHED ME. I THOUGHT THEY WANTED WHAT I DID. TO HELP ANIMALS.
"MR. CRAWLY WAS VERY... CONVINCING.
"HE TOLD ME WE WERE GIVING STRAYS A HOME. PEOPLE WOULD BRING THEM TO US, AND WE'D MAKE THEIR LIVES BETTER.
"AT FIRST, EVERYTHING SEEMED PERFECTLY NORMAL.
"TOO PERFECT, I GUESS.
"I STARTED TO NOTICE CATS GOING MISSING. ALWAYS THE ONES THAT WEREN'T PERFECTLY CUTE.
"CRAWLY PROMISED ME THEY WERE JUST MOVED TO ANOTHER FACILITY FOR CARE AND THEN ADOPTION.
"HE WAS SORT OF TELLING THE TRUTH.
"I COULDN'T FIND OUT WHAT THEY WERE DOING TO THEM, BUT THE CATS CLEARLY WEREN'T GETTING THE HAPPY HOMES I'D IMAGINED."

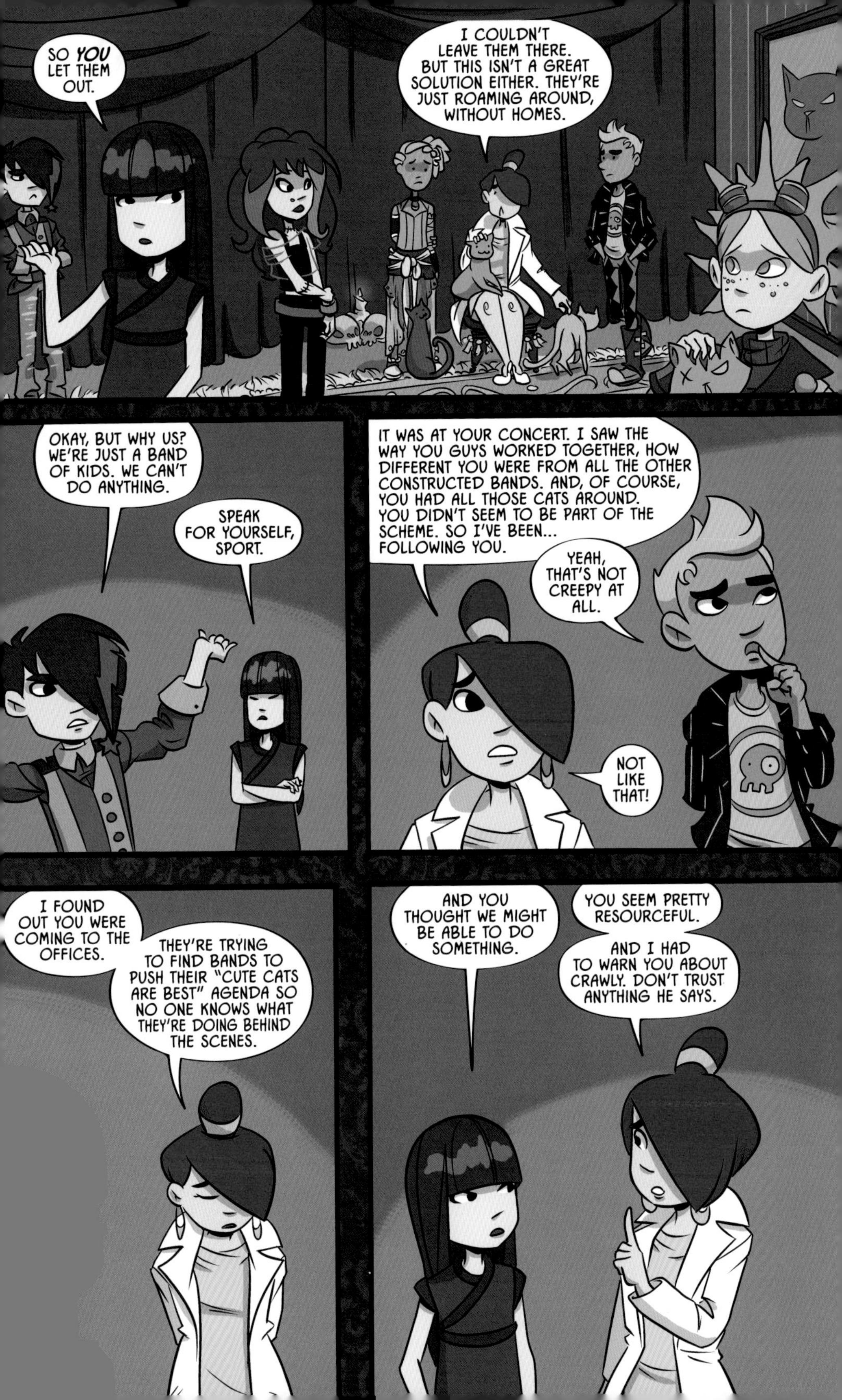
SO *YOU* LET THEM OUT.
I COULDN'T LEAVE THEM THERE. BUT THIS ISN'T A GREAT SOLUTION EITHER. THEY'RE JUST ROAMING AROUND, WITHOUT HOMES.
OKAY, BUT WHY US? WE'RE JUST A BAND OF KIDS. WE CAN'T DO ANYTHING.
SPEAK FOR YOURSELF, SPORT.
IT WAS AT YOUR CONCERT. I SAW THE WAY YOU GUYS WORKED TOGETHER, HOW DIFFERENT YOU WERE FROM ALL THE OTHER CONSTRUCTED BANDS. AND, OF COURSE, YOU HAD ALL THOSE CATS AROUND. YOU DIDN'T SEEM TO BE PART OF THE SCHEME. SO I'VE BEEN... FOLLOWING YOU.
YEAH, THAT'S NOT CREEPY AT ALL.
NOT LIKE THAT!
I FOUND OUT YOU WERE COMING TO THE OFFICES.
THEY'RE TRYING TO FIND BANDS TO PUSH THEIR "CUTE CATS ARE BEST" AGENDA SO NO ONE KNOWS WHAT THEY'RE DOING BEHIND THE SCENES.
AND YOU THOUGHT WE MIGHT BE ABLE TO DO SOMETHING.
YOU SEEM PRETTY RESOURCEFUL.
AND I HAD TO WARN YOU ABOUT CRAWLY. DON'T TRUST ANYTHING HE SAYS.

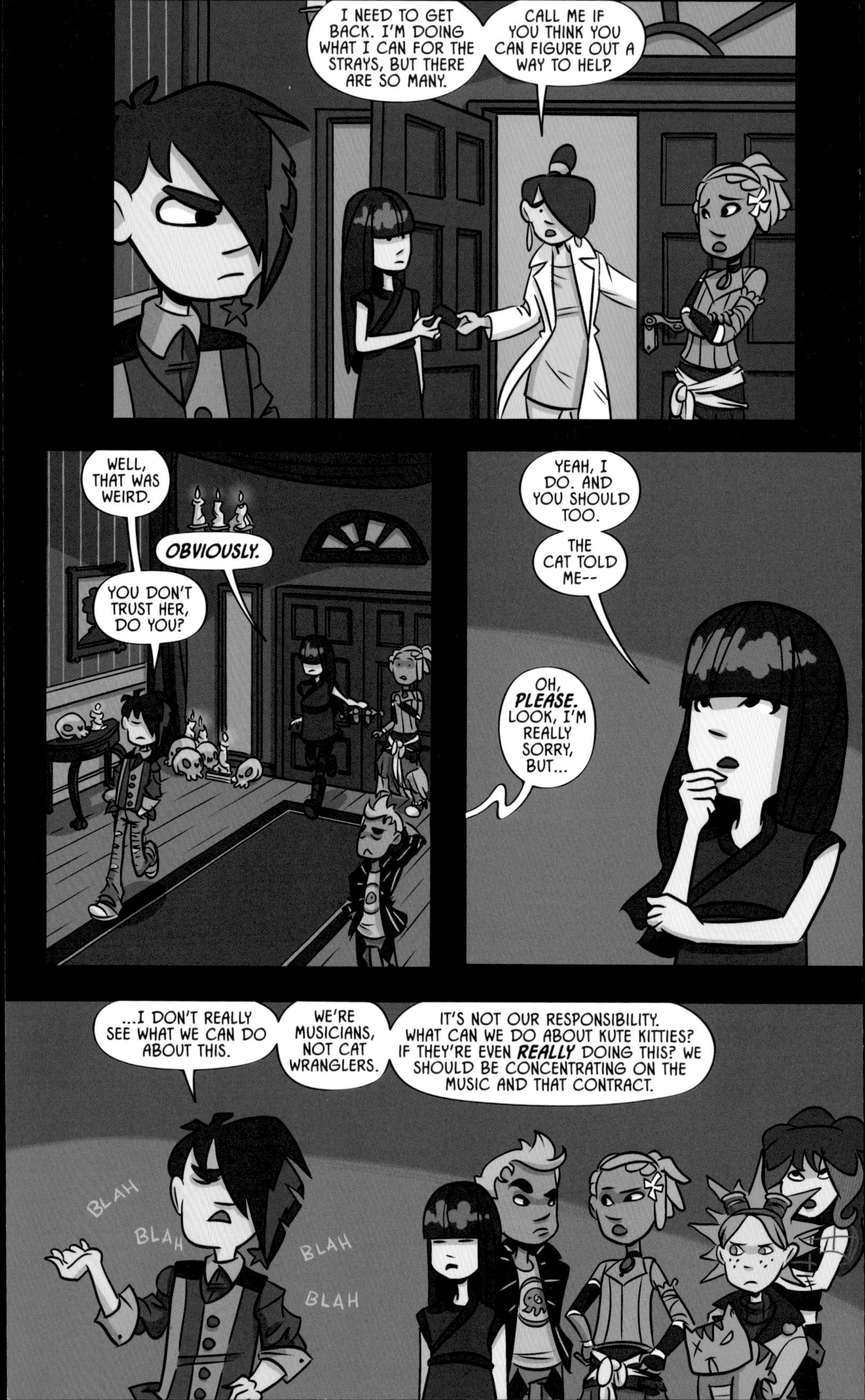
I NEED TO GET BACK. I'M DOING WHAT I CAN FOR THE STRAYS, BUT THERE ARE SO MANY.
CALL ME IF YOU THINK YOU CAN FIGURE OUT A WAY TO HELP.
WELL, THAT WAS WEIRD.
YOU DON'T TRUST HER, DO YOU?
OBVIOUSLY.
YEAH, I DO. AND YOU SHOULD TOO.
THE CAT TOLD ME--
OH, ***PLEASE.*** LOOK, I'M REALLY SORRY, BUT...
...I DON'T REALLY SEE WHAT WE CAN DO ABOUT THIS.
WE'RE MUSICIANS, NOT CAT WRANGLERS.
IT'S NOT OUR RESPONSIBILITY. WHAT CAN WE DO ABOUT KUTE KITTIES? IF THEY'RE EVEN ***REALLY*** DOING THIS? WE SHOULD BE CONCENTRATING ON THE MUSIC AND THAT CONTRACT.
BLAH
BLAH
BLAH
BLAH

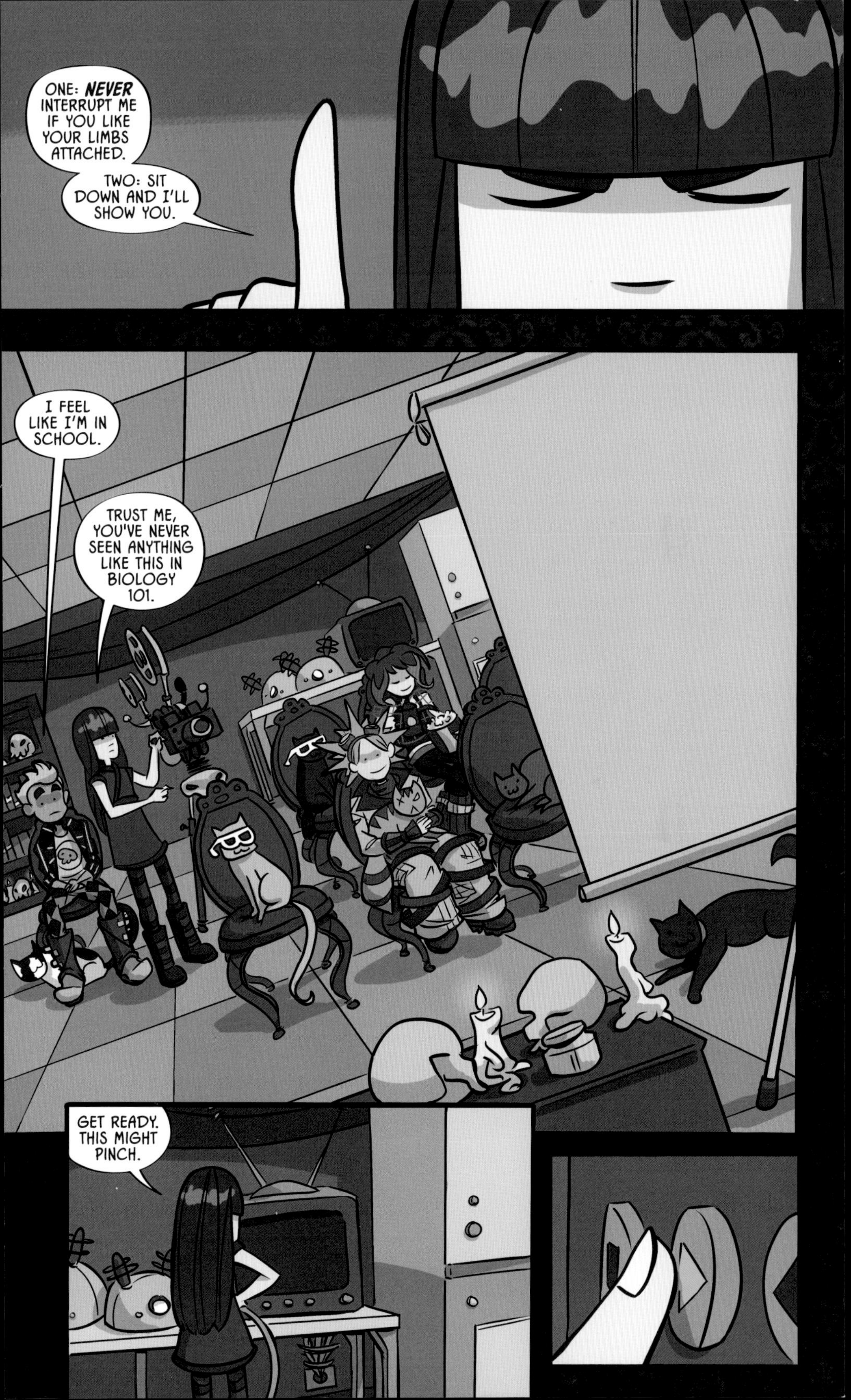
ONE: **NEVER** INTERRUPT ME IF YOU LIKE YOUR LIMBS ATTACHED.
TWO: SIT DOWN AND I'LL SHOW YOU.
I FEEL LIKE I'M IN SCHOOL.
TRUST ME, YOU'VE NEVER SEEN ANYTHING LIKE THIS IN BIOLOGY 101.
GET READY. THIS MIGHT PINCH.

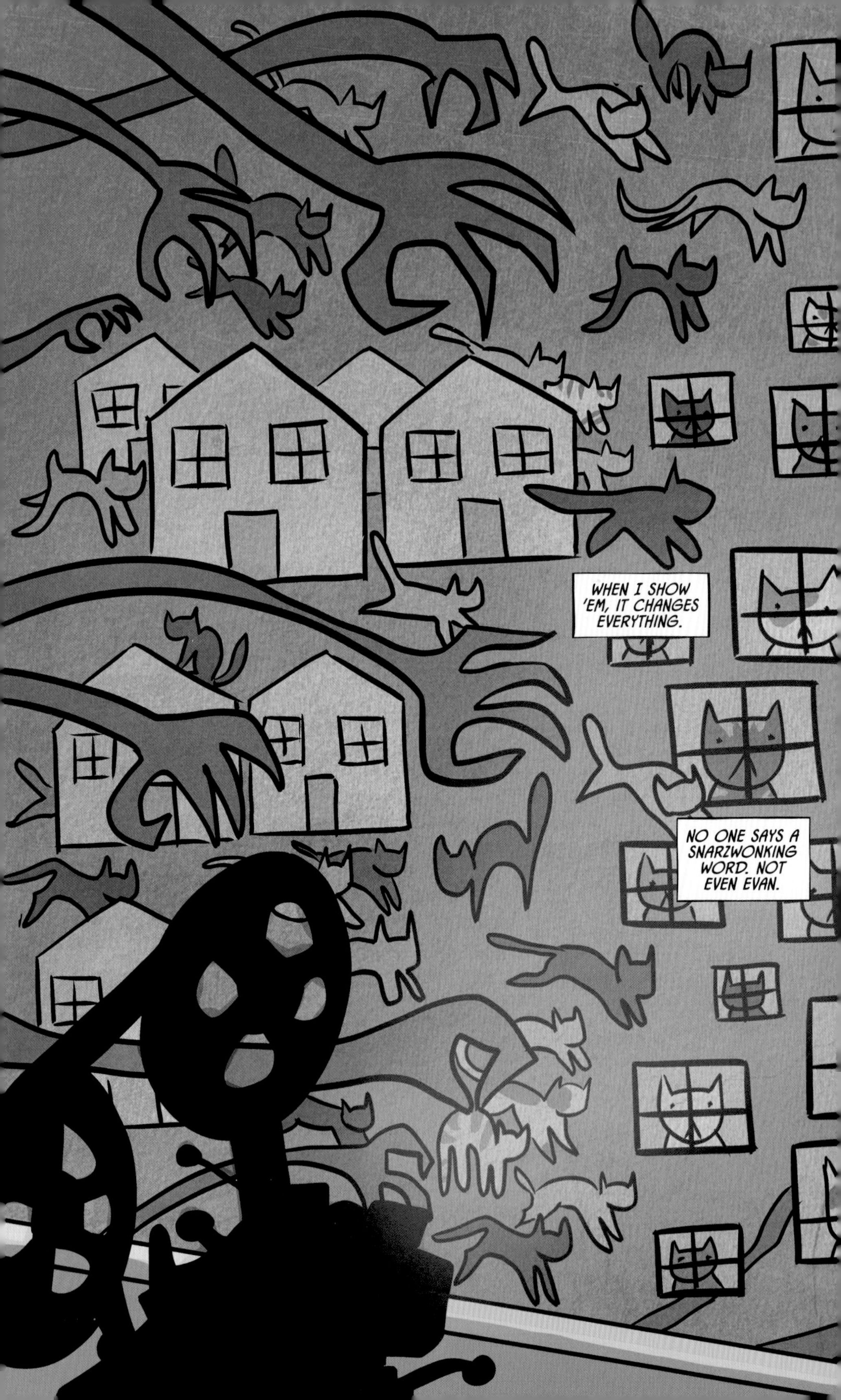
WHEN I SHOW 'EM, IT CHANGES EVERYTHING.
NO ONE SAYS A SNARZWONKING WORD. NOT EVEN EVAN.

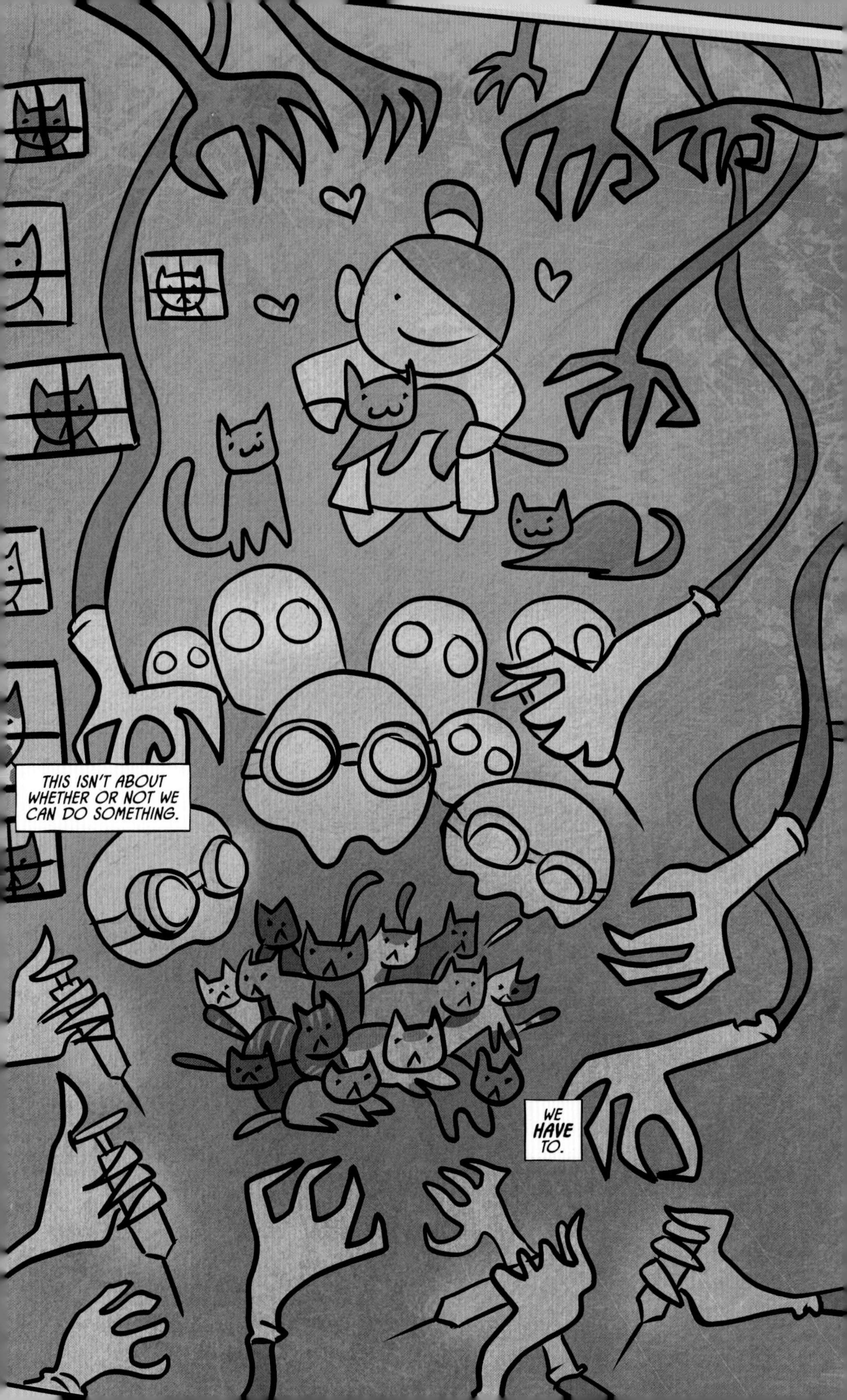
THIS ISN'T ABOUT WHETHER OR NOT WE CAN DO SOMETHING.
WE HAVE TO.

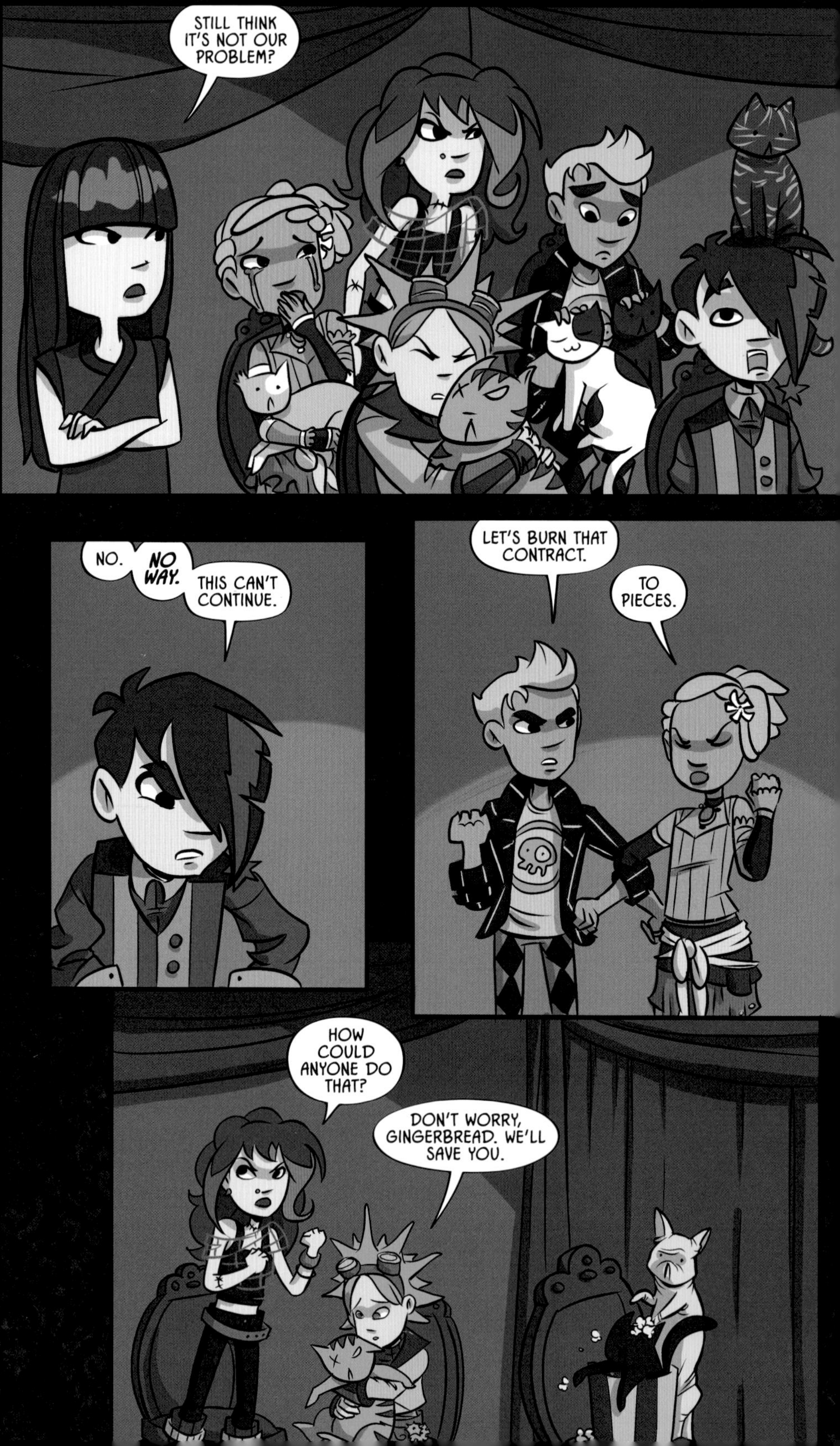
STILL THINK IT'S NOT OUR PROBLEM?
NO.
NO WAY.
THIS CAN'T CONTINUE.
LET'S BURN THAT CONTRACT.
TO PIECES.
HOW COULD ANYONE DO THAT?
DON'T WORRY, GINGERBREAD. WE'LL SAVE YOU.

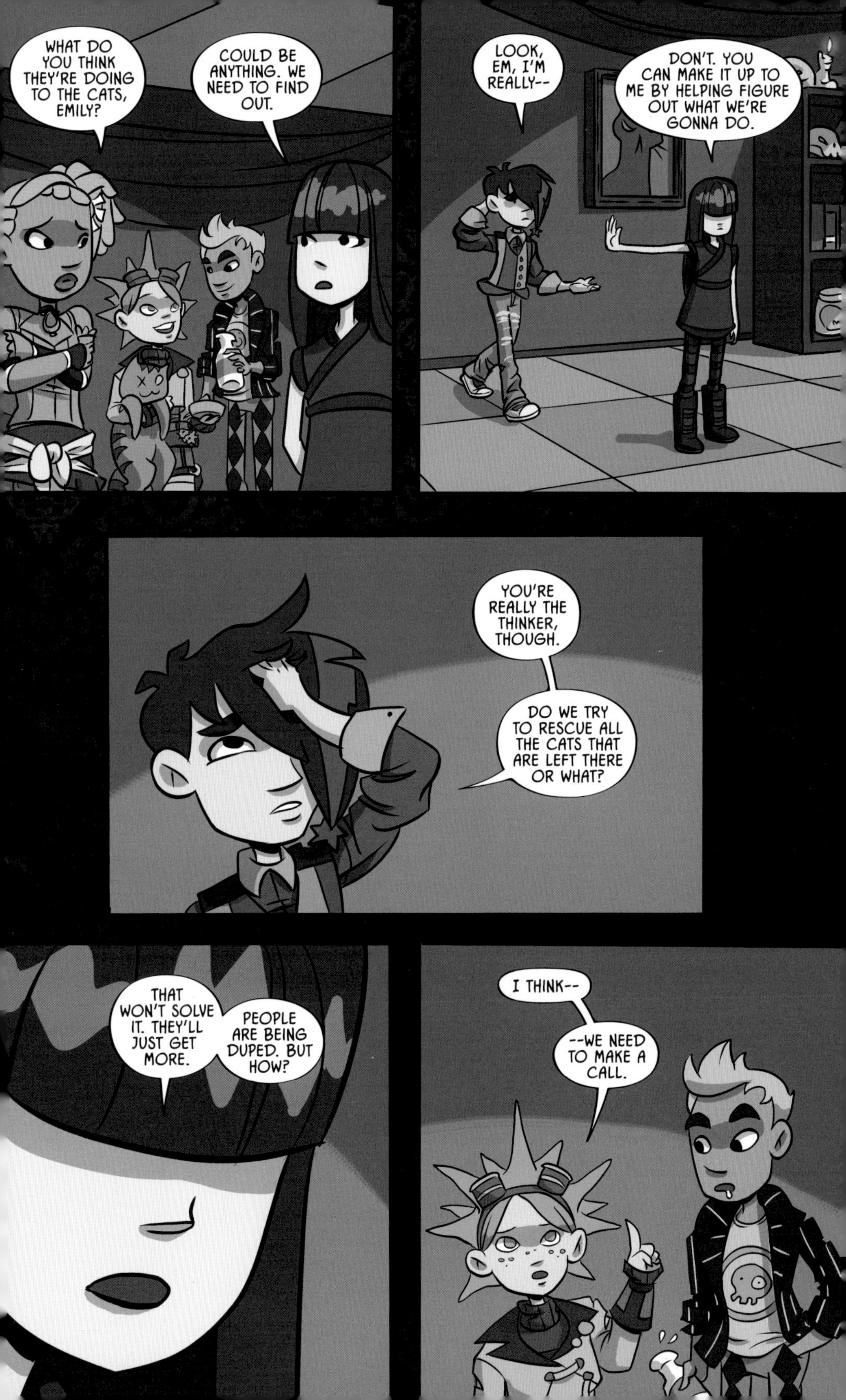
WHAT DO YOU THINK THEY'RE DOING TO THE CATS, EMILY?
COULD BE ANYTHING. WE NEED TO FIND OUT.
LOOK, EM, I'M REALLY--
DON'T. YOU CAN MAKE IT UP TO ME BY HELPING FIGURE OUT WHAT WE'RE GONNA DO.
YOU'RE REALLY THE THINKER, THOUGH.
DO WE TRY TO RESCUE ALL THE CATS THAT ARE LEFT THERE OR WHAT?
THAT WON'T SOLVE IT. THEY'LL JUST GET MORE.
PEOPLE ARE BEING DUPED. BUT HOW?
I THINK--
--WE NEED TO MAKE A CALL.

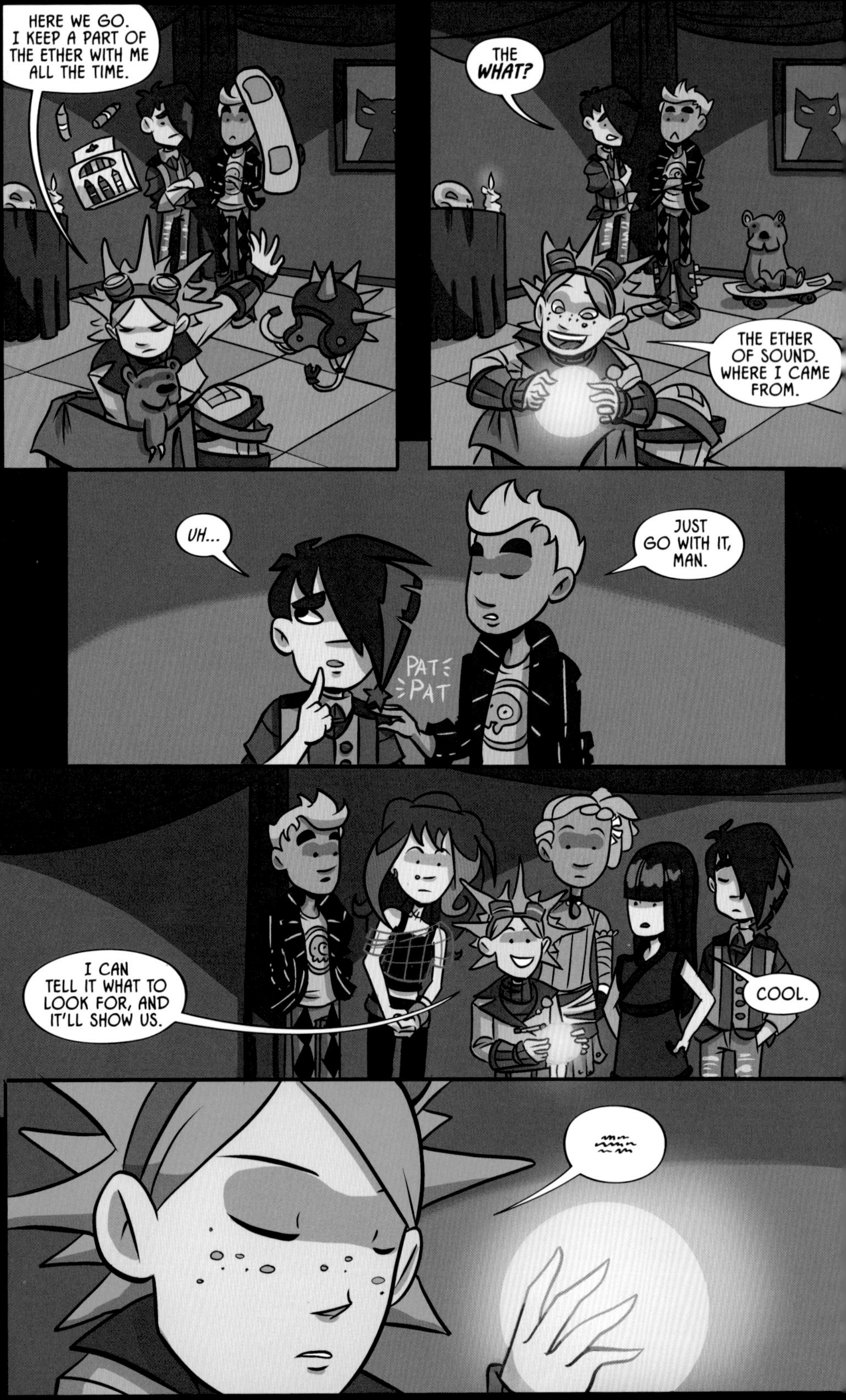
HERE WE GO. I KEEP A PART OF THE ETHER WITH ME ALL THE TIME.
THE *WHAT?*
THE ETHER OF SOUND. WHERE I CAME FROM.
UH...
JUST GO WITH IT, MAN.
PAT PAT
I CAN TELL IT WHAT TO LOOK FOR, AND IT'LL SHOW US.
COOL.

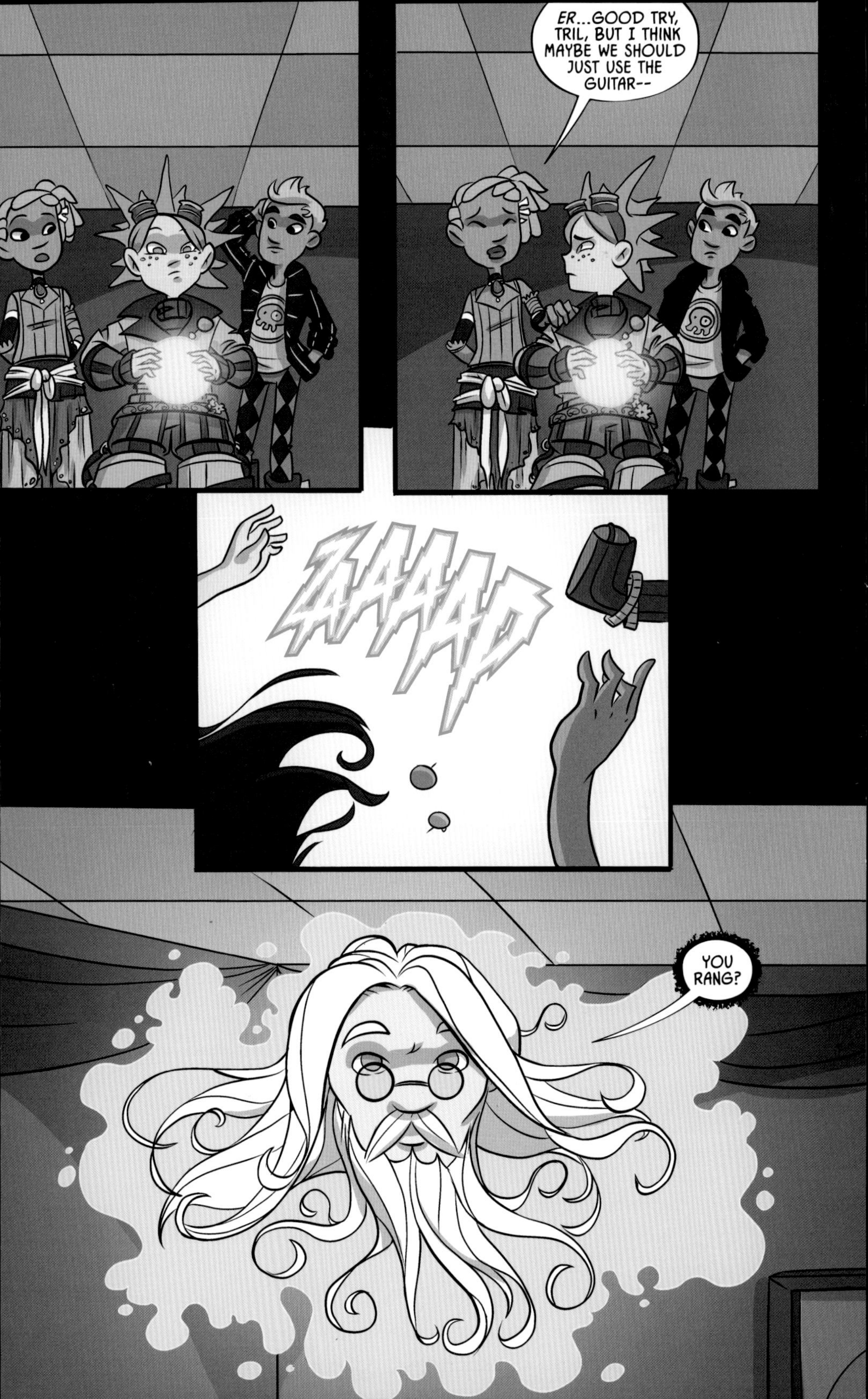
ER...GOOD TRY, TRIL, BUT I THINK MAYBE WE SHOULD JUST USE THE GUITAR--
ZAAAAD
YOU RANG?

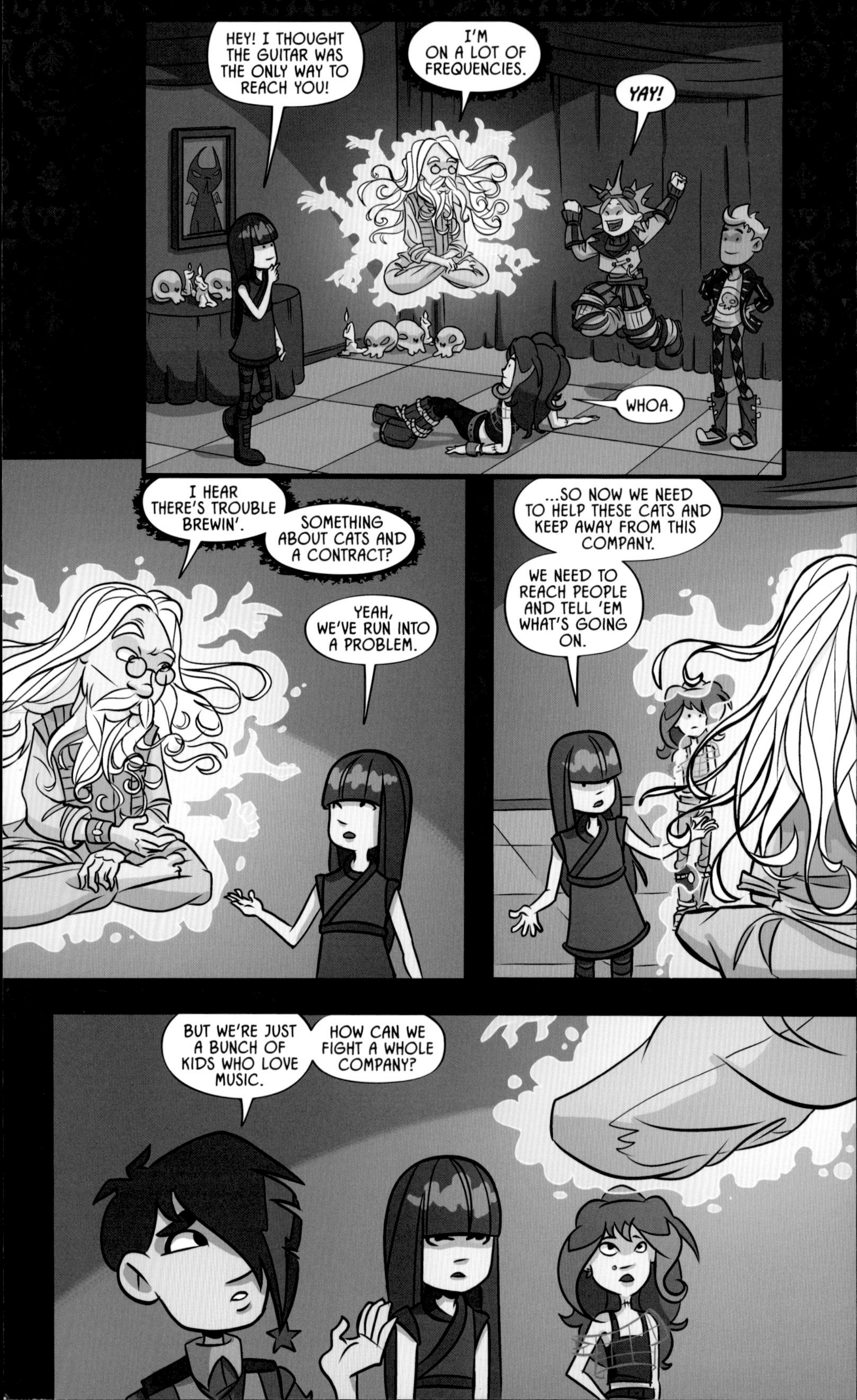
HEY! I THOUGHT THE GUITAR WAS THE ONLY WAY TO REACH YOU!
I'M ON A LOT OF FREQUENCIES.
YAY!
WHOA.
I HEAR THERE'S TROUBLE BREWIN'.
SOMETHING ABOUT CATS AND A CONTRACT?
YEAH, WE'VE RUN INTO A PROBLEM.
...SO NOW WE NEED TO HELP THESE CATS AND KEEP AWAY FROM THIS COMPANY.
WE NEED TO REACH PEOPLE AND TELL 'EM WHAT'S GOING ON.
BUT WE'RE JUST A BUNCH OF KIDS WHO LOVE MUSIC.
HOW CAN WE FIGHT A WHOLE COMPANY?

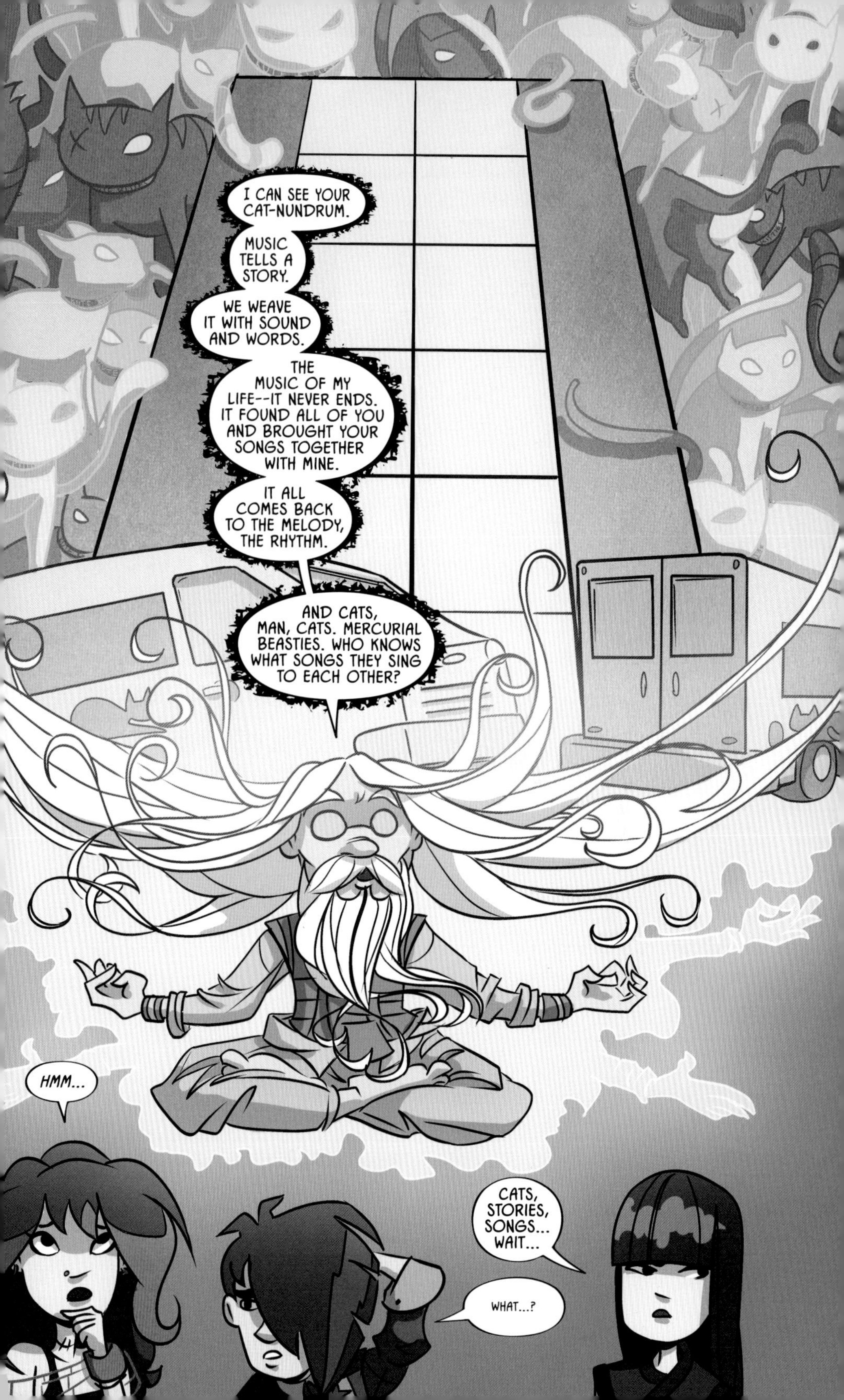
I CAN SEE YOUR CAT-NUNDRUM.
MUSIC TELLS A STORY.
WE WEAVE IT WITH SOUND AND WORDS.
THE MUSIC OF MY LIFE--IT NEVER ENDS. IT FOUND ALL OF YOU AND BROUGHT YOUR SONGS TOGETHER WITH MINE.
IT ALL COMES BACK TO THE MELODY, THE RHYTHM.
AND CATS, MAN, CATS. MERCURIAL BEASTIES. WHO KNOWS WHAT SONGS THEY SING TO EACH OTHER?
HMM...
CATS, STORIES, SONGS... WAIT...
WHAT...?

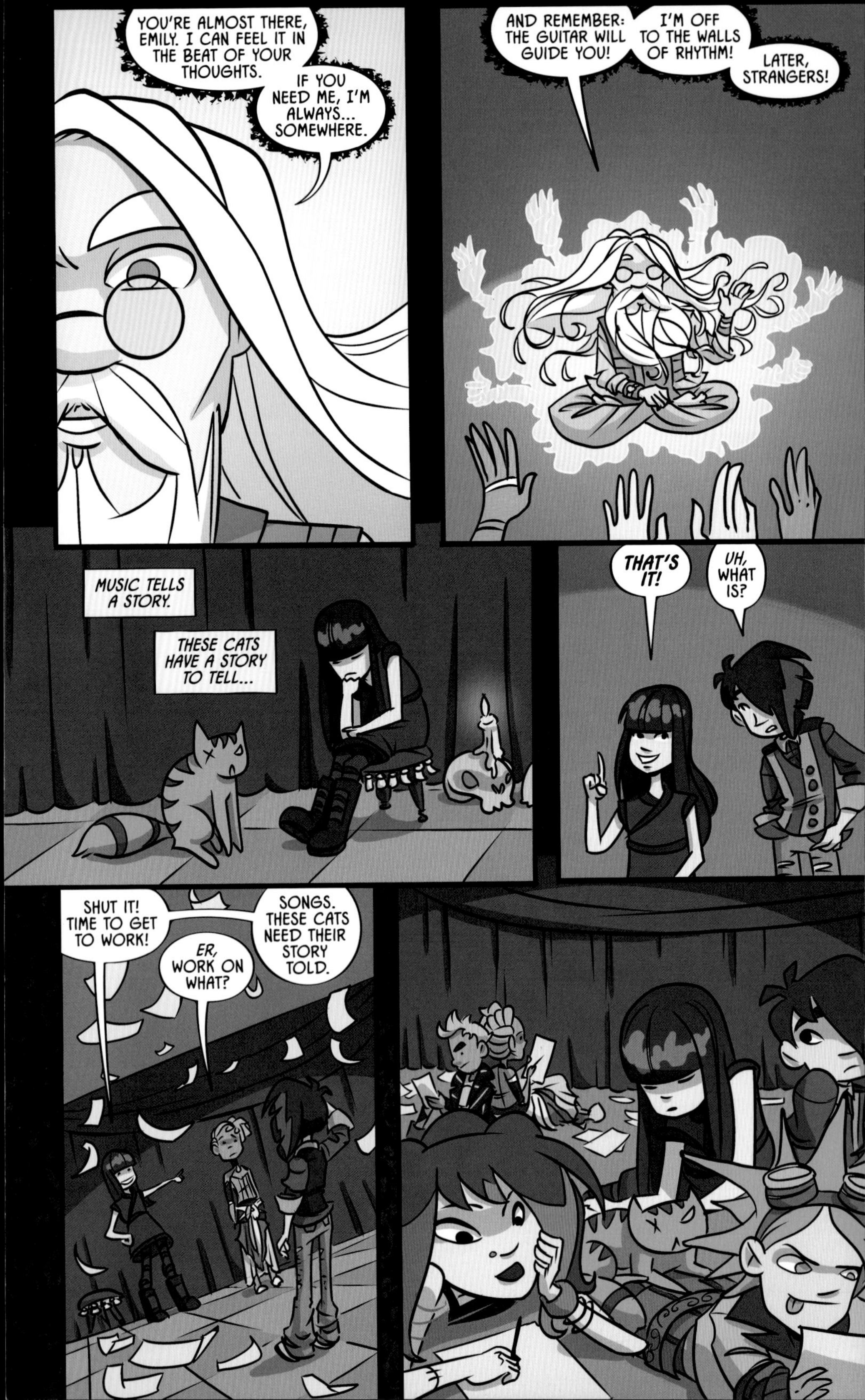
YOU'RE ALMOST THERE, EMILY. I CAN FEEL IT IN THE BEAT OF YOUR THOUGHTS.
IF YOU NEED ME, I'M ALWAYS... SOMEWHERE.
AND REMEMBER: THE GUITAR WILL GUIDE YOU!
I'M OFF TO THE WALLS OF RHYTHM!
LATER, STRANGERS!
MUSIC TELLS A STORY.
THESE CATS HAVE A STORY TO TELL...
THAT'S IT!
UH, WHAT IS?
SHUT IT! TIME TO GET TO WORK!
ER, WORK ON WHAT?
SONGS. THESE CATS NEED THEIR STORY TOLD.

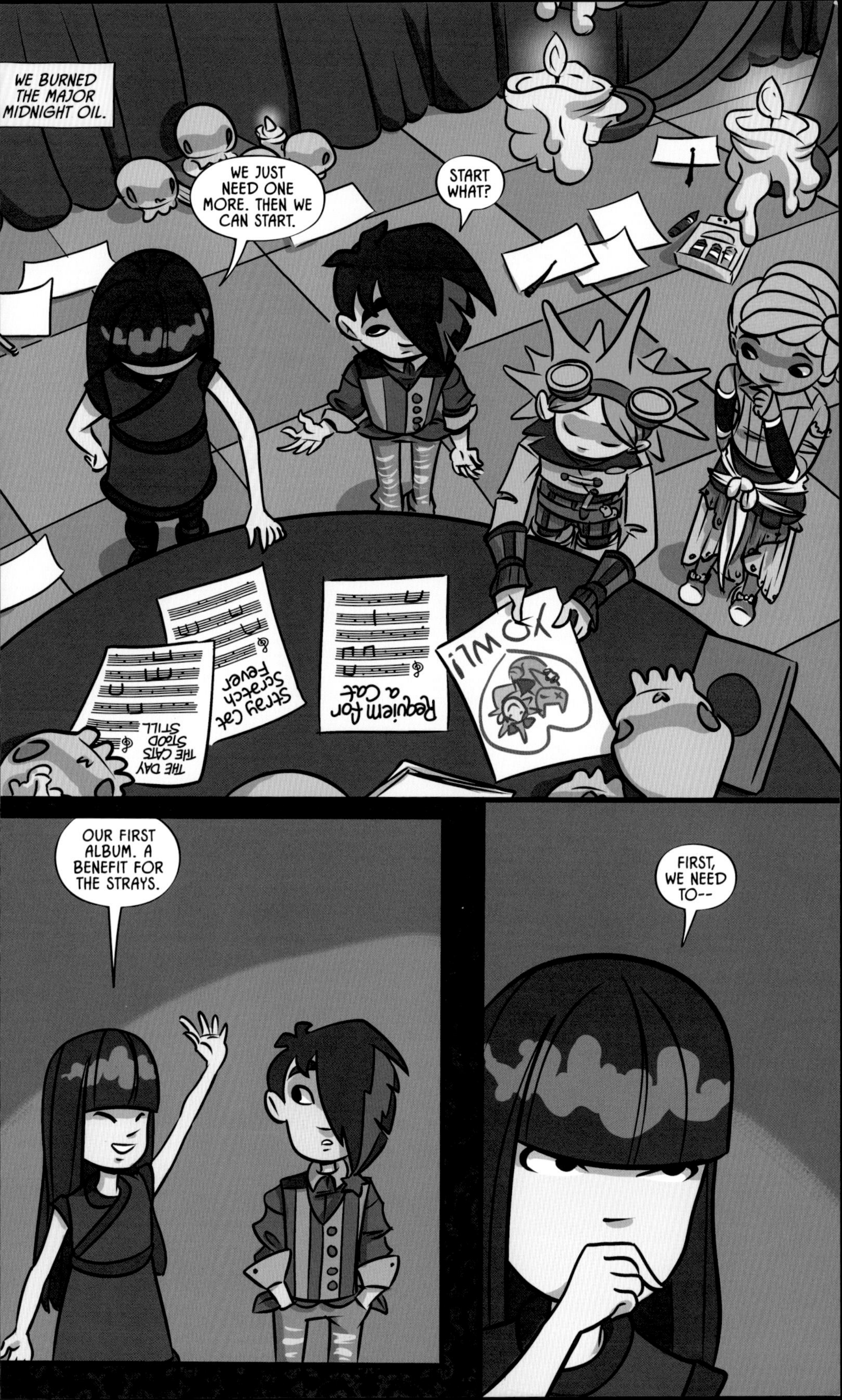
WE BURNED THE MAJOR MIDNIGHT OIL.
WE JUST NEED ONE MORE. THEN WE CAN START.
START WHAT?
THE DAY THE CATS STOOD STILL
Stray Cat Scratch Fever
Requiem for a Cat
YO WL!
OUR FIRST ALBUM. A BENEFIT FOR THE STRAYS.
FIRST, WE NEED TO--

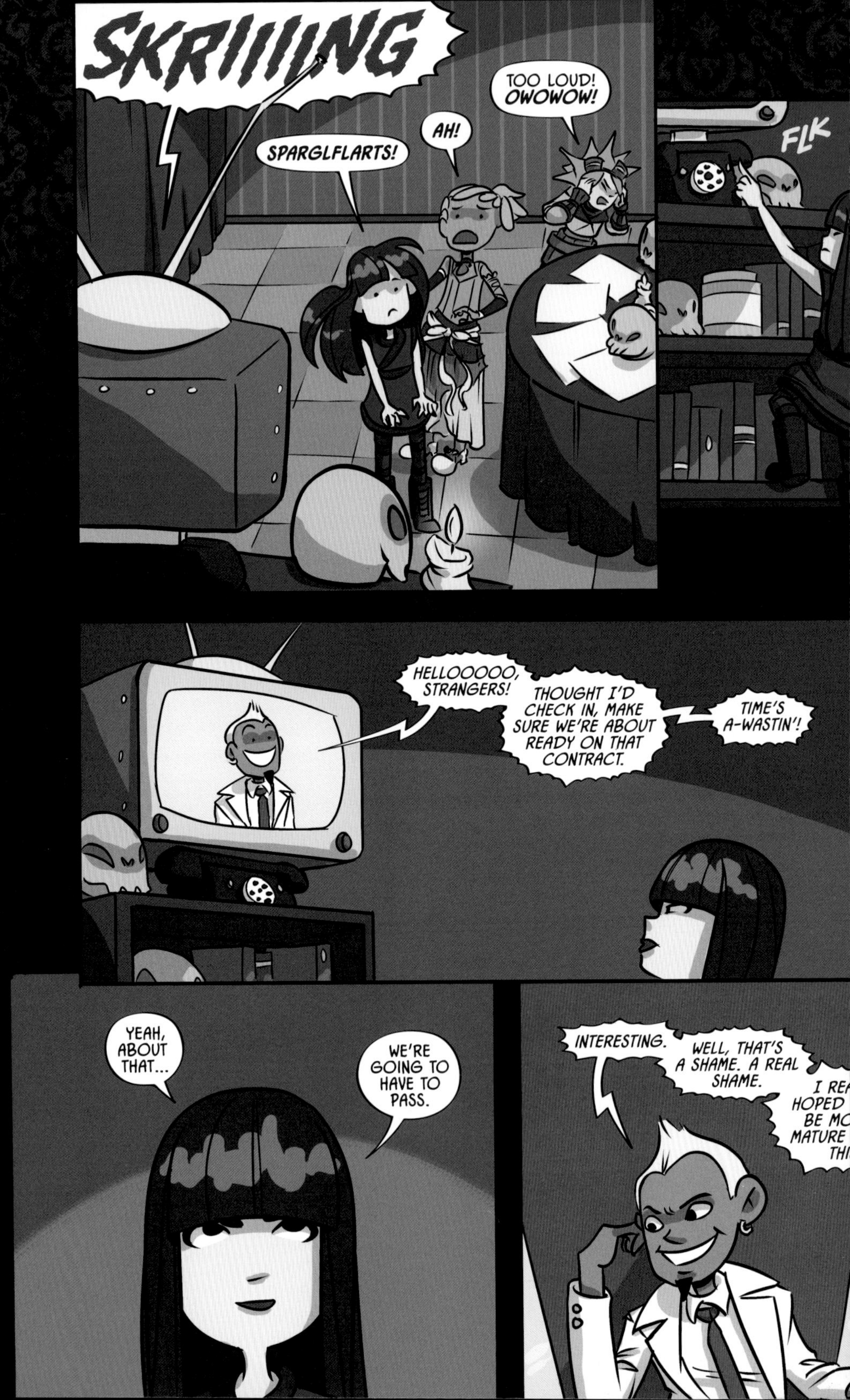
SKRIIIING
SPARGLFLARTS!
AH!
TOO LOUD! OWOWOW!
FLK
HELLOOOOO, STRANGERS!
THOUGHT I'D CHECK IN, MAKE SURE WE'RE ABOUT READY ON THAT CONTRACT.
TIME'S A-WASTIN'!
YEAH, ABOUT THAT...
WE'RE GOING TO HAVE TO PASS.
INTERESTING.
WELL, THAT'S A SHAME. A REAL SHAME.

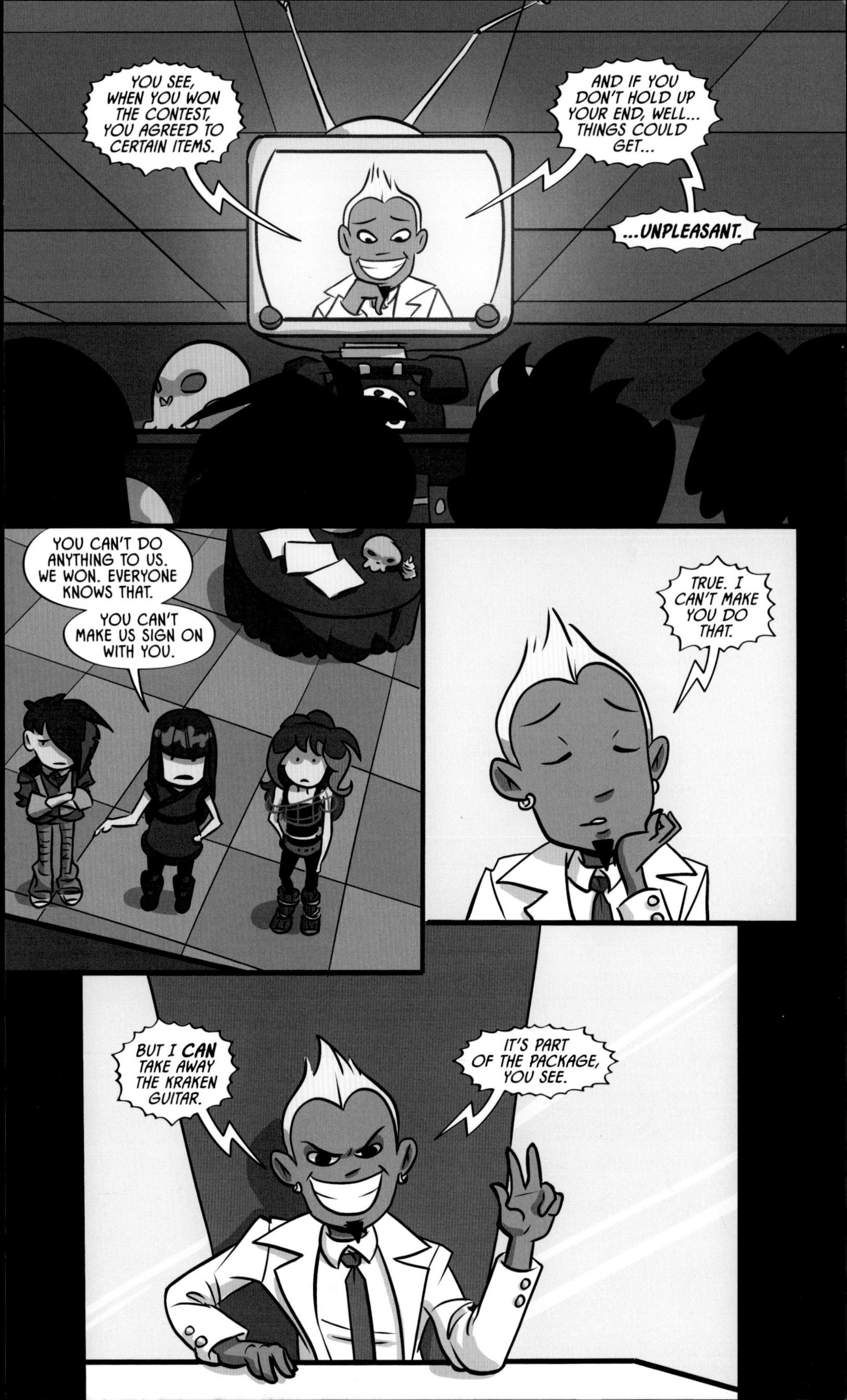
YOU SEE, WHEN YOU WON THE CONTEST, YOU AGREED TO CERTAIN ITEMS.
AND IF YOU DON'T HOLD UP YOUR END, WELL... THINGS COULD GET...
...UNPLEASANT.
YOU CAN'T DO ANYTHING TO US. WE WON. EVERYONE KNOWS THAT.
YOU CAN'T MAKE US SIGN ON WITH YOU.
TRUE. I CAN'T MAKE YOU DO THAT.
BUT I CAN TAKE AWAY THE KRAKEN GUITAR.
IT'S PART OF THE PACKAGE, YOU SEE.

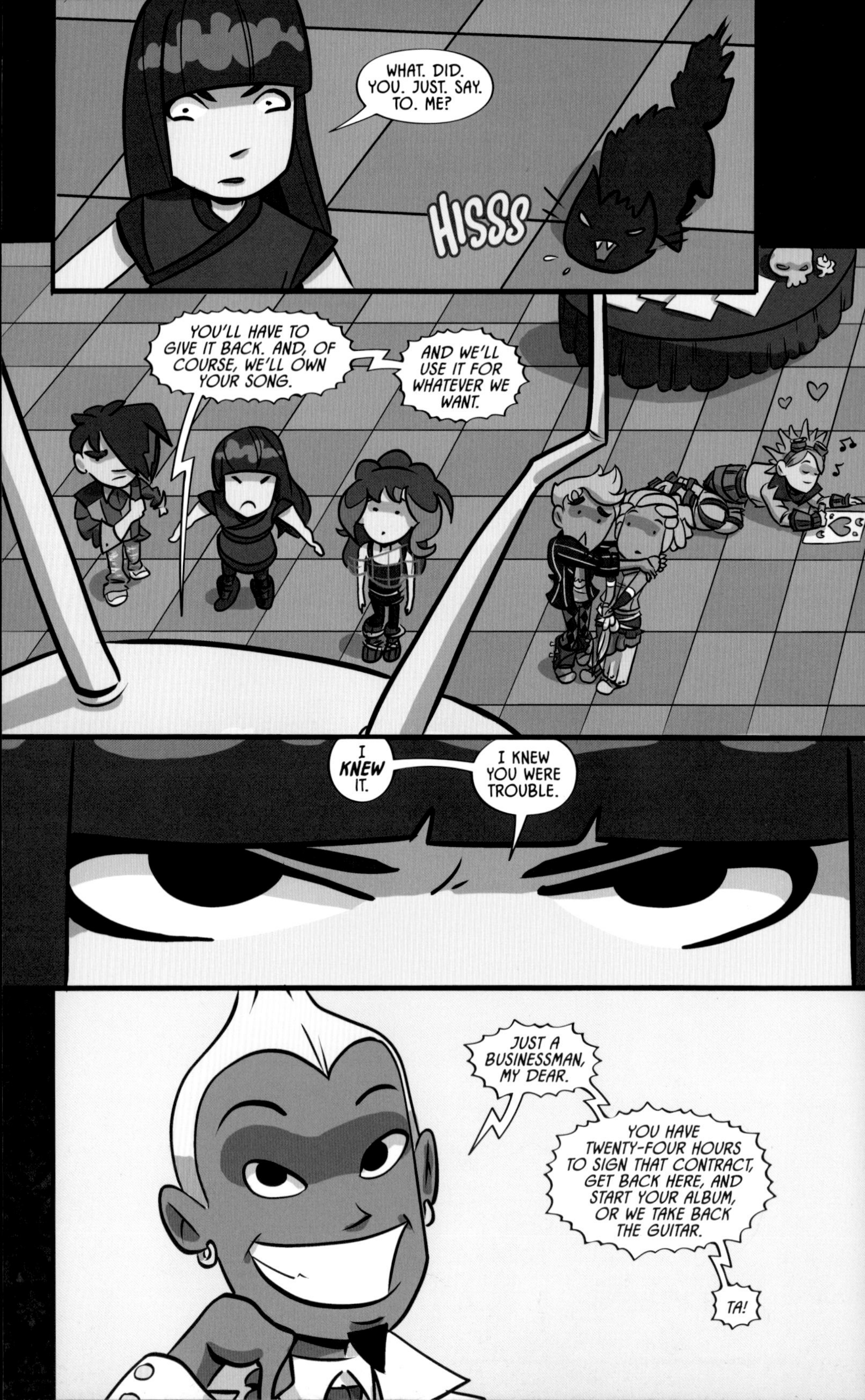
WHAT. DID. YOU. JUST. SAY. TO. ME?
HISSS
YOU'LL HAVE TO GIVE IT BACK. AND, OF COURSE, WE'LL OWN YOUR SONG.
AND WE'LL USE IT FOR WHATEVER WE WANT.
I KNEW IT.
I KNEW YOU WERE TROUBLE.
JUST A BUSINESSMAN, MY DEAR.
YOU HAVE TWENTY-FOUR HOURS TO SIGN THAT CONTRACT, GET BACK HERE, AND START YOUR ALBUM, OR WE TAKE BACK THE GUITAR.
TA!

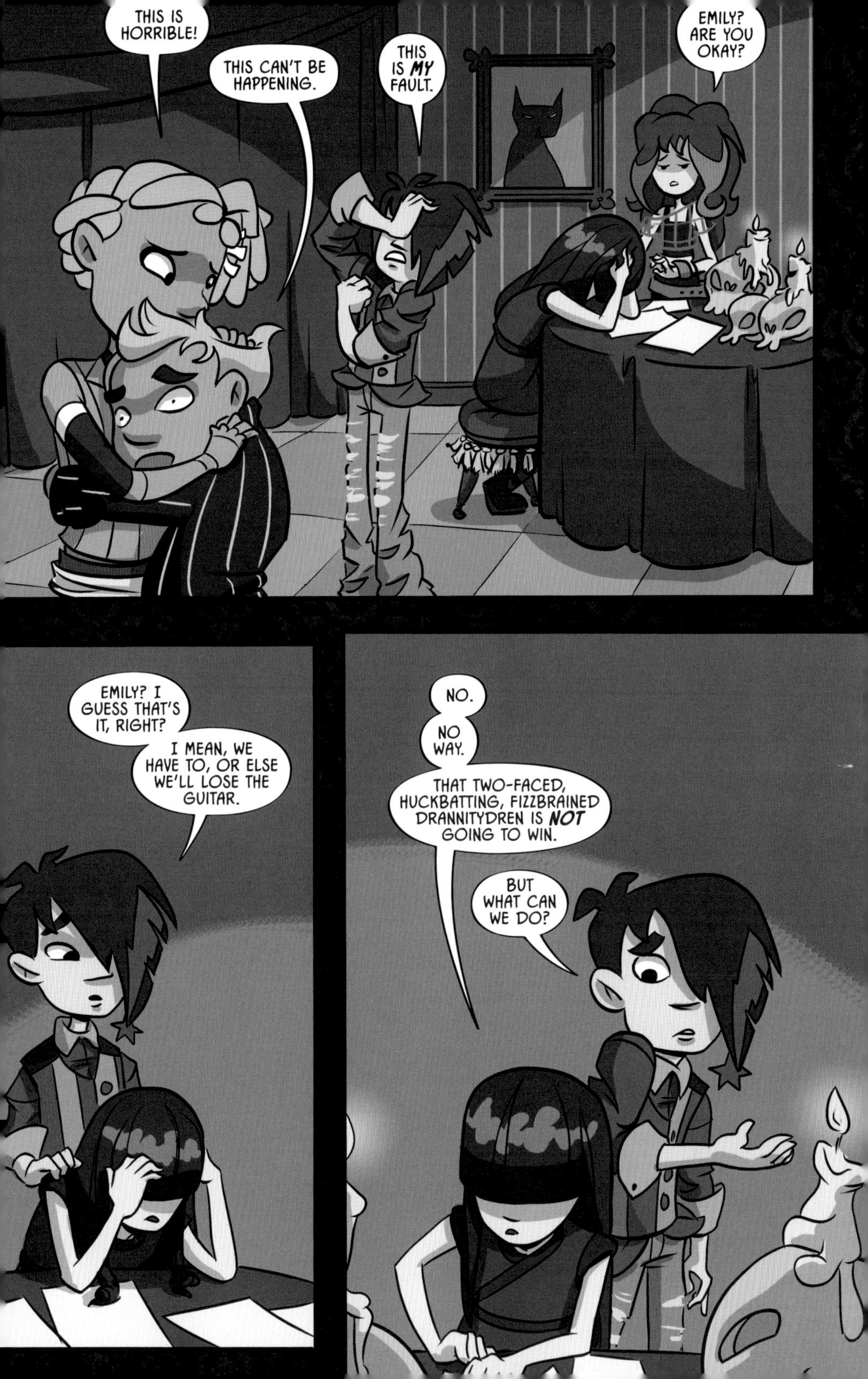
THIS IS HORRIBLE!
THIS CAN'T BE HAPPENING.
THIS IS *MY* FAULT.
EMILY? ARE YOU OKAY?
EMILY? I GUESS THAT'S IT, RIGHT?
I MEAN, WE HAVE TO, OR ELSE WE'LL LOSE THE GUITAR.
NO.
NO WAY.
THAT TWO-FACED, HUCKBATTING, FIZZBRAINED DRANNITYDREN IS *NOT* GOING TO WIN.
BUT WHAT CAN WE DO?

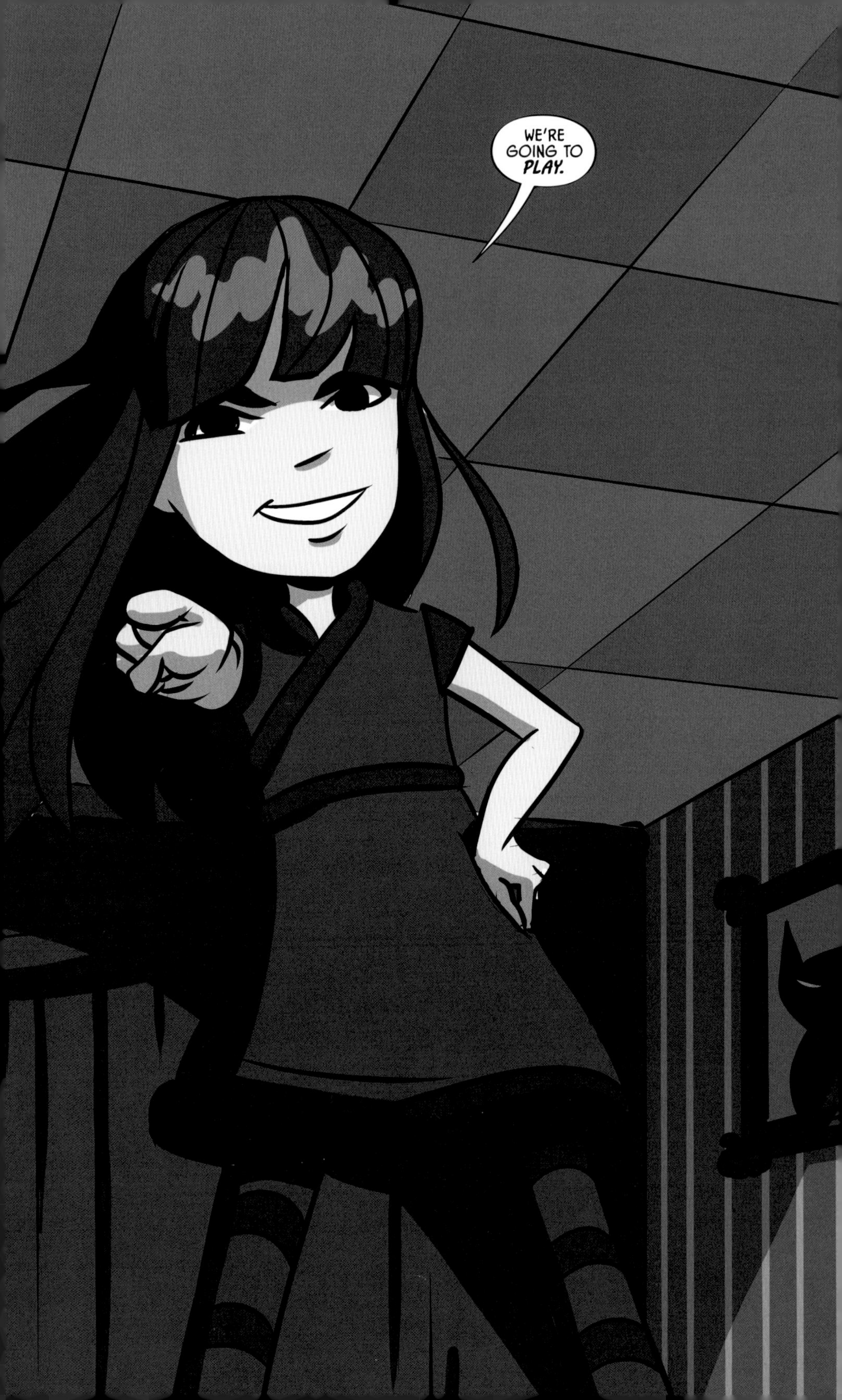
WE'RE GOING TO PLAY.

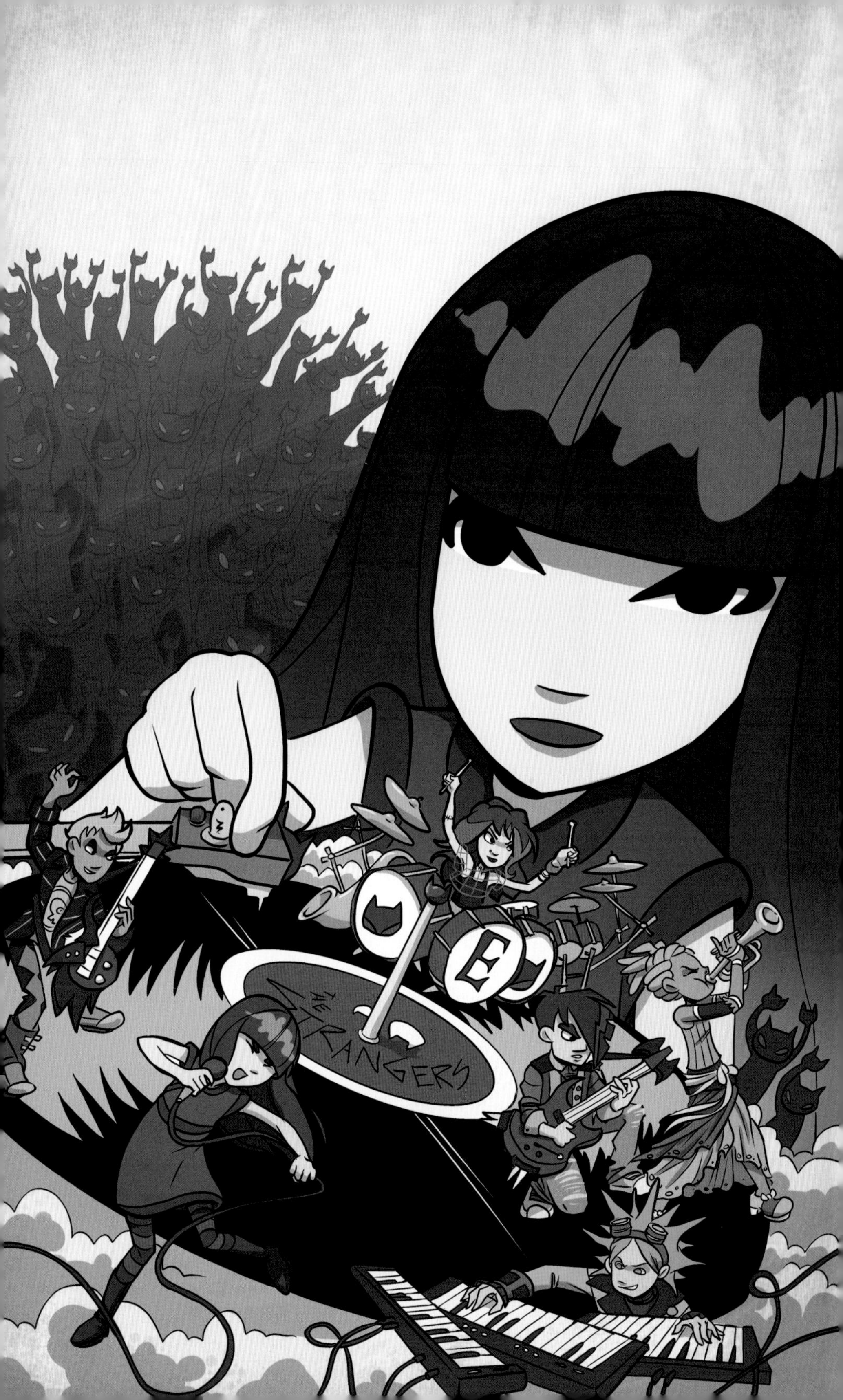
THE STRANGERS

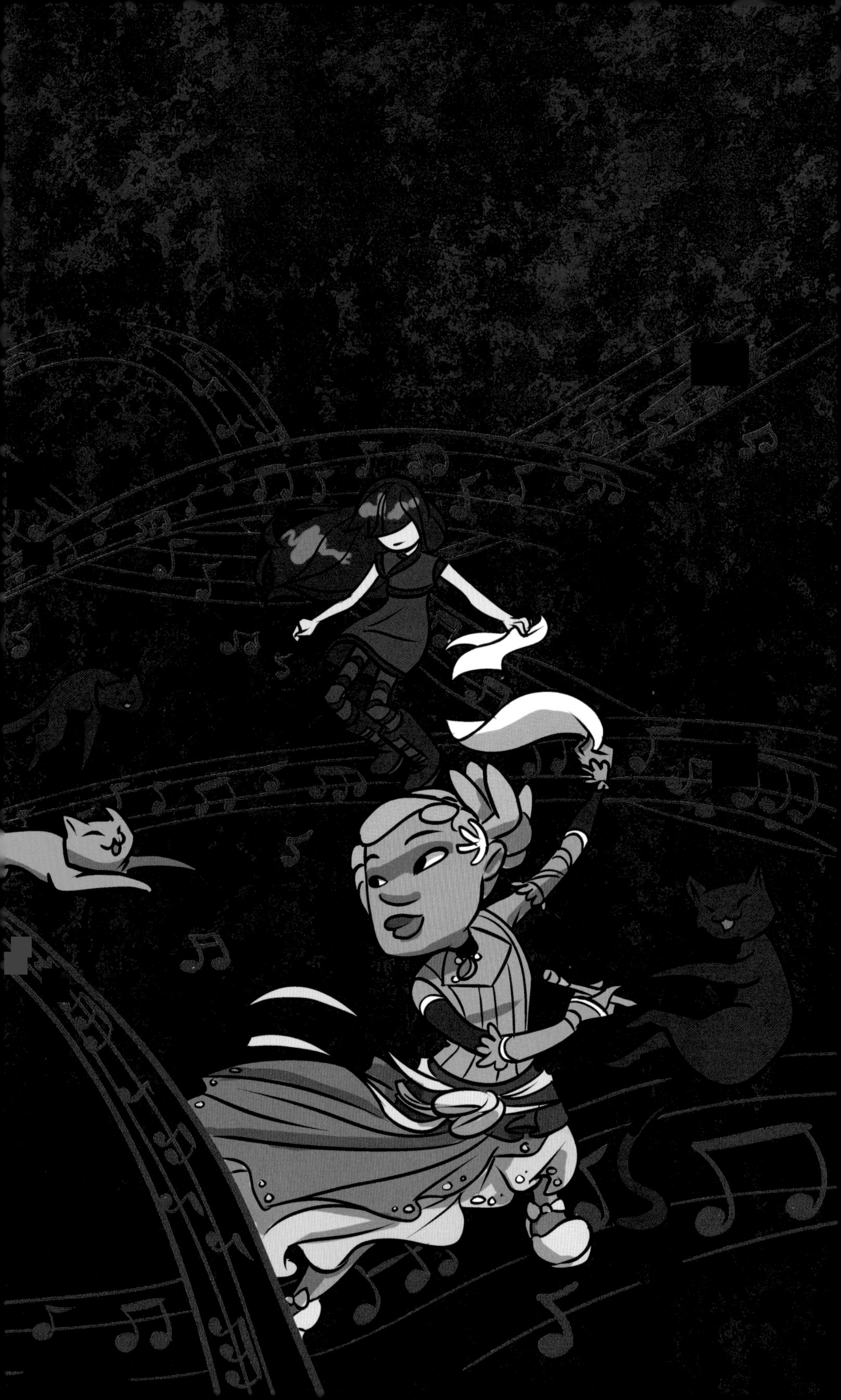

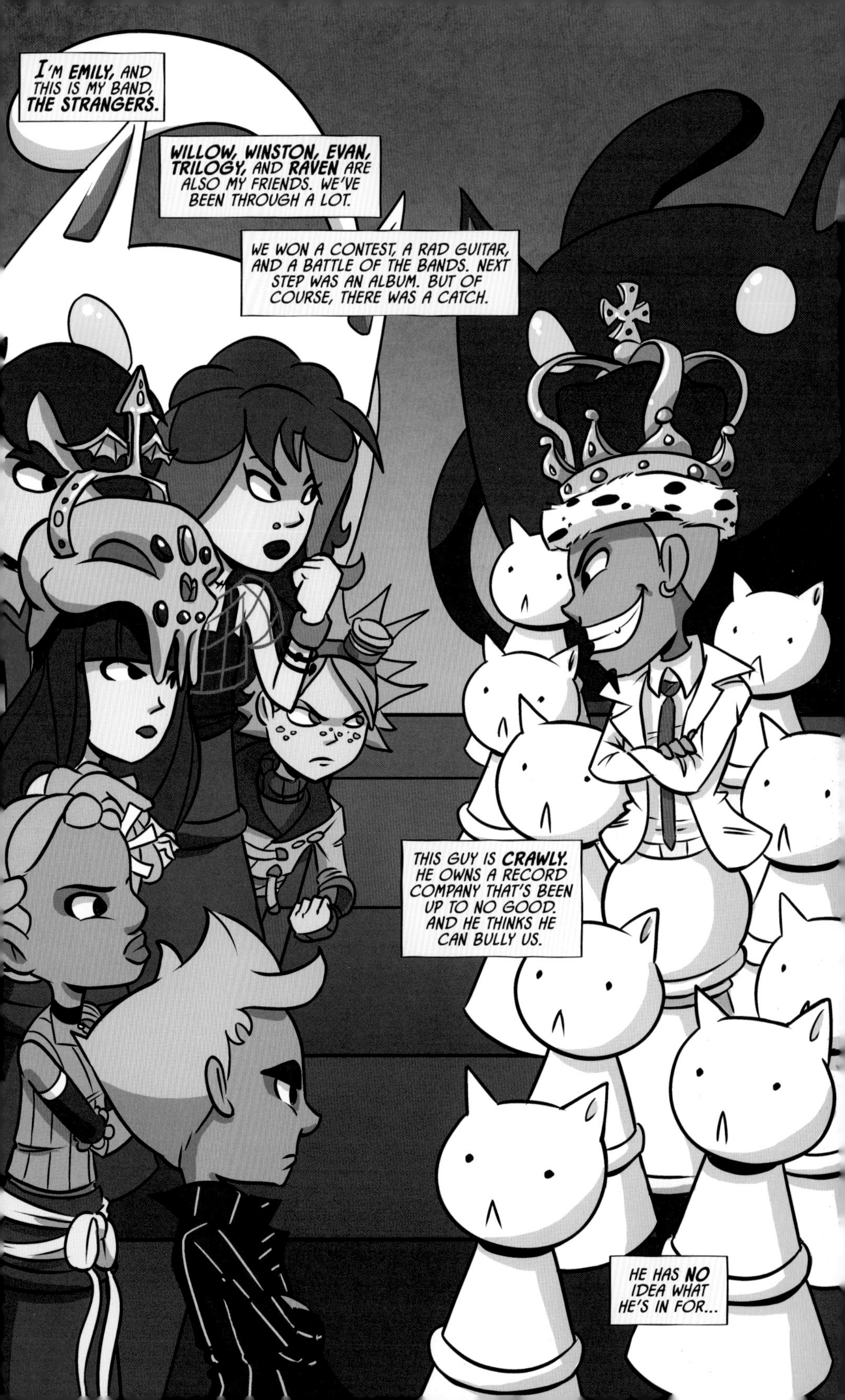
I'M EMILY, AND THIS IS MY BAND, THE STRANGERS.
WILLOW, WINSTON, EVAN, TRILOGY, AND RAVEN ARE ALSO MY FRIENDS. WE'VE BEEN THROUGH A LOT.
WE WON A CONTEST, A RAD GUITAR, AND A BATTLE OF THE BANDS. NEXT STEP WAS AN ALBUM. BUT OF COURSE, THERE WAS A CATCH.
THIS GUY IS CRAWLY. HE OWNS A RECORD COMPANY THAT'S BEEN UP TO NO GOOD. AND HE THINKS HE CAN BULLY US.
HE HAS NO IDEA WHAT HE'S IN FOR...

EVERYONE'S HEAD IS LIKE A JUNK PILE.

MEMORIES, HOPES, DREAMS...WE ALL WANT A LOT OUT OF THIS WHOLE BAND THING.

WISH I COULD SEE WHAT THE OTHERS ARE THINKIN', BUT RIGHT NOW I'VE GOT ENOUGH ON MY MIND.

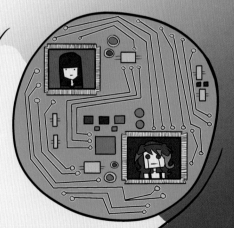

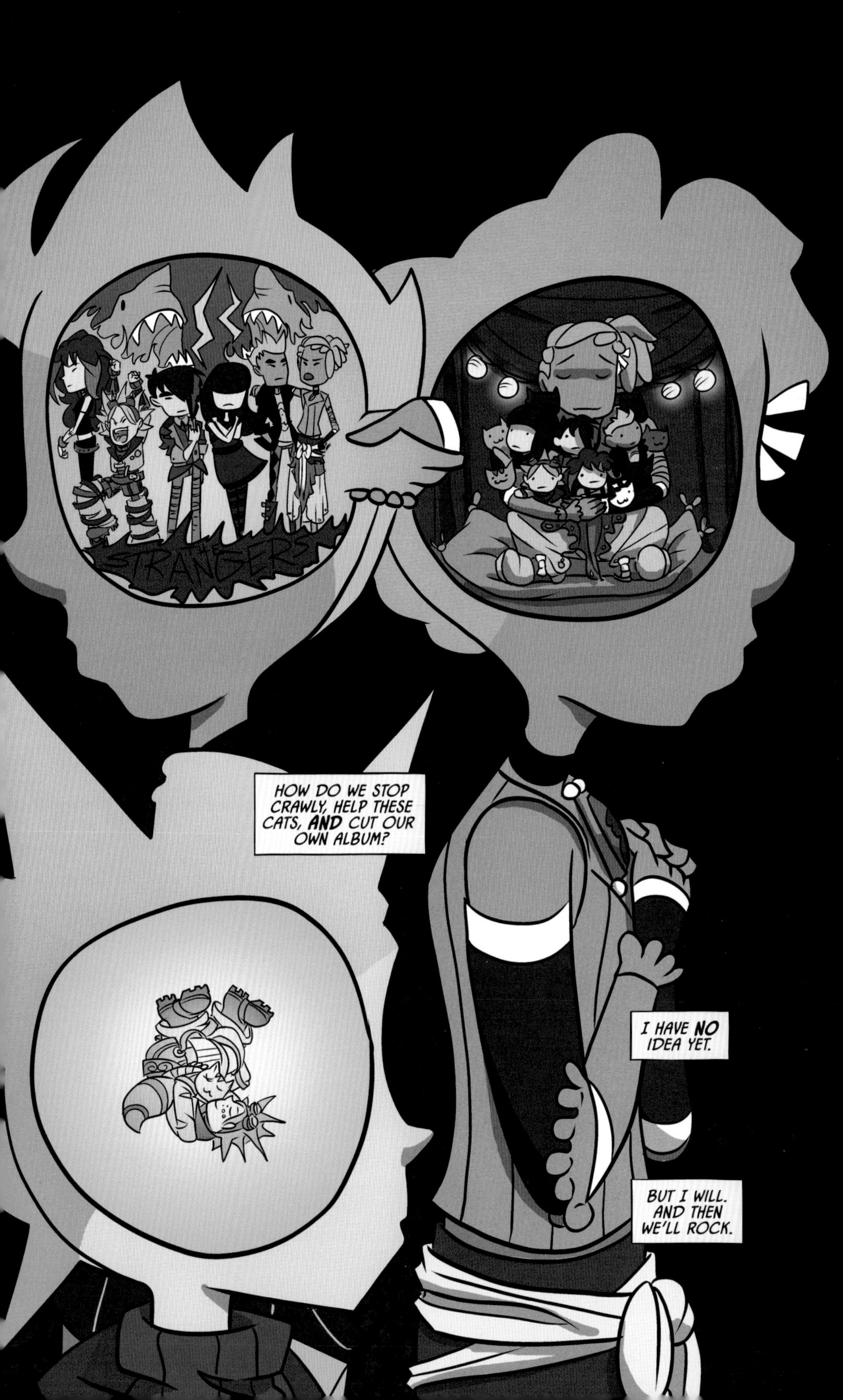

STRANGERS
HOW DO WE STOP CRAWLY, HELP THESE CATS, **AND** CUT OUR OWN ALBUM?
I HAVE **NO** IDEA YET.
BUT I WILL. AND THEN WE'LL ROCK.

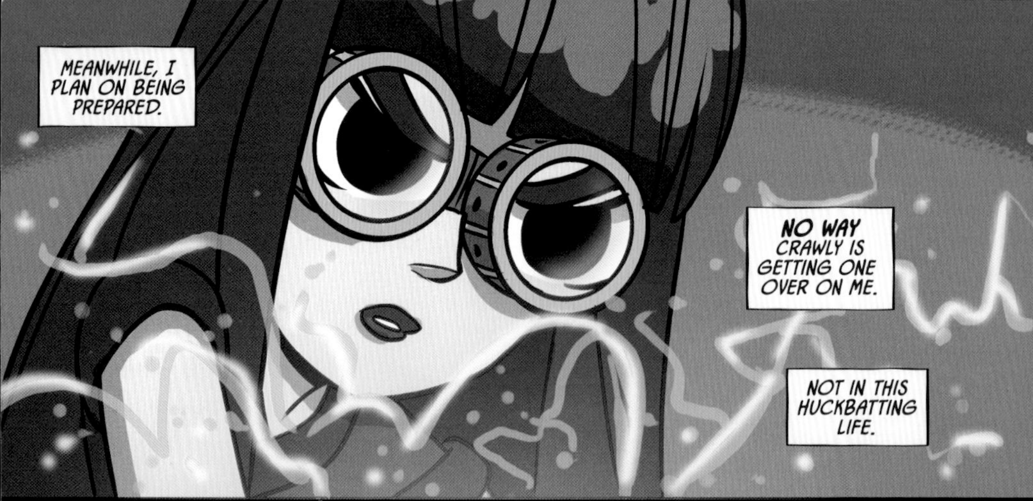
MEANWHILE, I PLAN ON BEING PREPARED.
NO WAY CRAWLY IS GETTING ONE OVER ON ME.
NOT IN THIS HUCKBATTING LIFE.

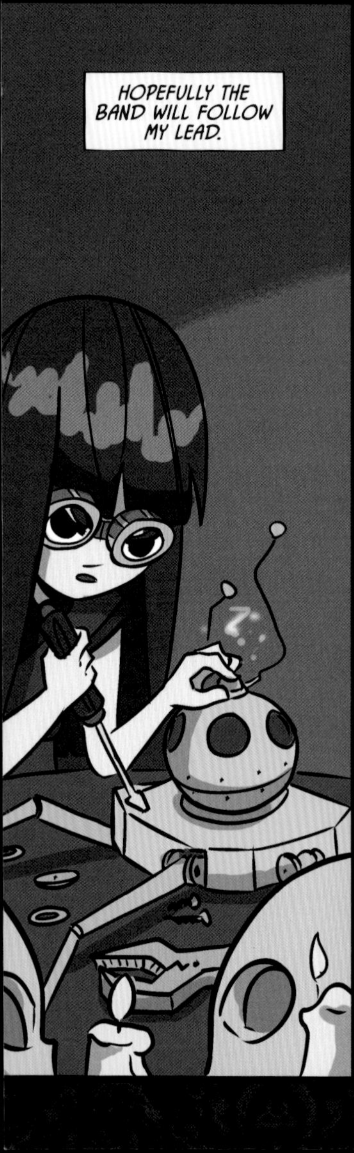
HOPEFULLY THE BAND WILL FOLLOW MY LEAD.

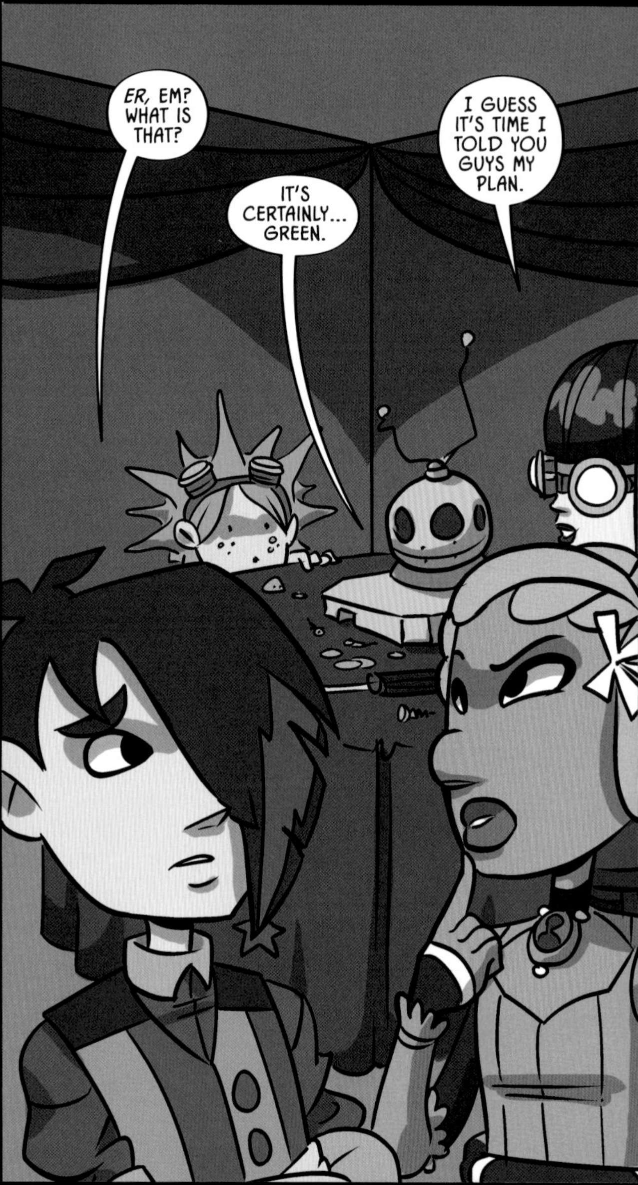
ER, EM? WHAT IS THAT?
IT'S CERTAINLY... GREEN.
I GUESS IT'S TIME I TOLD YOU GUYS MY PLAN.

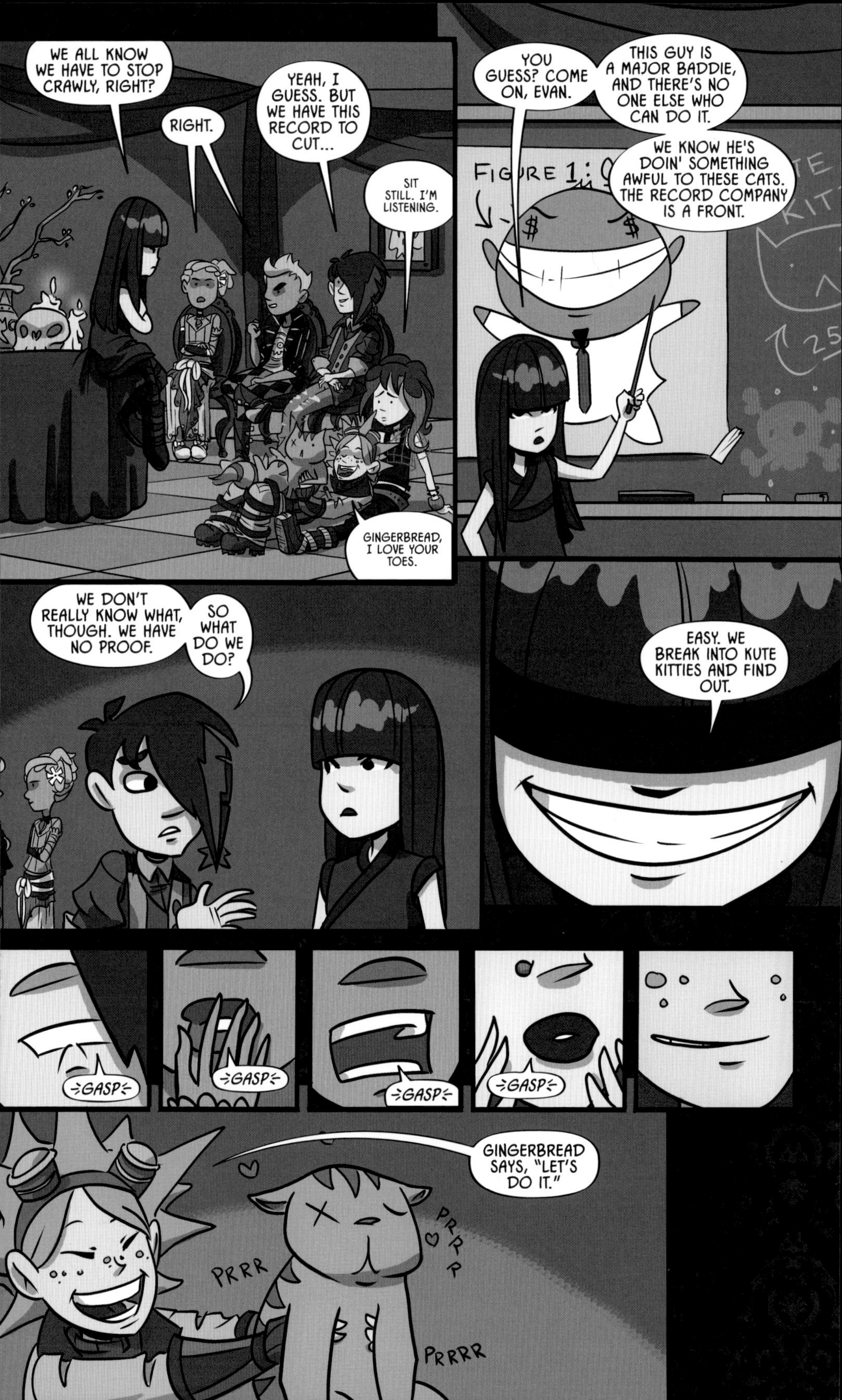
WE ALL KNOW WE HAVE TO STOP CRAWLY, RIGHT?
RIGHT.
YEAH, I GUESS. BUT WE HAVE THIS RECORD TO CUT...
SIT STILL. I'M LISTENING.
GINGERBREAD, I LOVE YOUR TOES.
YOU GUESS? COME ON, EVAN.
THIS GUY IS A MAJOR BADDIE, AND THERE'S NO ONE ELSE WHO CAN DO IT.
WE KNOW HE'S DOIN' SOMETHING AWFUL TO THESE CATS. THE RECORD COMPANY IS A FRONT.
FIGURE 1:
WE DON'T REALLY KNOW WHAT, THOUGH. WE HAVE NO PROOF.
SO WHAT DO WE DO?
EASY. WE BREAK INTO KUTE KITTIES AND FIND OUT.
GASP
GASP
GASP
GASP
GINGERBREAD SAYS, "LET'S DO IT."
PRRR
PRRR
PRRRR

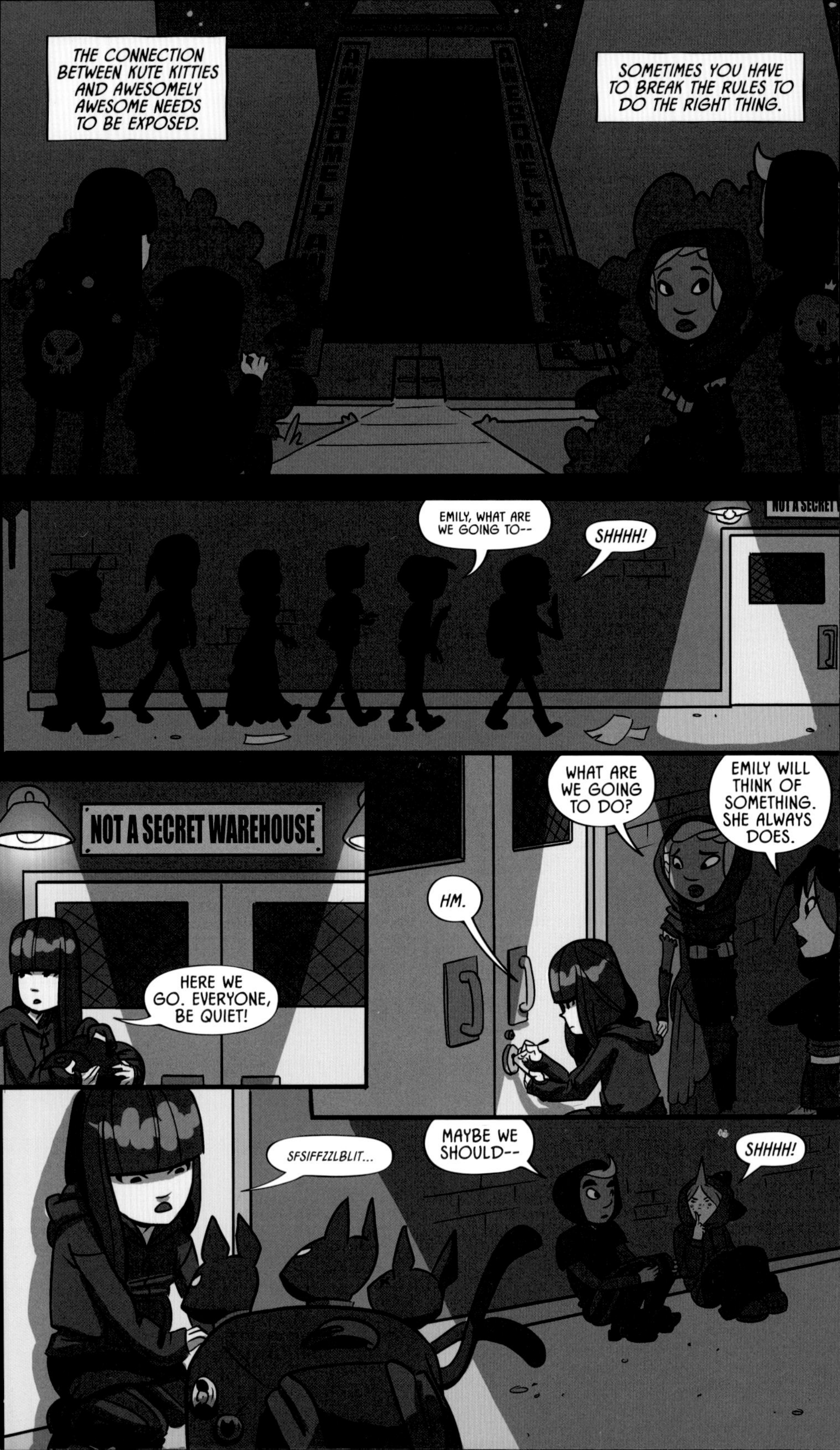
THE CONNECTION BETWEEN KUTE KITTIES AND AWESOMELY AWESOME NEEDS TO BE EXPOSED.
SOMETIMES YOU HAVE TO BREAK THE RULES TO DO THE RIGHT THING.
EMILY, WHAT ARE WE GOING TO--
SHHHH!
NOT A SECRET WAREHOUSE
HERE WE GO. EVERYONE, BE QUIET!
WHAT ARE WE GOING TO DO?
EMILY WILL THINK OF SOMETHING. SHE ALWAYS DOES.
HM.
SFSIFFZZLBLIT...
MAYBE WE SHOULD--
SHHHH!

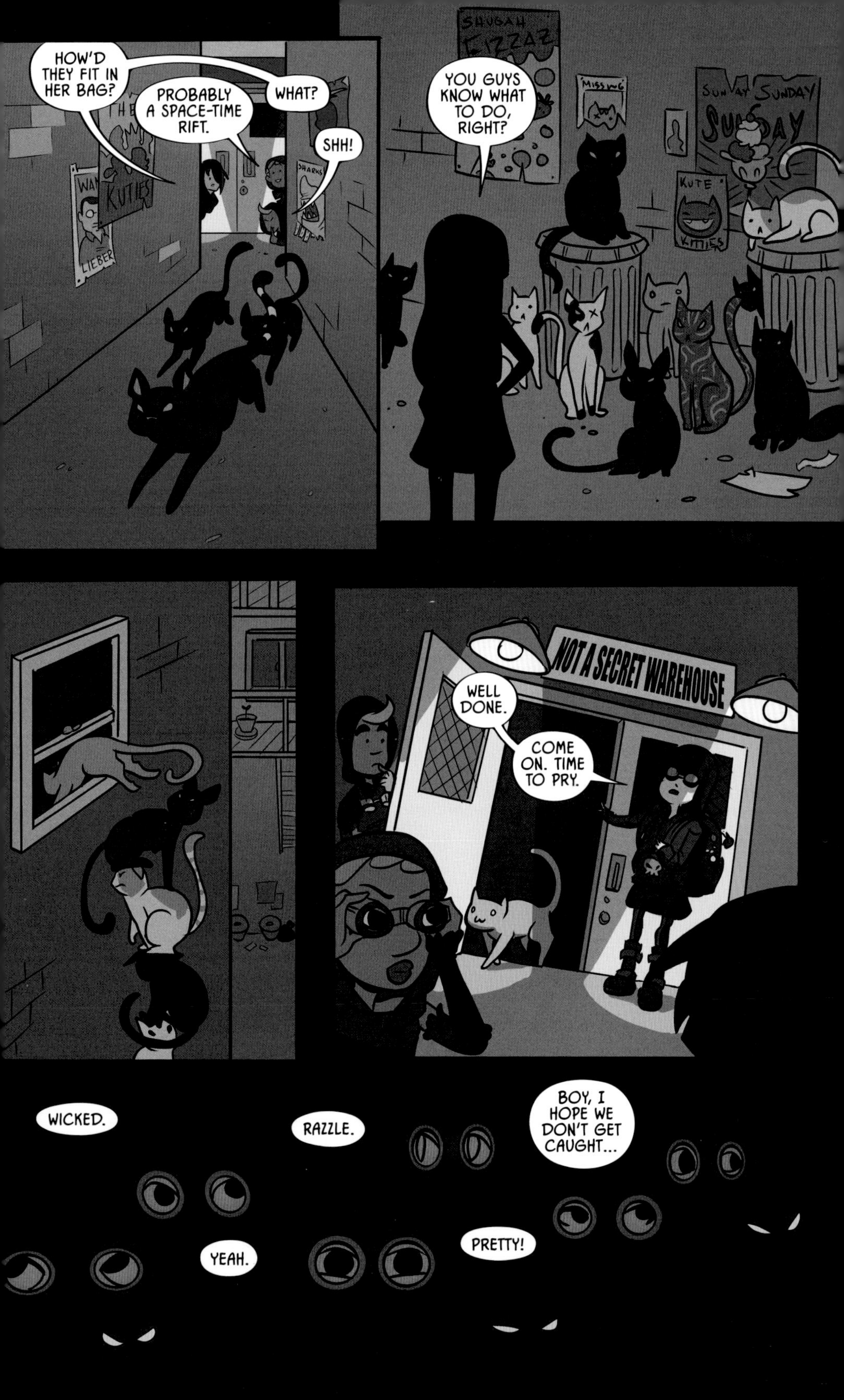
HOW'D THEY FIT IN HER BAG?
PROBABLY A SPACE-TIME RIFT.
WHAT?
SHH!
YOU GUYS KNOW WHAT TO DO, RIGHT?
KUTE KITTIES
NOT A SECRET WAREHOUSE
WELL DONE.
COME ON. TIME TO PRY.
WICKED.
RAZZLE.
BOY, I HOPE WE DON'T GET CAUGHT...
YEAH.
PRETTY!

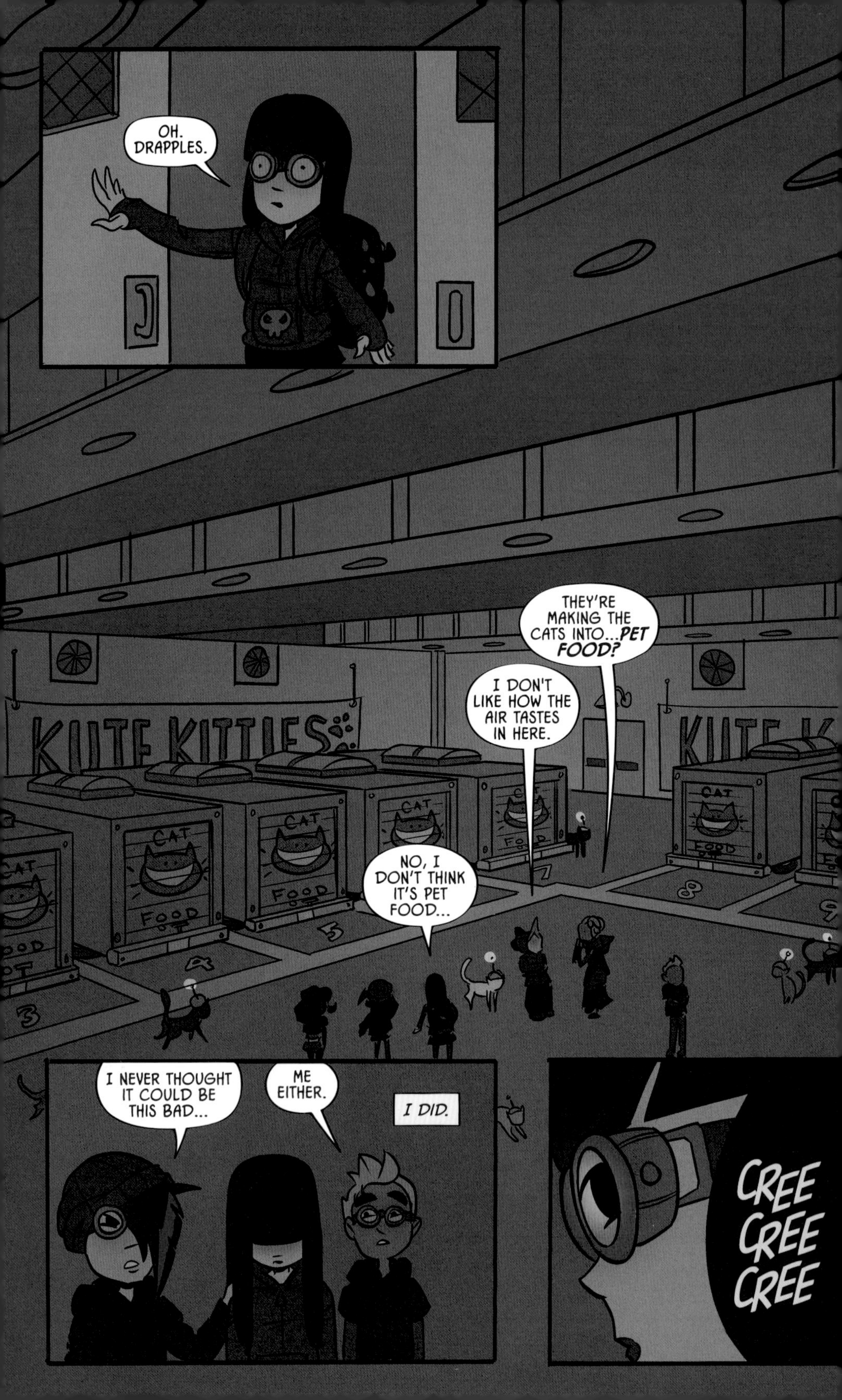
OH. DRAPPLES.
KUTE KITTIES
CAT FOOD
THEY'RE MAKING THE CATS INTO...*PET FOOD?*
I DON'T LIKE HOW THE AIR TASTES IN HERE.
NO, I DON'T THINK IT'S PET FOOD...
I NEVER THOUGHT IT COULD BE THIS BAD...
ME EITHER.
I DID.
CREE CREE CREE

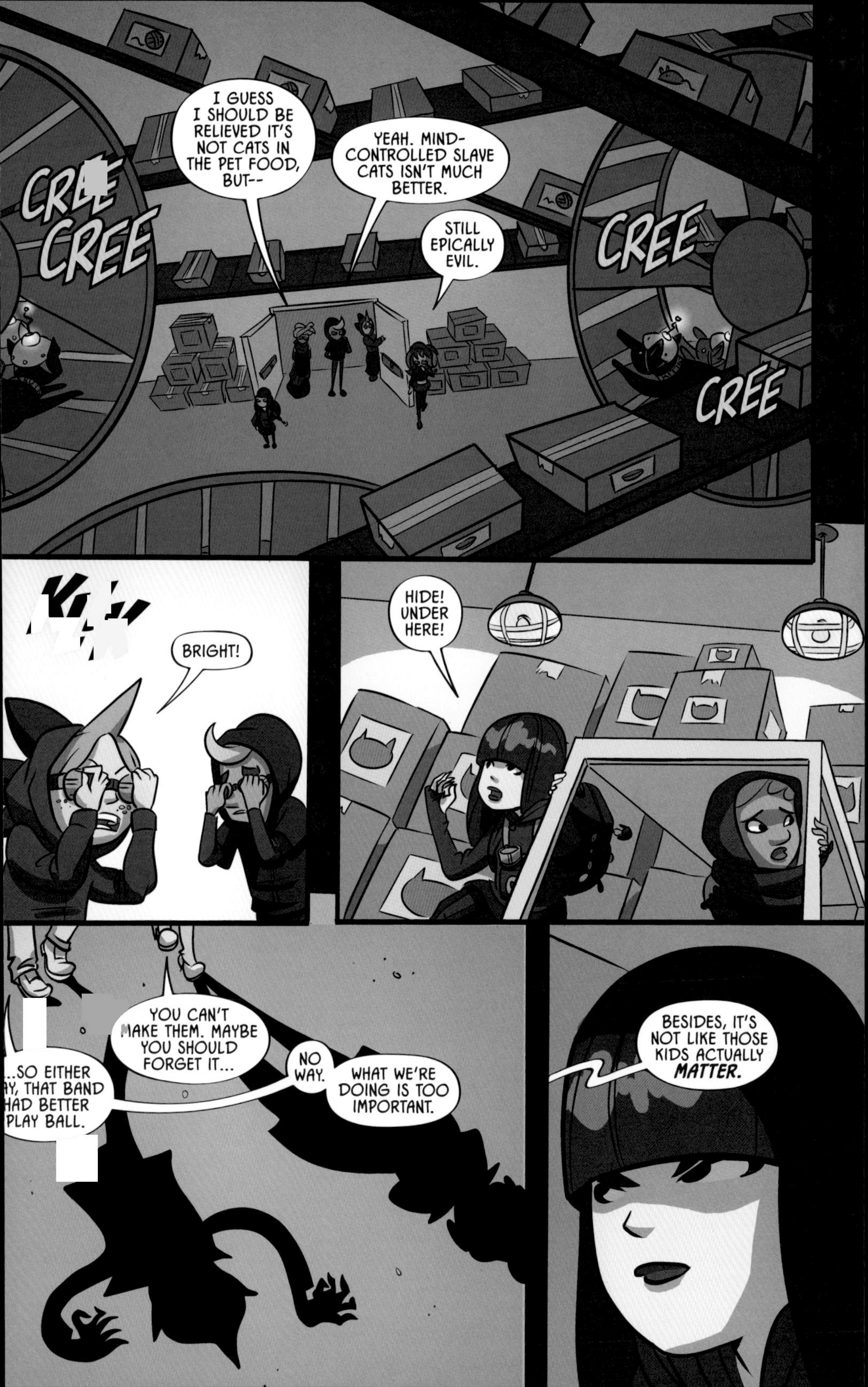
CREE
I GUESS I SHOULD BE RELIEVED IT'S NOT CATS IN THE PET FOOD, BUT--
YEAH. MIND-CONTROLLED SLAVE CATS ISN'T MUCH BETTER.
STILL EPICALLY EVIL.
CREE
CREE
BRIGHT!
HIDE! UNDER HERE!
...SO EITHER
AY, THAT BAND
HAD BETTER
PLAY BALL.
YOU CAN'T MAKE THEM. MAYBE YOU SHOULD FORGET IT...
NO WAY.
WHAT WE'RE DOING IS TOO IMPORTANT.
BESIDES, IT'S NOT LIKE THOSE KIDS ACTUALLY *MATTER.*

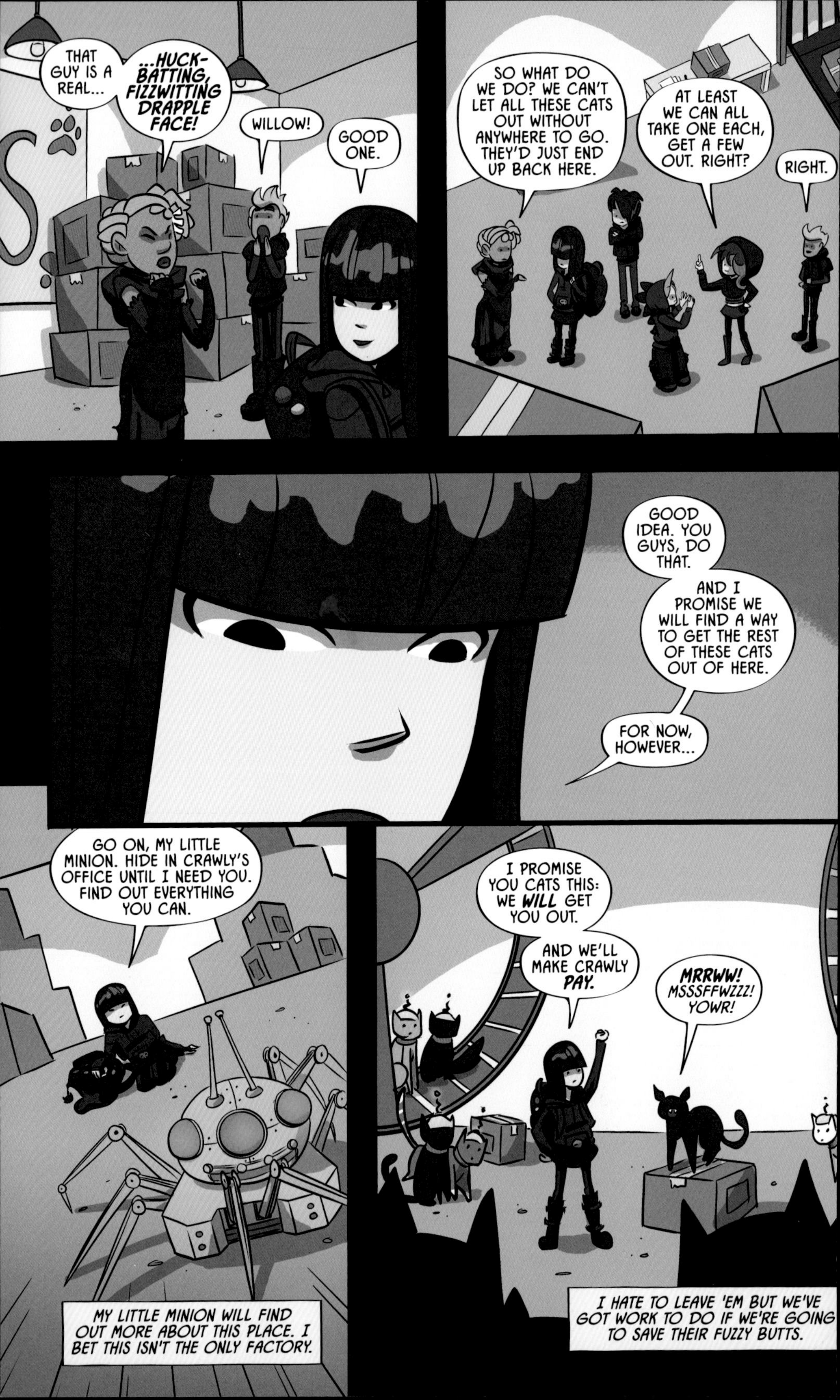
THAT GUY IS A REAL...
...HUCK-BATTING, FIZZWITTING DRAPPLE FACE!
WILLOW!
GOOD ONE.
SO WHAT DO WE DO? WE CAN'T LET ALL THESE CATS OUT WITHOUT ANYWHERE TO GO. THEY'D JUST END UP BACK HERE.
AT LEAST WE CAN ALL TAKE ONE EACH, GET A FEW OUT. RIGHT?
RIGHT.
GOOD IDEA. YOU GUYS, DO THAT.
AND I PROMISE WE WILL FIND A WAY TO GET THE REST OF THESE CATS OUT OF HERE.
FOR NOW, HOWEVER...
GO ON, MY LITTLE MINION. HIDE IN CRAWLY'S OFFICE UNTIL I NEED YOU. FIND OUT EVERYTHING YOU CAN.
MY LITTLE MINION WILL FIND OUT MORE ABOUT THIS PLACE. I BET THIS ISN'T THE ONLY FACTORY.
I PROMISE YOU CATS THIS: WE WILL GET YOU OUT.
AND WE'LL MAKE CRAWLY PAY.
MRRWW! MSSSFFWZZZ! YOWR!
I HATE TO LEAVE 'EM BUT WE'VE GOT WORK TO DO IF WE'RE GOING TO SAVE THEIR FUZZY BUTTS.

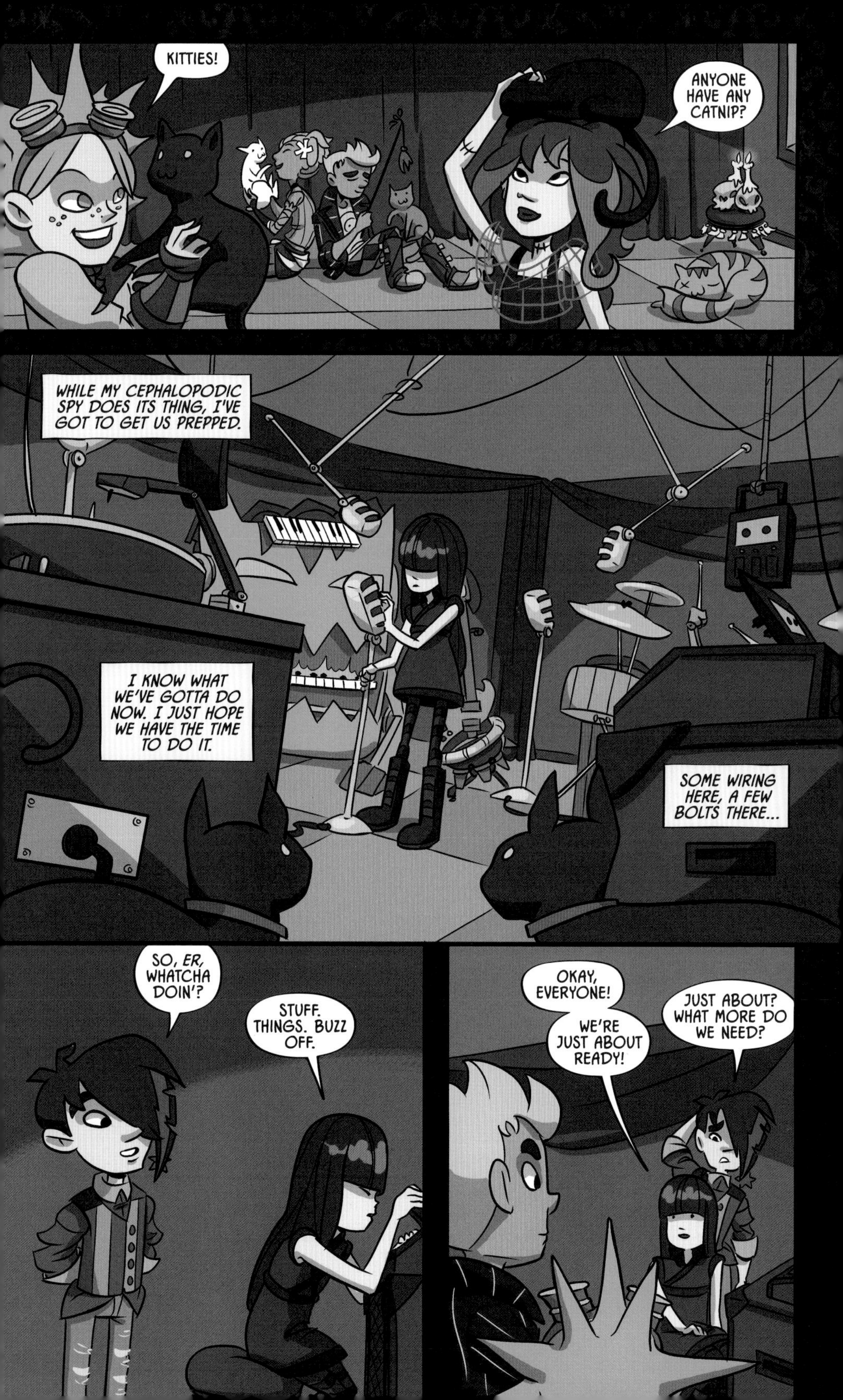
KITTIES!
ANYONE HAVE ANY CATNIP?
WHILE MY CEPHALOPODIC SPY DOES ITS THING, I'VE GOT TO GET US PREPPED.
I KNOW WHAT WE'VE GOTTA DO NOW. I JUST HOPE WE HAVE THE TIME TO DO IT.
SOME WIRING HERE, A FEW BOLTS THERE...
SO, ER, WHATCHA DOIN'?
STUFF. THINGS. BUZZ OFF.
OKAY, EVERYONE!
WE'RE JUST ABOUT READY!
JUST ABOUT? WHAT MORE DO WE NEED?

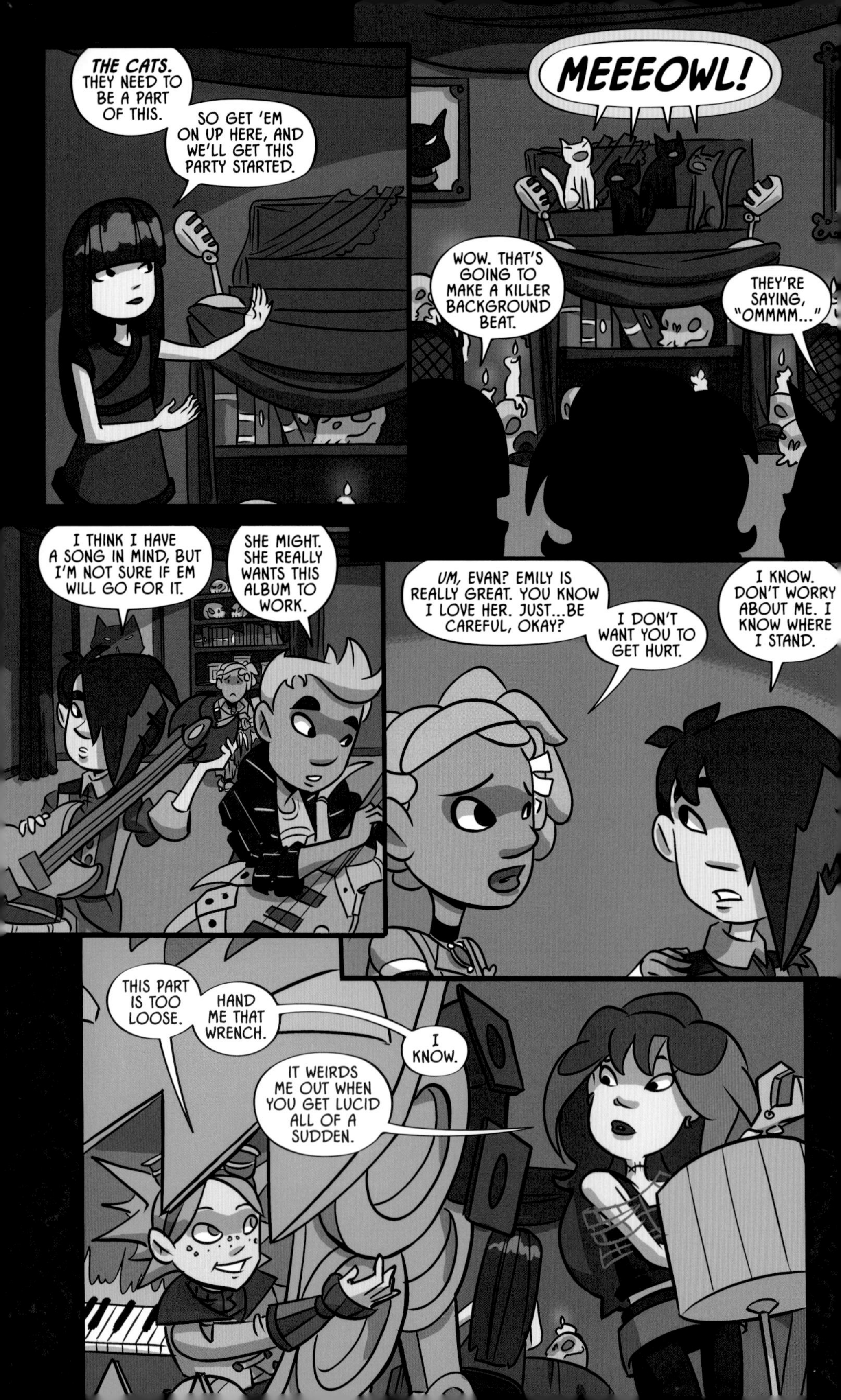

THE CATS. THEY NEED TO BE A PART OF THIS.
SO GET 'EM ON UP HERE, AND WE'LL GET THIS PARTY STARTED.
MEEEOWL!
WOW. THAT'S GOING TO MAKE A KILLER BACKGROUND BEAT.
THEY'RE SAYING, "OMMMM..."
I THINK I HAVE A SONG IN MIND, BUT I'M NOT SURE IF EM WILL GO FOR IT.
SHE MIGHT. SHE REALLY WANTS THIS ALBUM TO WORK.
UM, EVAN? EMILY IS REALLY GREAT. YOU KNOW I LOVE HER. JUST...BE CAREFUL, OKAY?
I DON'T WANT YOU TO GET HURT.
I KNOW. DON'T WORRY ABOUT ME. I KNOW WHERE I STAND.
THIS PART IS TOO LOOSE.
HAND ME THAT WRENCH.
I KNOW.
IT WEIRDS ME OUT WHEN YOU GET LUCID ALL OF A SUDDEN.

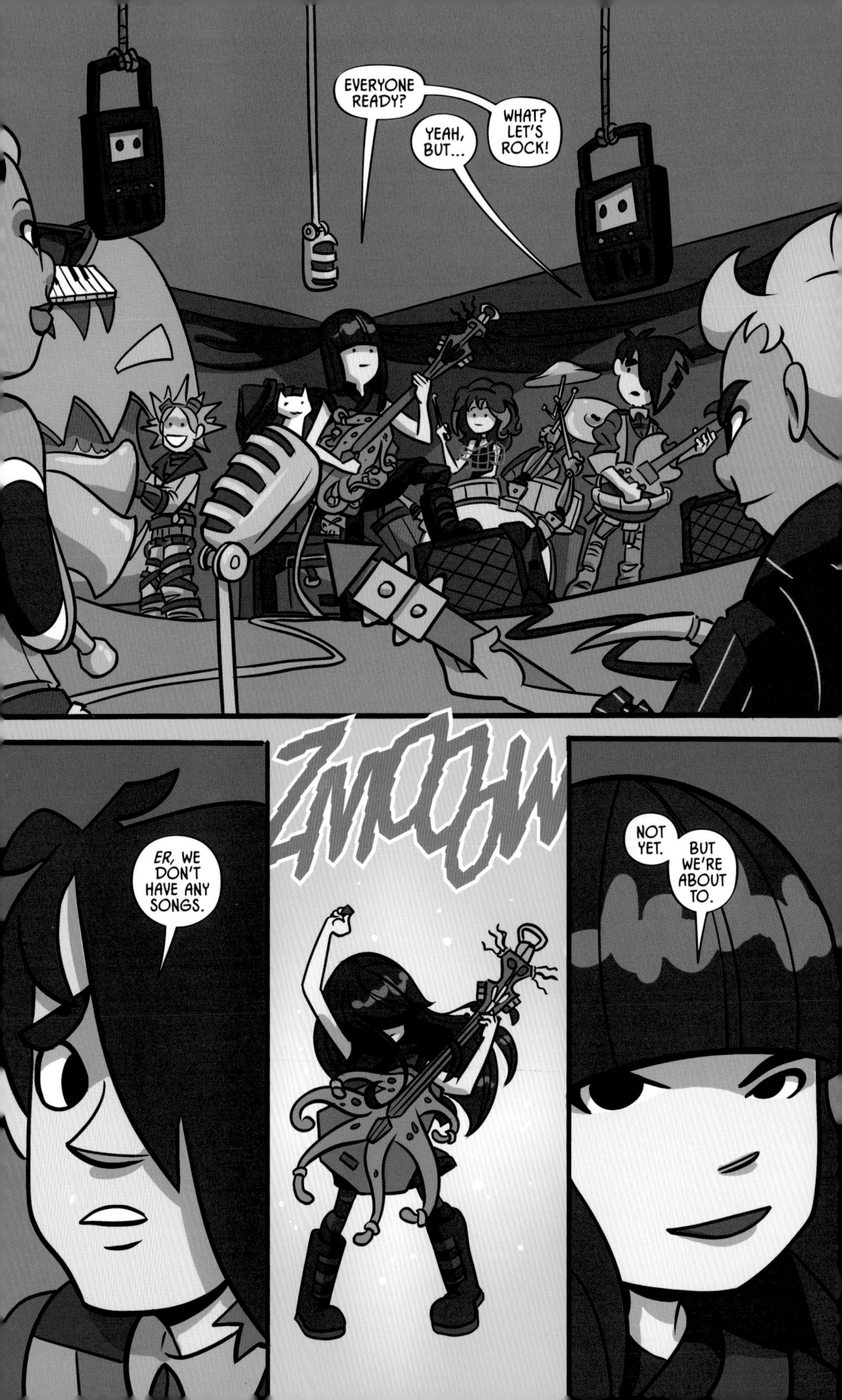
EVERYONE READY?
YEAH, BUT...
WHAT? LET'S ROCK!
ER, WE DON'T HAVE ANY SONGS.
ZMOOW
NOT YET.
BUT WE'RE ABOUT TO.

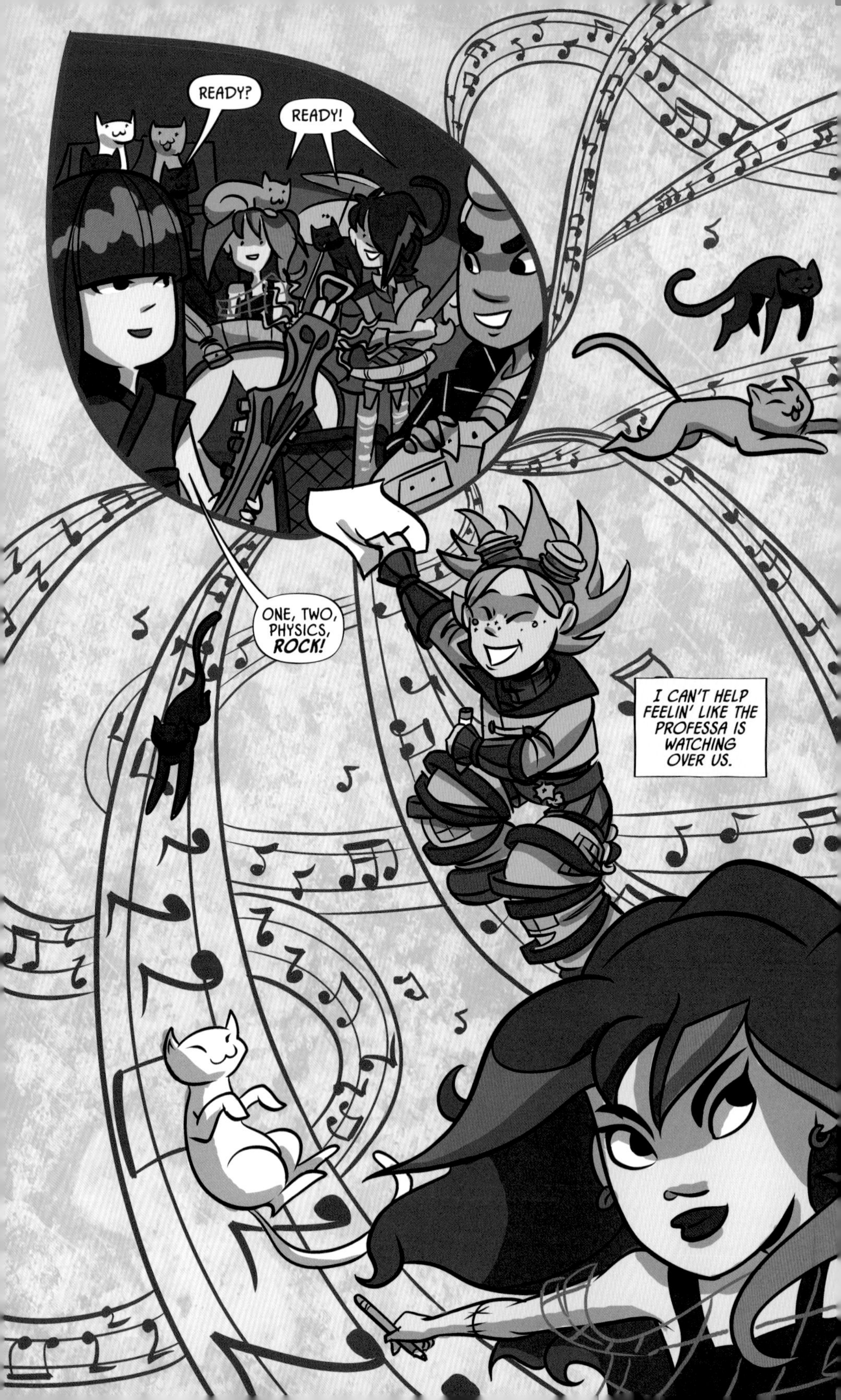
READY?
READY!
ONE, TWO, PHYSICS, ROCK!
I CAN'T HELP FEELIN' LIKE THE PROFESSA IS WATCHING OVER US.

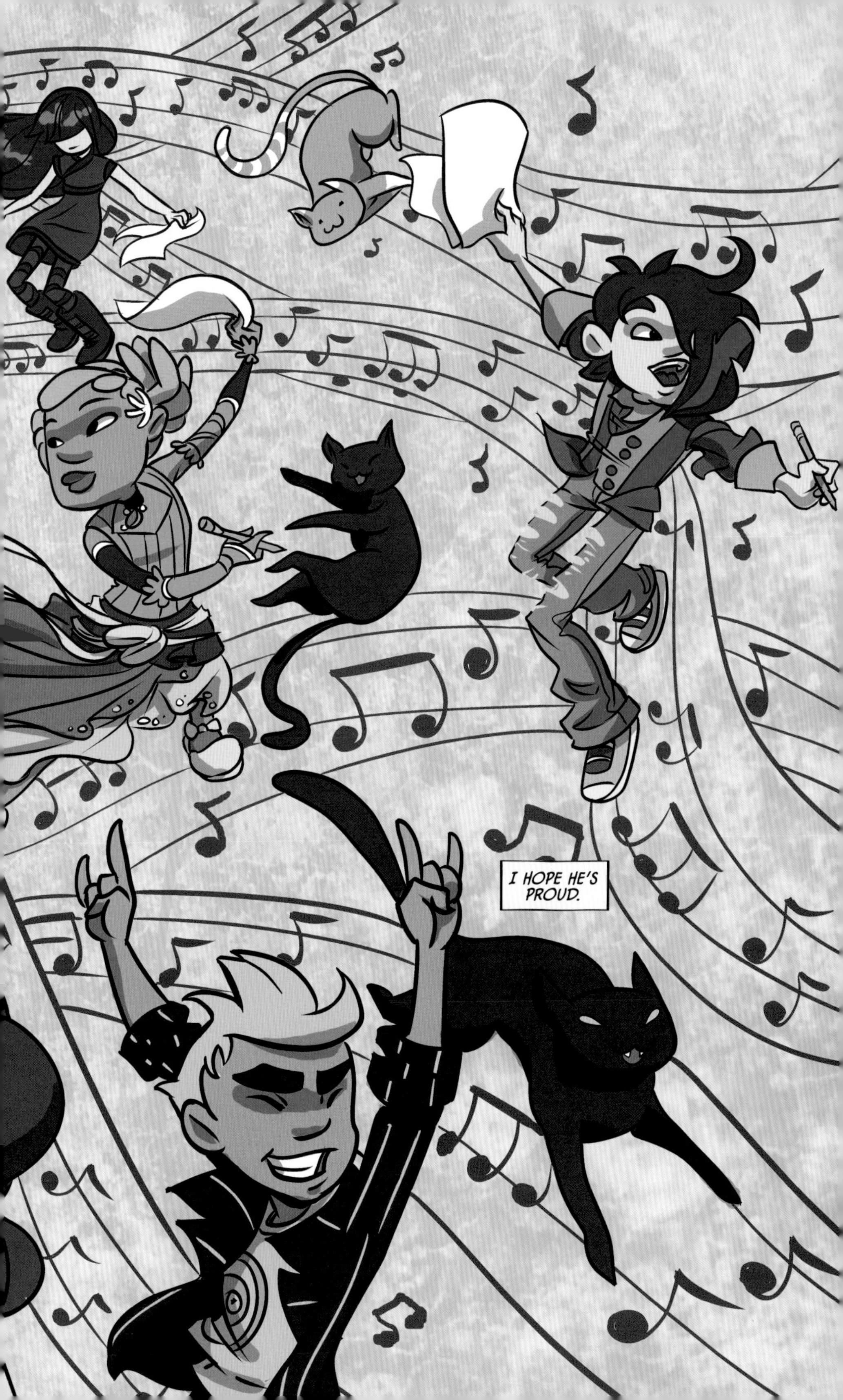
I HOPE HE'S PROUD.

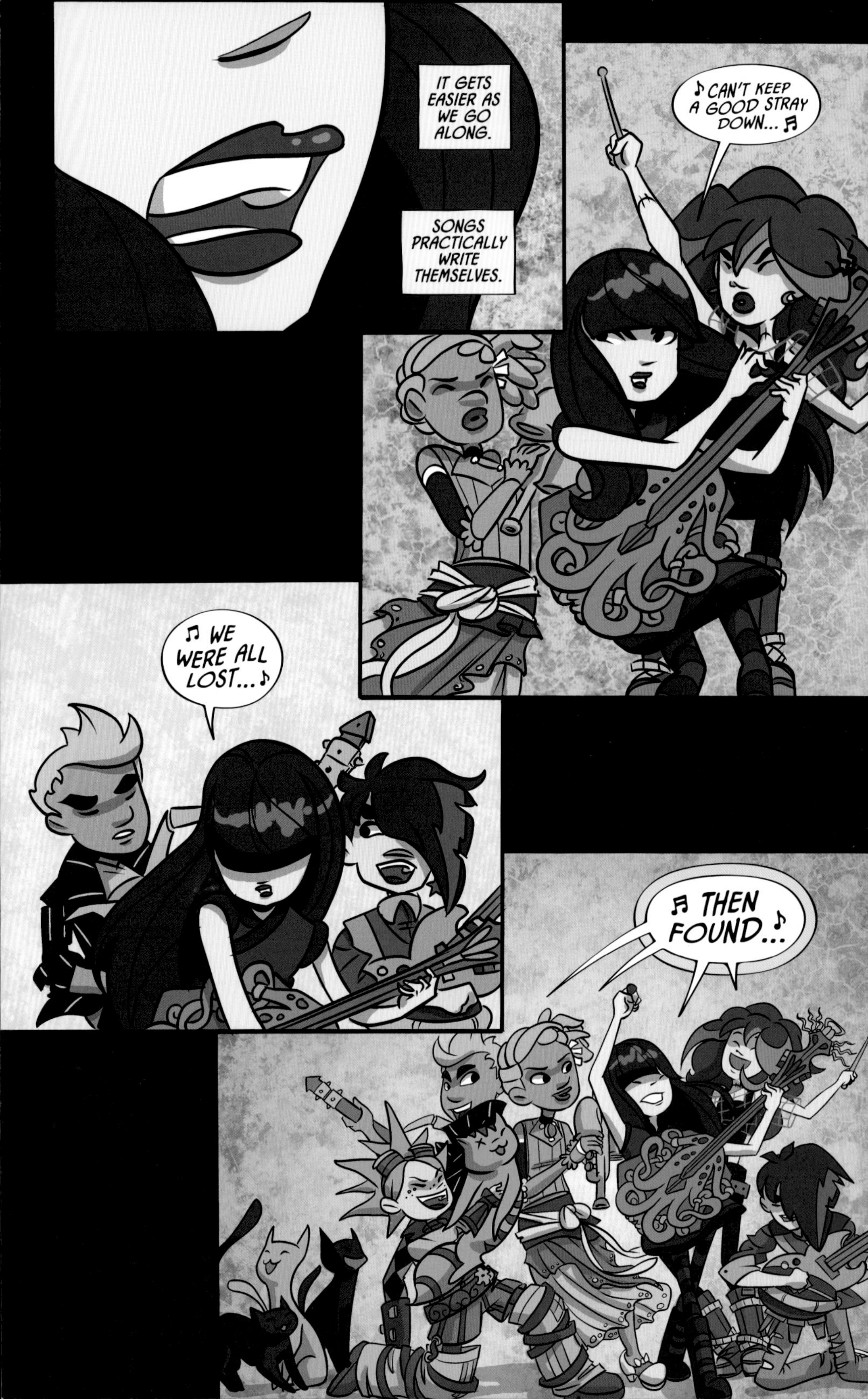
IT GETS EASIER AS WE GO ALONG.
SONGS PRACTICALLY WRITE THEMSELVES.
♪ CAN'T KEEP A GOOD STRAY DOWN... ♫
♫ WE WERE ALL LOST... ♪
♫ THEN FOUND... ♪

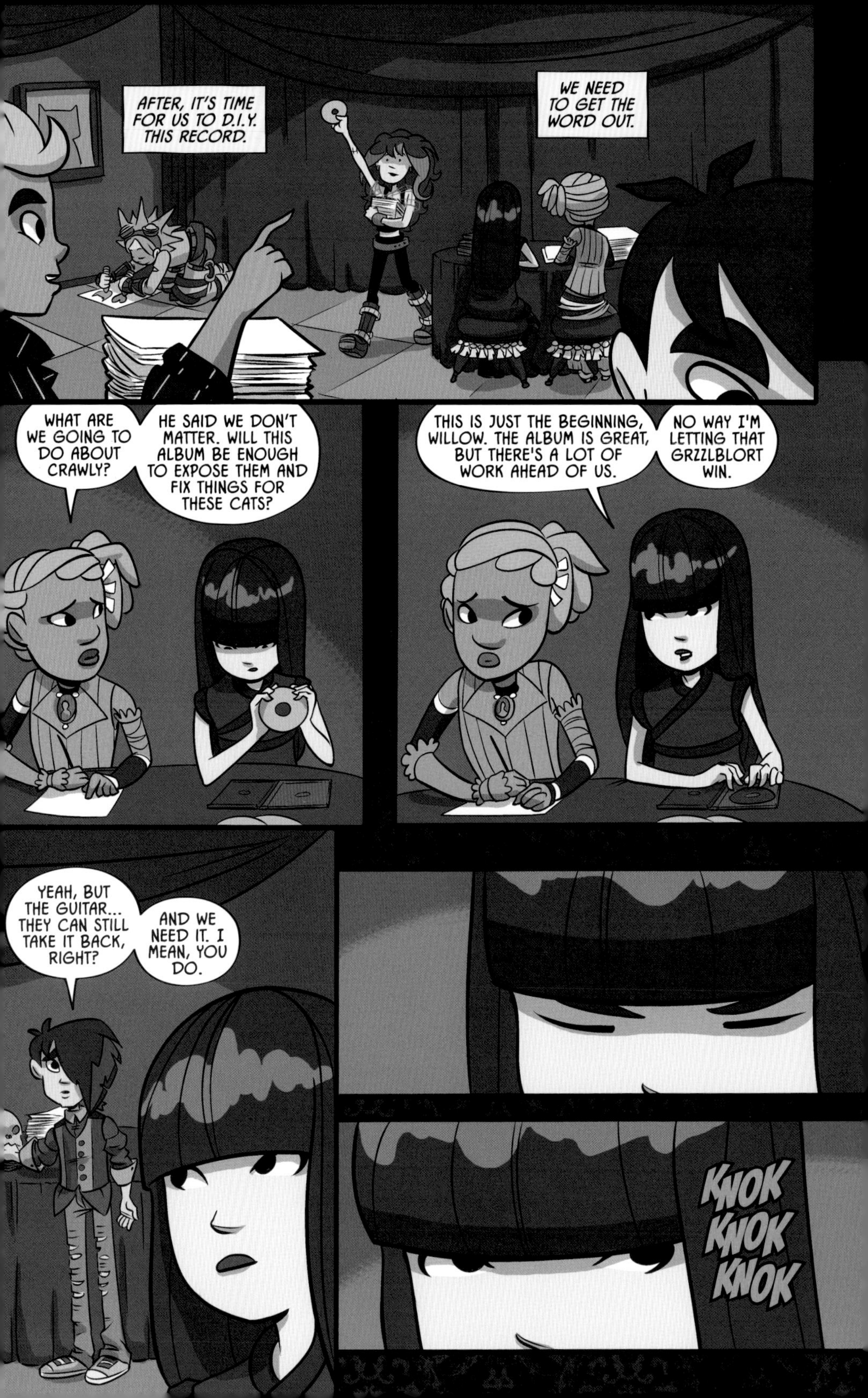

AFTER, IT'S TIME FOR US TO D.I.Y. THIS RECORD.
WE NEED TO GET THE WORD OUT.
WHAT ARE WE GOING TO DO ABOUT CRAWLY?
HE SAID WE DON'T MATTER. WILL THIS ALBUM BE ENOUGH TO EXPOSE THEM AND FIX THINGS FOR THESE CATS?
THIS IS JUST THE BEGINNING, WILLOW. THE ALBUM IS GREAT, BUT THERE'S A LOT OF WORK AHEAD OF US.
NO WAY I'M LETTING THAT GRZZLBLORT WIN.
YEAH, BUT THE GUITAR... THEY CAN STILL TAKE IT BACK, RIGHT?
AND WE NEED IT. I MEAN, YOU DO.
KNOK KNOK KNOK

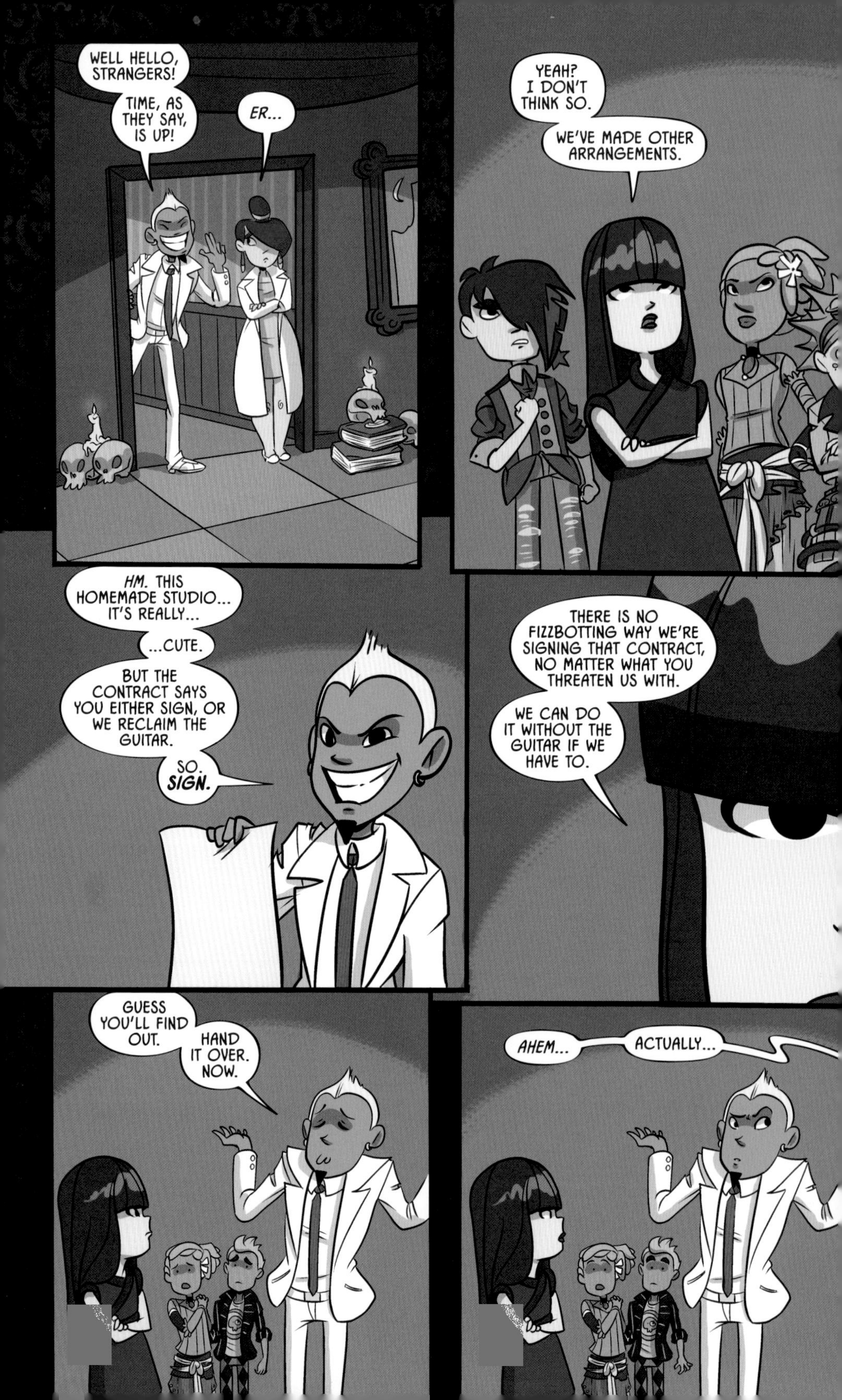
WELL HELLO, STRANGERS!
TIME, AS THEY SAY, IS UP!
ER...
YEAH? I DON'T THINK SO.
WE'VE MADE OTHER ARRANGEMENTS.
HM. THIS HOMEMADE STUDIO... IT'S REALLY...
...CUTE.
BUT THE CONTRACT SAYS YOU EITHER SIGN, OR WE RECLAIM THE GUITAR.
SO. SIGN.
THERE IS NO FIZZBOTTING WAY WE'RE SIGNING THAT CONTRACT, NO MATTER WHAT YOU THREATEN US WITH.
WE CAN DO IT WITHOUT THE GUITAR IF WE HAVE TO.
GUESS YOU'LL FIND OUT.
HAND IT OVER. NOW.
AHEM...
ACTUALLY...

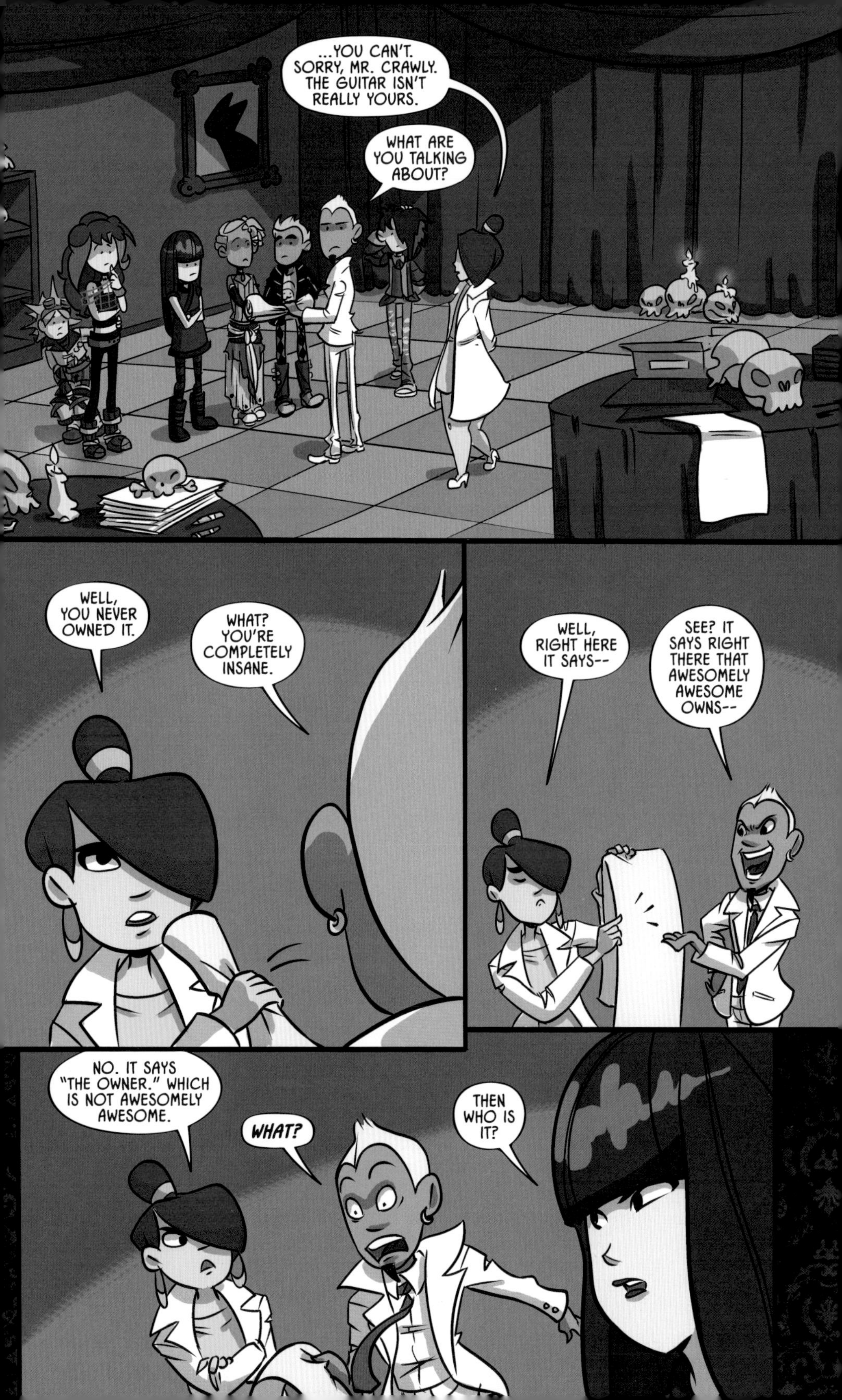
...YOU CAN'T. SORRY, MR. CRAWLY. THE GUITAR ISN'T REALLY YOURS.
WHAT ARE YOU TALKING ABOUT?
WELL, YOU NEVER OWNED IT.
WHAT? YOU'RE COMPLETELY INSANE.
WELL, RIGHT HERE IT SAYS--
SEE? IT SAYS RIGHT THERE THAT AWESOMELY AWESOME OWNS--
NO. IT SAYS "THE OWNER." WHICH IS NOT AWESOMELY AWESOME.
WHAT?
THEN WHO IS IT?

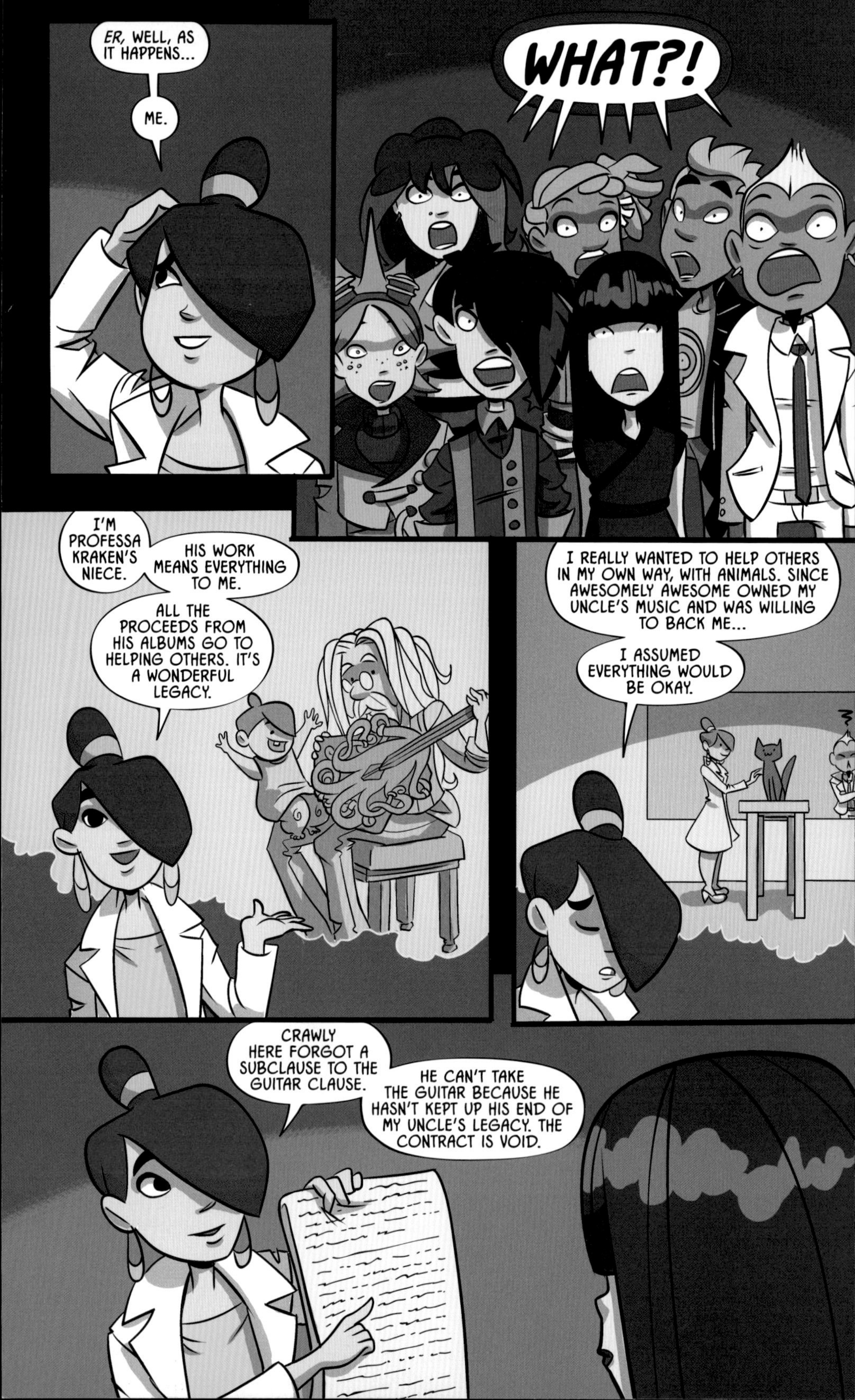
ER, WELL, AS IT HAPPENS...
ME.
WHAT?!
I'M PROFESSA KRAKEN'S NIECE.
HIS WORK MEANS EVERYTHING TO ME.
ALL THE PROCEEDS FROM HIS ALBUMS GO TO HELPING OTHERS. IT'S A WONDERFUL LEGACY.
I REALLY WANTED TO HELP OTHERS IN MY OWN WAY, WITH ANIMALS. SINCE AWESOMELY AWESOME OWNED MY UNCLE'S MUSIC AND WAS WILLING TO BACK ME...
I ASSUMED EVERYTHING WOULD BE OKAY.
CRAWLY HERE FORGOT A SUBCLAUSE TO THE GUITAR CLAUSE.
HE CAN'T TAKE THE GUITAR BECAUSE HE HASN'T KEPT UP HIS END OF MY UNCLE'S LEGACY. THE CONTRACT IS VOID.

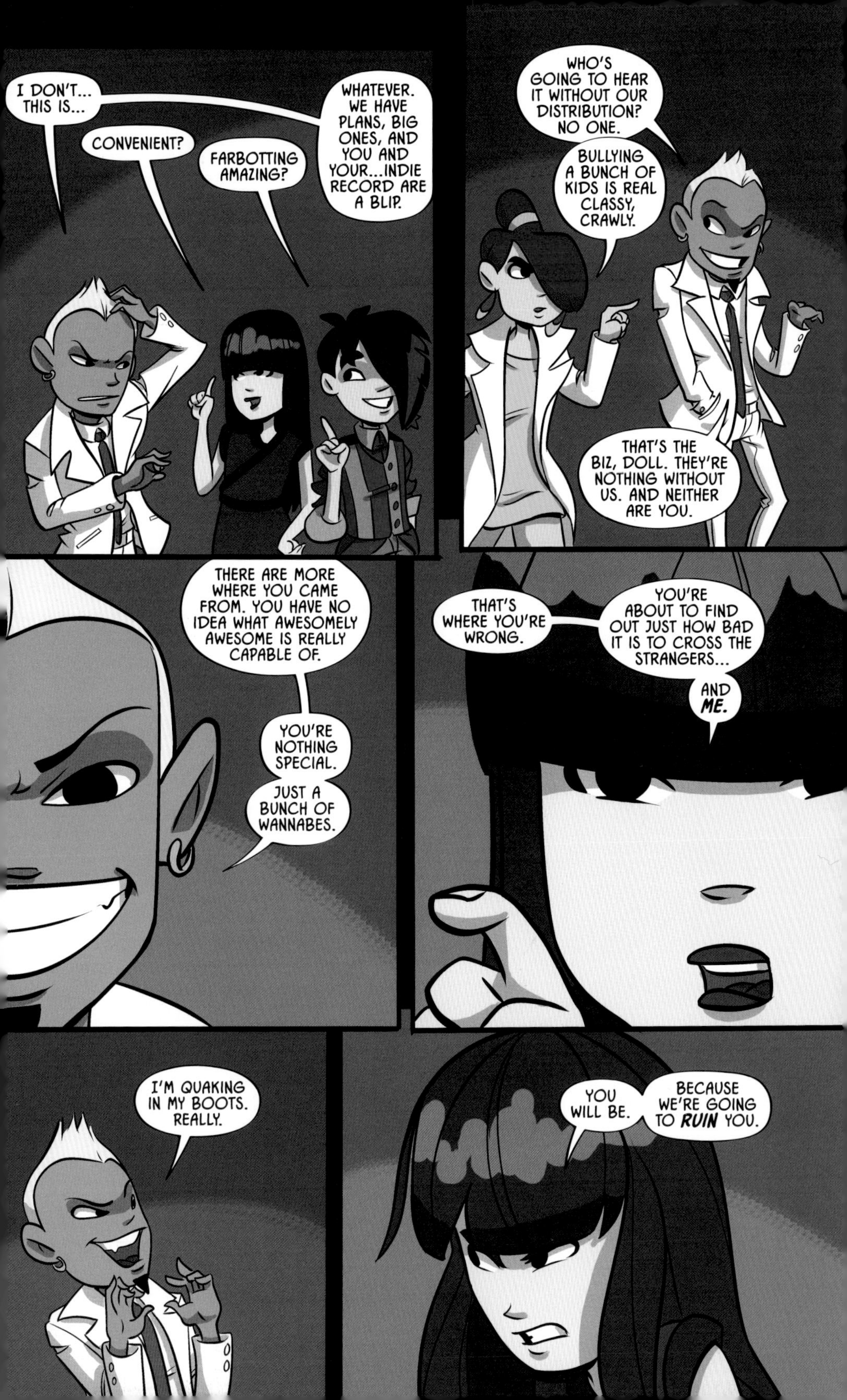
I DON'T... THIS IS...
CONVENIENT?
FARBOTTING AMAZING?
WHATEVER. WE HAVE PLANS, BIG ONES, AND YOU AND YOUR...INDIE RECORD ARE A BLIP.
WHO'S GOING TO HEAR IT WITHOUT OUR DISTRIBUTION? NO ONE.
BULLYING A BUNCH OF KIDS IS REAL CLASSY, CRAWLY.
THAT'S THE BIZ, DOLL. THEY'RE NOTHING WITHOUT US. AND NEITHER ARE YOU.
THERE ARE MORE WHERE YOU CAME FROM. YOU HAVE NO IDEA WHAT AWESOMELY AWESOME IS REALLY CAPABLE OF.
YOU'RE NOTHING SPECIAL.
JUST A BUNCH OF WANNABES.
THAT'S WHERE YOU'RE WRONG.
YOU'RE ABOUT TO FIND OUT JUST HOW BAD IT IS TO CROSS THE STRANGERS...
AND ME.
I'M QUAKING IN MY BOOTS. REALLY.
YOU WILL BE.
BECAUSE WE'RE GOING TO RUIN YOU.

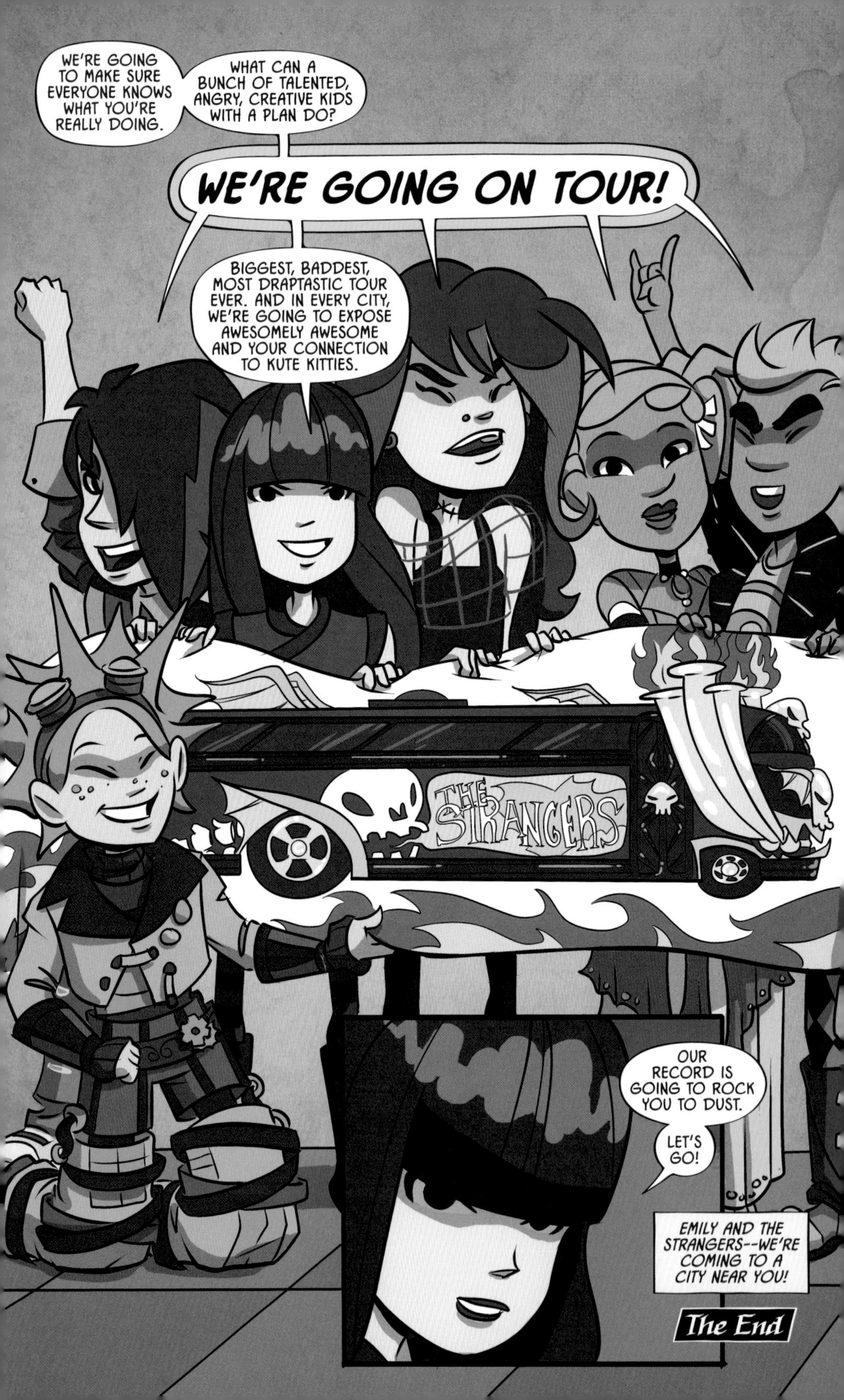
WE'RE GOING TO MAKE SURE EVERYONE KNOWS WHAT YOU'RE REALLY DOING.
WHAT CAN A BUNCH OF TALENTED, ANGRY, CREATIVE KIDS WITH A PLAN DO?
WE'RE GOING ON TOUR!
BIGGEST, BADDEST, MOST DRAPTASTIC TOUR EVER. AND IN EVERY CITY, WE'RE GOING TO EXPOSE AWESOMELY AWESOME AND YOUR CONNECTION TO KUTE KITTIES.
THE STRANGERS
OUR RECORD IS GOING TO ROCK YOU TO DUST.
LET'S GO!
EMILY AND THE STRANGERS--WE'RE COMING TO A CITY NEAR YOU!
The End

THE FOLLOWING STORY WAS FEATURED IN THE COMIC BOOK LEGAL DEFENSE FUND BENEFIT BOOK

LIBERTY ANNUAL 2014

PUBLISHED BY IMAGE COMICS

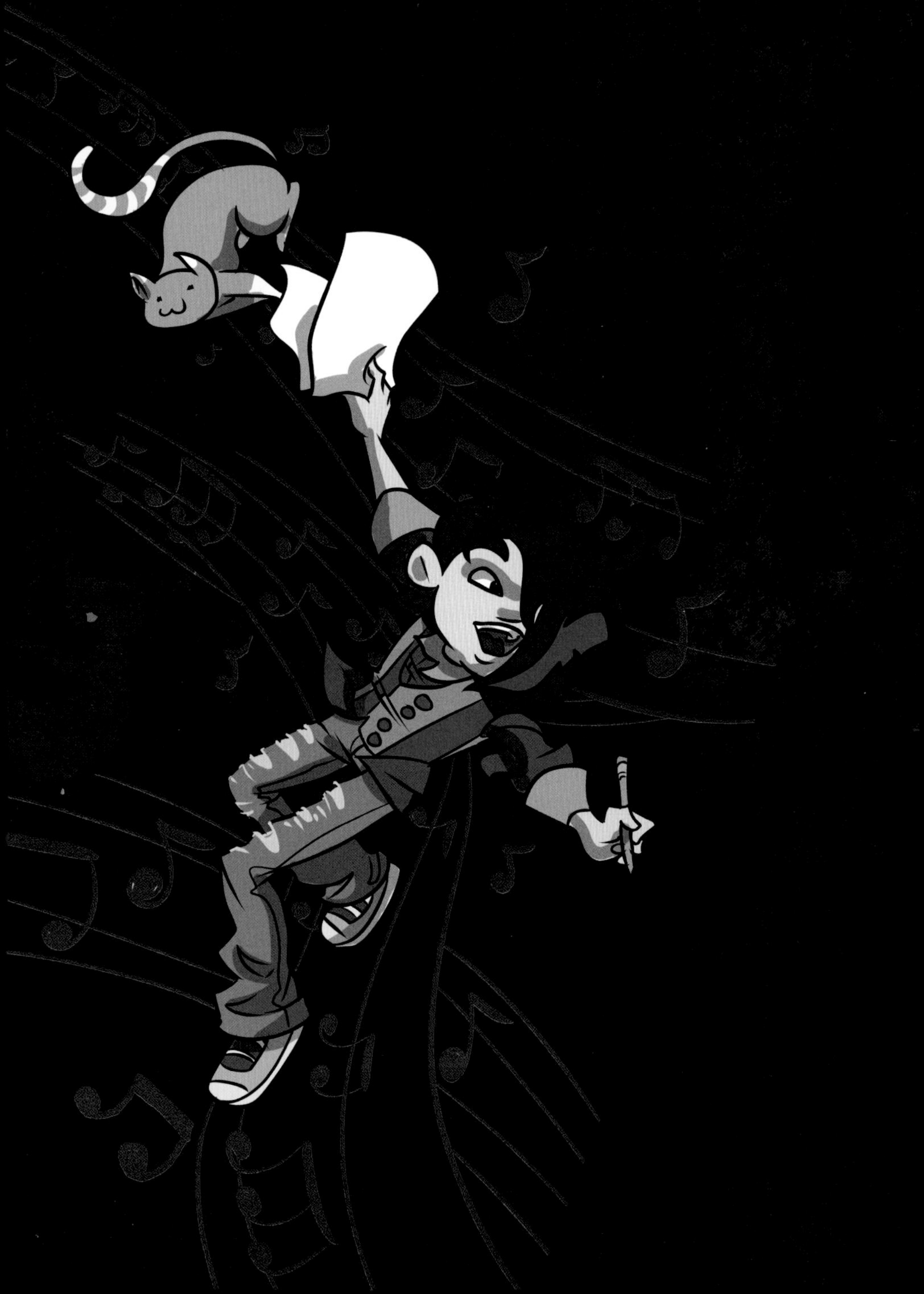

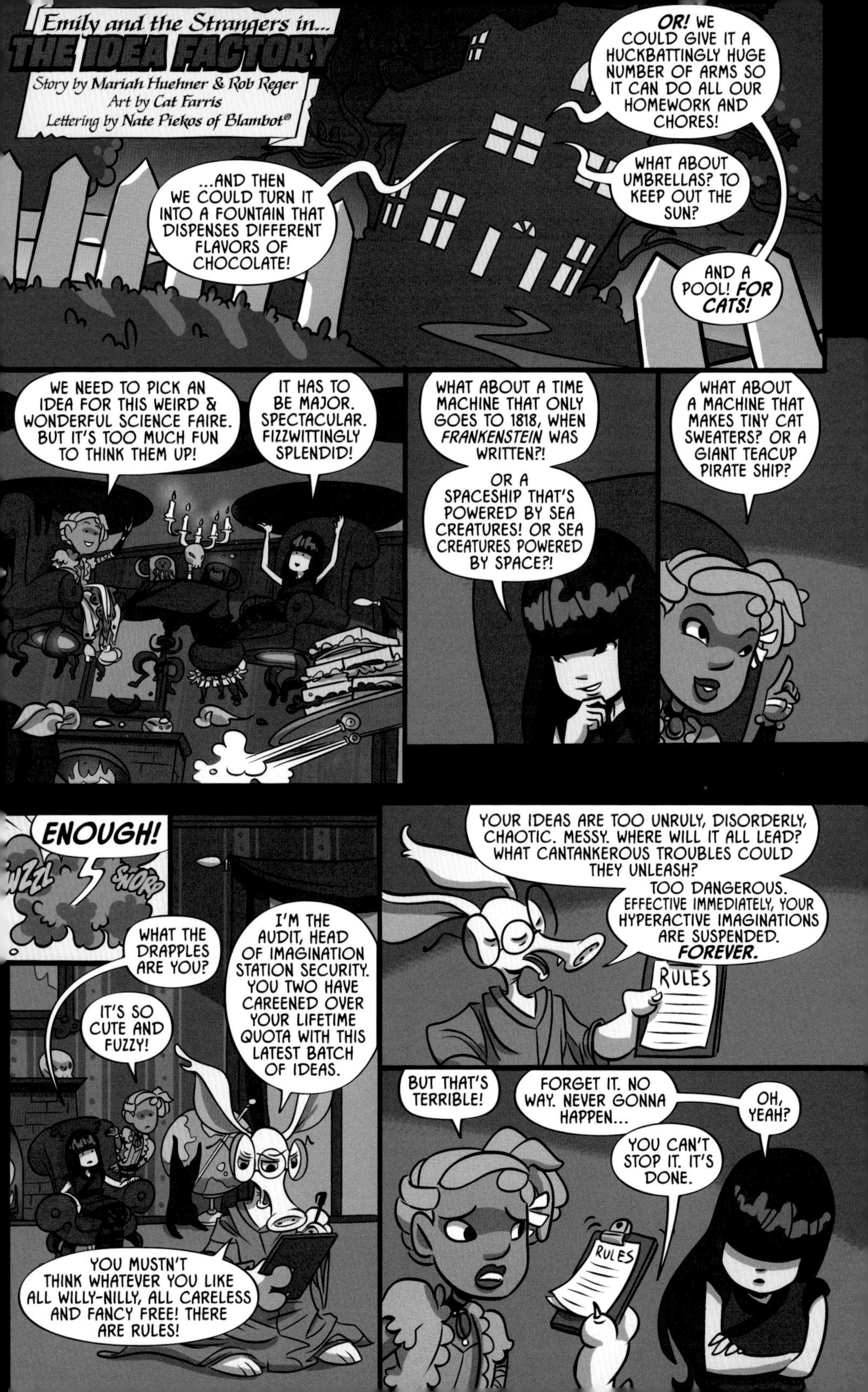
Emily and the Strangers in...
THE IDEA FACTORY
Story by Mariah Huehner & Rob Reger
Art by Cat Farris
Lettering by Nate Piekos of Blambot®
...AND THEN WE COULD TURN IT INTO A FOUNTAIN THAT DISPENSES DIFFERENT FLAVORS OF CHOCOLATE!
OR! WE COULD GIVE IT A HUCKBATTINGLY HUGE NUMBER OF ARMS SO IT CAN DO ALL OUR HOMEWORK AND CHORES!
WHAT ABOUT UMBRELLAS? TO KEEP OUT THE SUN?
AND A POOL! FOR CATS!
WE NEED TO PICK AN IDEA FOR THIS WEIRD & WONDERFUL SCIENCE FAIRE. BUT IT'S TOO MUCH FUN TO THINK THEM UP!
IT HAS TO BE MAJOR. SPECTACULAR. FIZZWITTINGLY SPLENDID!
WHAT ABOUT A TIME MACHINE THAT ONLY GOES TO 1818, WHEN FRANKENSTEIN WAS WRITTEN?!
OR A SPACESHIP THAT'S POWERED BY SEA CREATURES! OR SEA CREATURES POWERED BY SPACE?!
WHAT ABOUT A MACHINE THAT MAKES TINY CAT SWEATERS? OR A GIANT TEACUP PIRATE SHIP?
ENOUGH!
WHAT THE DRAPPLES ARE YOU?
IT'S SO CUTE AND FUZZY!
I'M THE AUDIT, HEAD OF IMAGINATION STATION SECURITY. YOU TWO HAVE CAREENED OVER YOUR LIFETIME QUOTA WITH THIS LATEST BATCH OF IDEAS.
YOU MUSTN'T THINK WHATEVER YOU LIKE ALL WILLY-NILLY, ALL CARELESS AND FANCY FREE! THERE ARE RULES!
YOUR IDEAS ARE TOO UNRULY, DISORDERLY, CHAOTIC. MESSY. WHERE WILL IT ALL LEAD? WHAT CANTANKEROUS TROUBLES COULD THEY UNLEASH?
TOO DANGEROUS. EFFECTIVE IMMEDIATELY, YOUR HYPERACTIVE IMAGINATIONS ARE SUSPENDED. FOREVER.
RULES
BUT THAT'S TERRIBLE!
FORGET IT. NO WAY. NEVER GONNA HAPPEN...
OH, YEAH?
YOU CAN'T STOP IT. IT'S DONE.
RULES

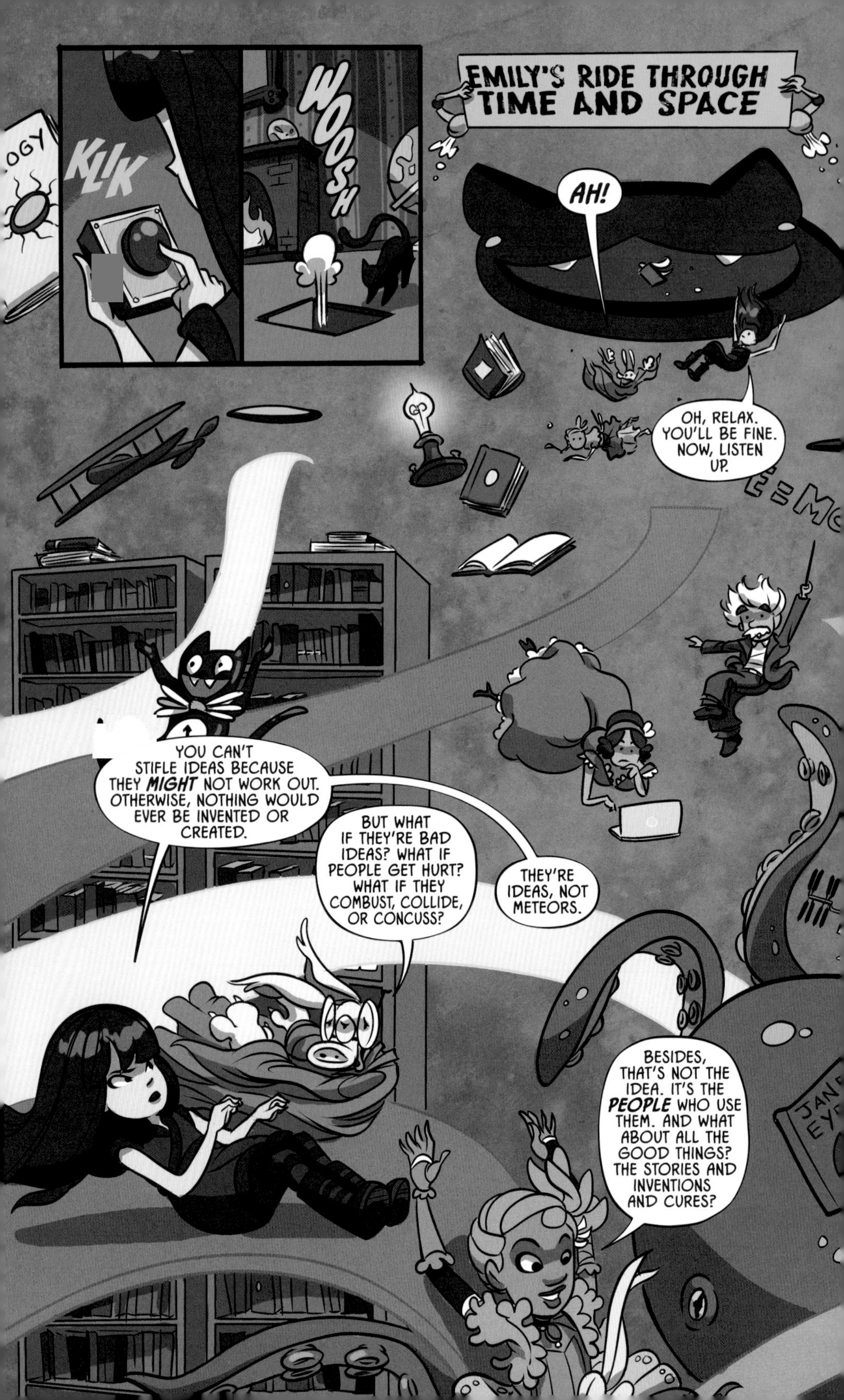
KLIK
WOOSH
EMILY'S RIDE THROUGH TIME AND SPACE
AH!
OH, RELAX. YOU'LL BE FINE. NOW, LISTEN UP.
YOU CAN'T STIFLE IDEAS BECAUSE THEY *MIGHT* NOT WORK OUT. OTHERWISE, NOTHING WOULD EVER BE INVENTED OR CREATED.
BUT WHAT IF THEY'RE BAD IDEAS? WHAT IF PEOPLE GET HURT? WHAT IF THEY COMBUST, COLLIDE, OR CONCUSS?
THEY'RE IDEAS, NOT METEORS.
BESIDES, THAT'S NOT THE IDEA. IT'S THE *PEOPLE* WHO USE THEM. AND WHAT ABOUT ALL THE GOOD THINGS? THE STORIES AND INVENTIONS AND CURES?

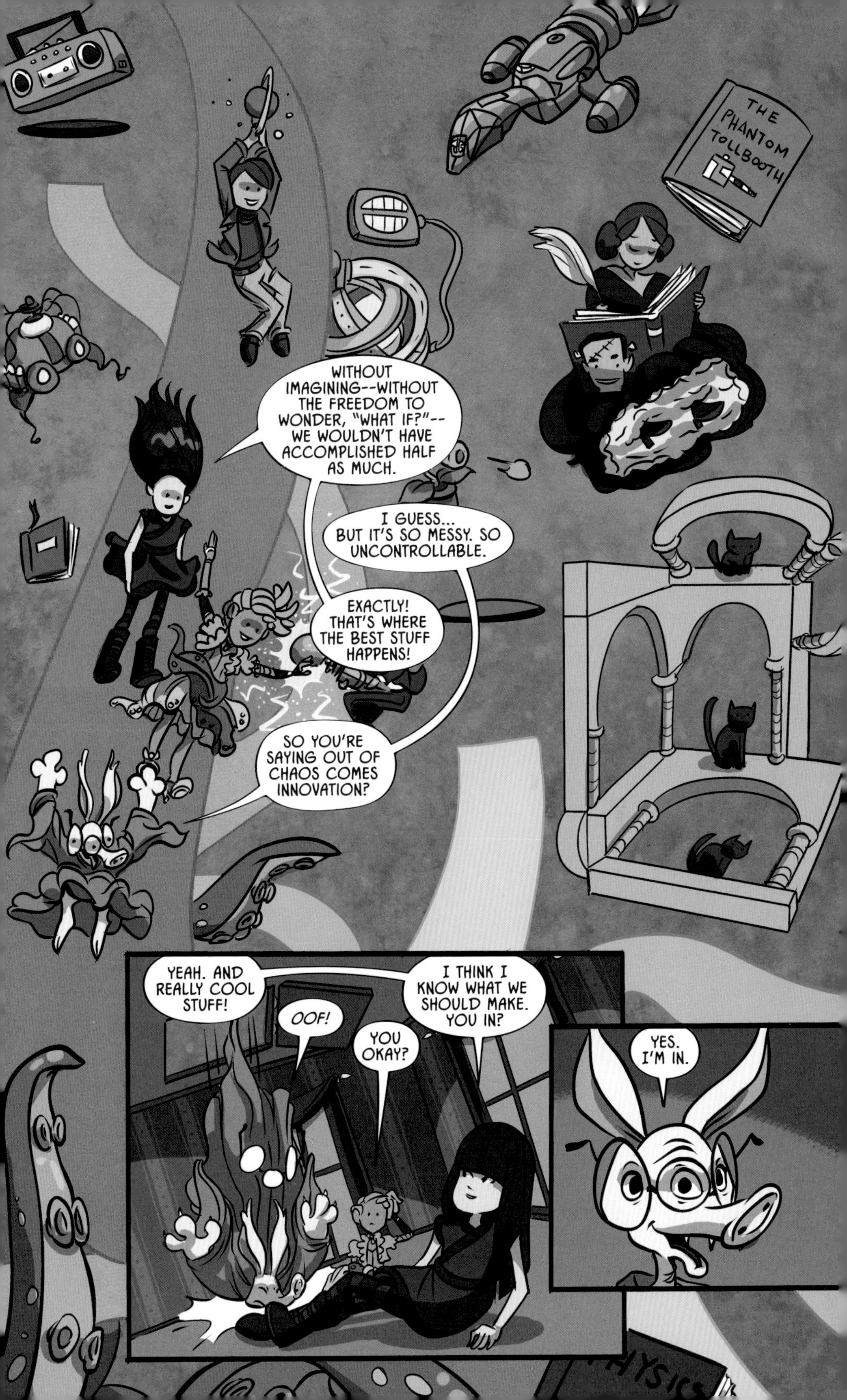
THE PHANTOM TOLLBOOTH
WITHOUT IMAGINING--WITHOUT THE FREEDOM TO WONDER, "WHAT IF?"--WE WOULDN'T HAVE ACCOMPLISHED HALF AS MUCH.
I GUESS... BUT IT'S SO MESSY. SO UNCONTROLLABLE.
EXACTLY! THAT'S WHERE THE BEST STUFF HAPPENS!
SO YOU'RE SAYING OUT OF CHAOS COMES INNOVATION?
YEAH. AND REALLY COOL STUFF!
I THINK I KNOW WHAT WE SHOULD MAKE. YOU IN?
OOF!
YOU OKAY?
YES. I'M IN.

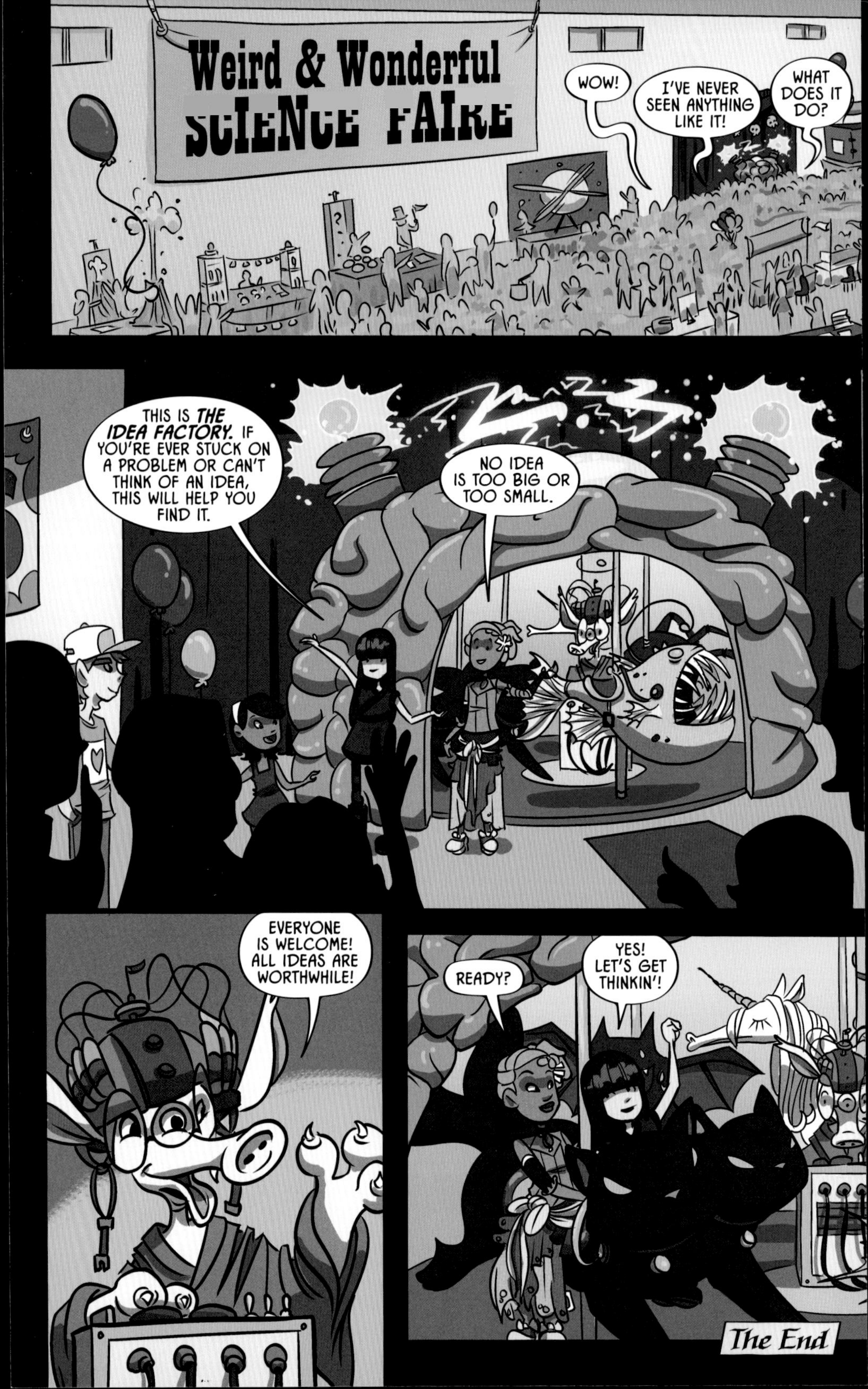
Weird & Wonderful
SCIENCE FAIRE
WOW!
I'VE NEVER SEEN ANYTHING LIKE IT!
WHAT DOES IT DO?
THIS IS *THE IDEA FACTORY.* IF YOU'RE EVER STUCK ON A PROBLEM OR CAN'T THINK OF AN IDEA, THIS WILL HELP YOU FIND IT.
NO IDEA IS TOO BIG OR TOO SMALL.
EVERYONE IS WELCOME! ALL IDEAS ARE WORTHWHILE!
READY?
YES! LET'S GET THINKIN'!
The End

Emily® and the Strangers

SKETCHBOOK

ART BY
CAT FARRIS
and **BUZZ PARKER**

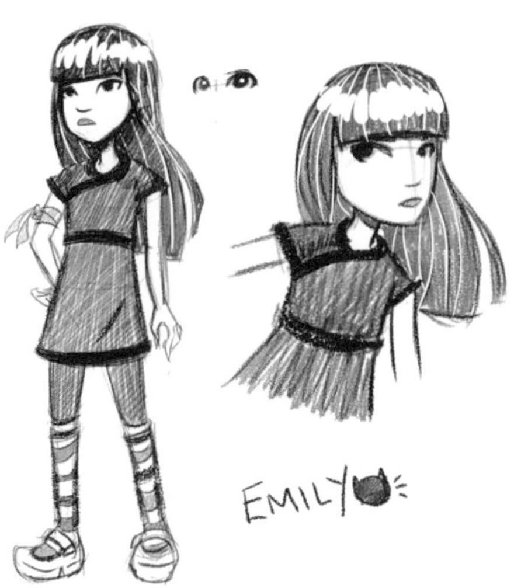
EMILY

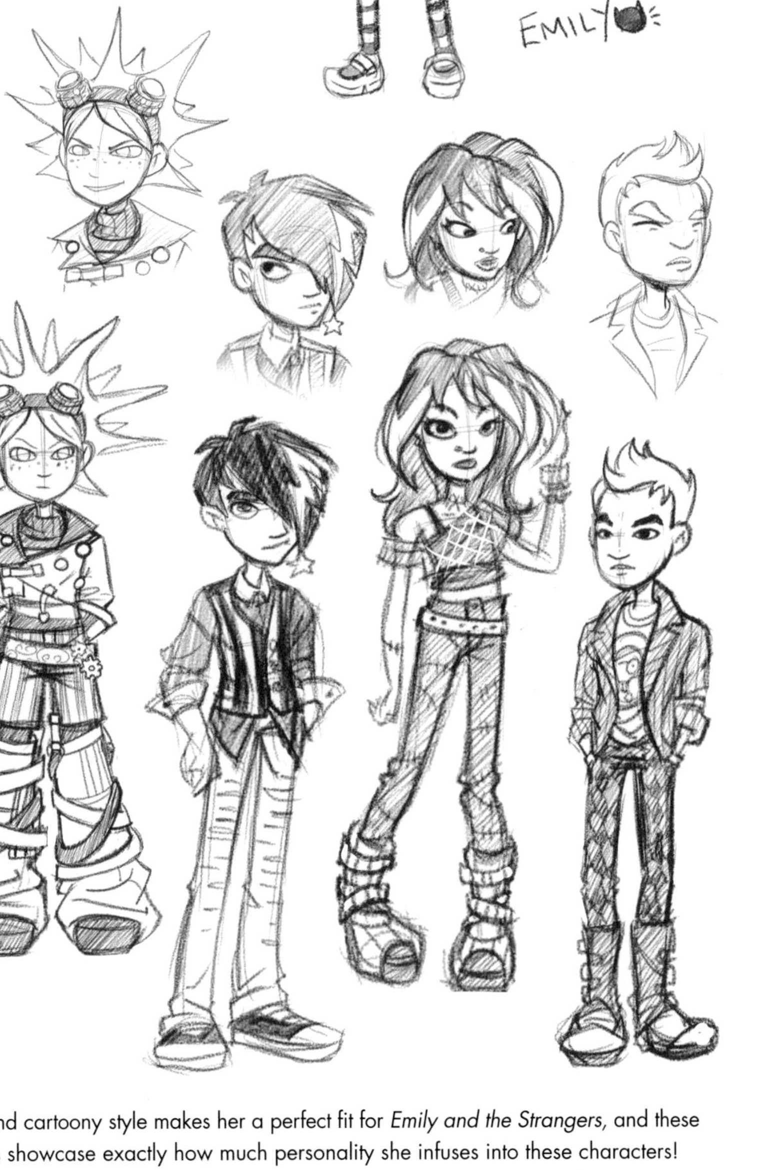

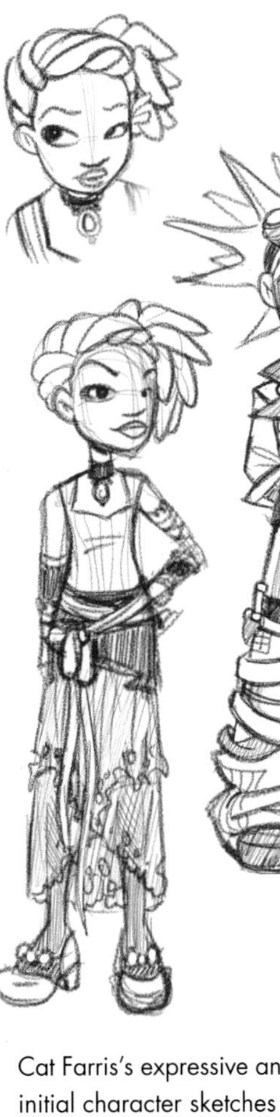

Cat Farris's expressive and cartoony style makes her a perfect fit for *Emily and the Strangers,* and these initial character sketches showcase exactly how much personality she infuses into these characters!

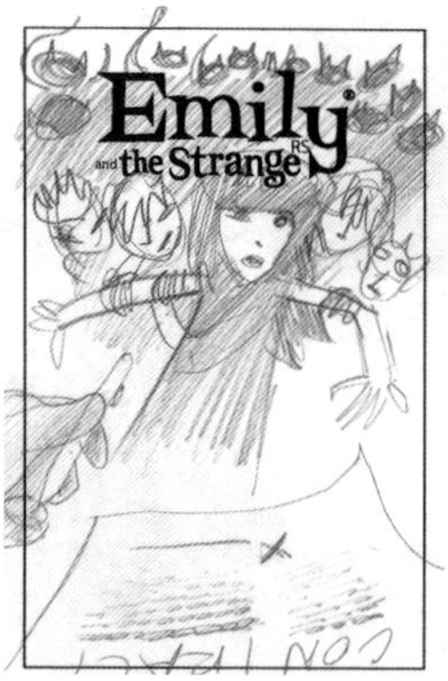
Emily
and the Strange
CONTRACT

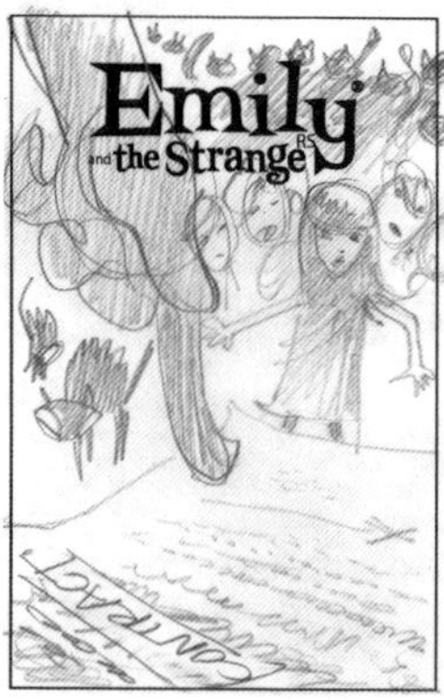
Emily
and the Strange
CONTRACT

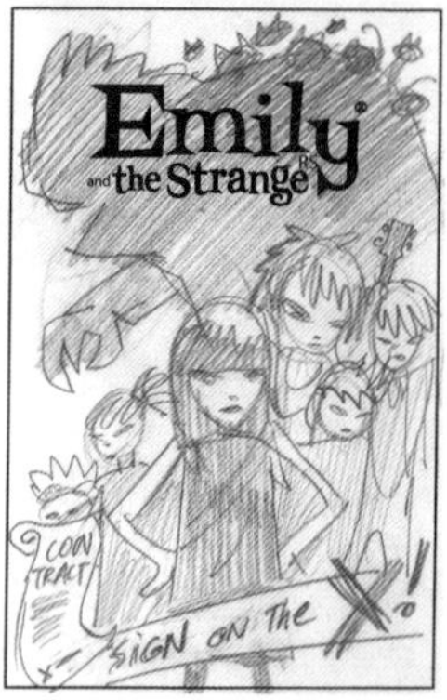
Emily
and the Strange
CONTRACT
SIGN ON THE X

The cover process for each issue begins with longtime Emily artist Buzz Parker sketching up a number of ideas. After discussion about which sketch best exemplifies the issue's story, Buzz tightens up his pencils and passes them on to Cat Farris.

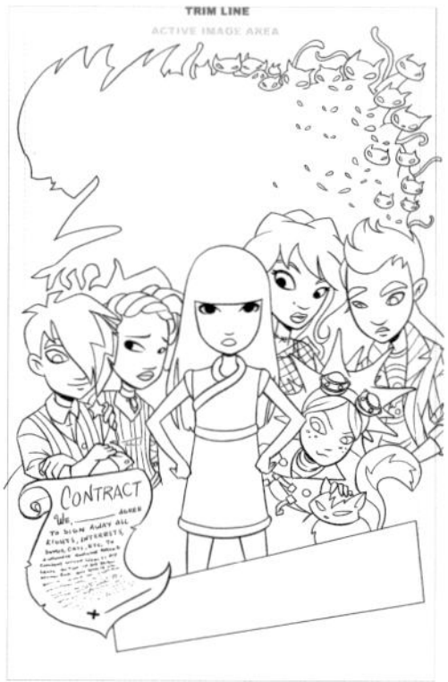
TRIM LINE
ACTIVE IMAGE AREA
CONTRACT

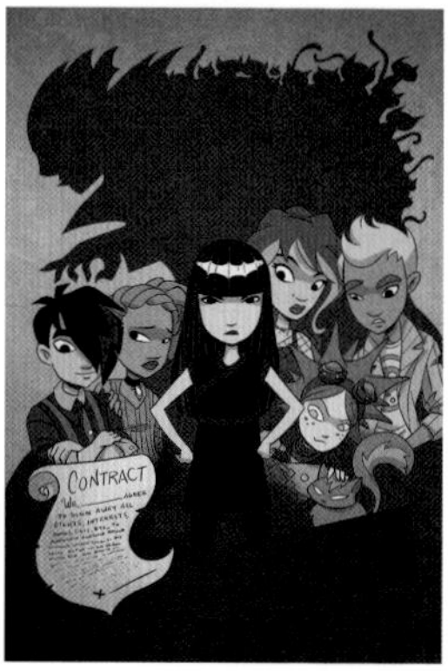
CONTRACT

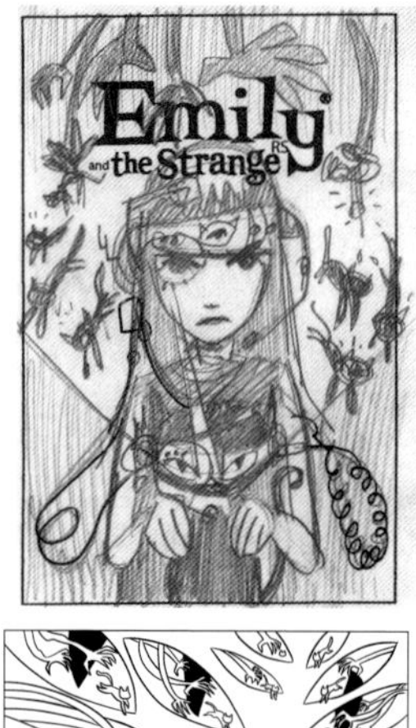
Emily
and the Strange

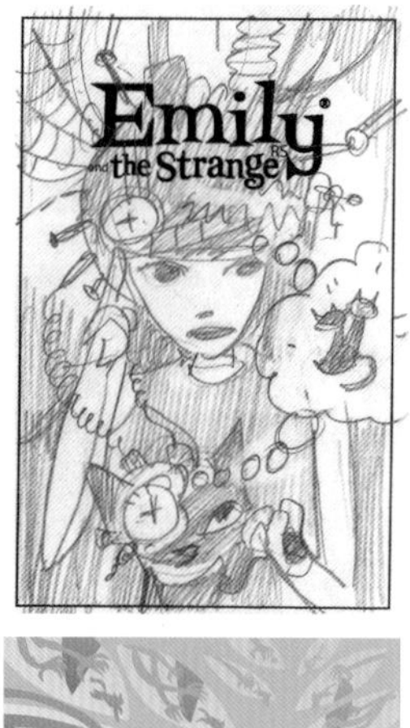
Emily
and the Strange

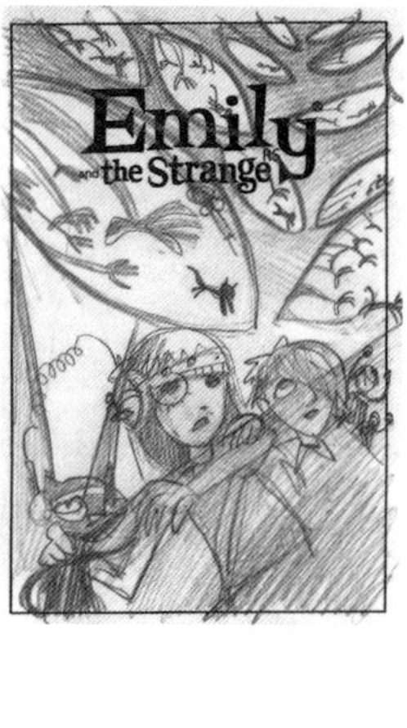
Emily
and the Strange

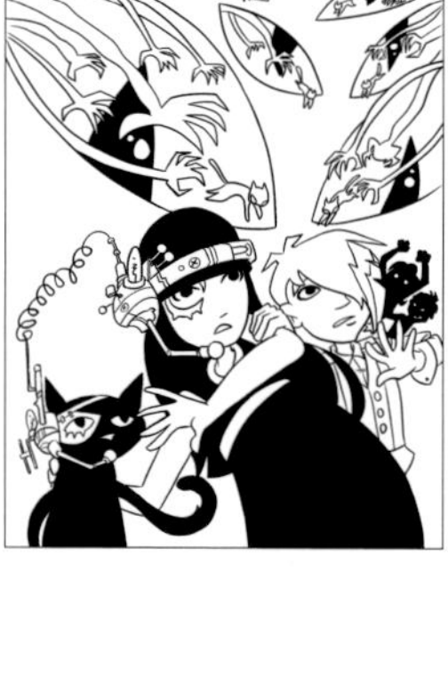

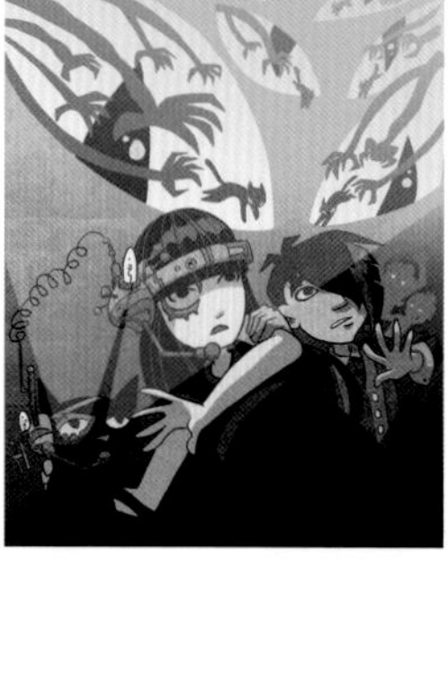

Cat then applies her style and additional details to flesh out the design for the inks.

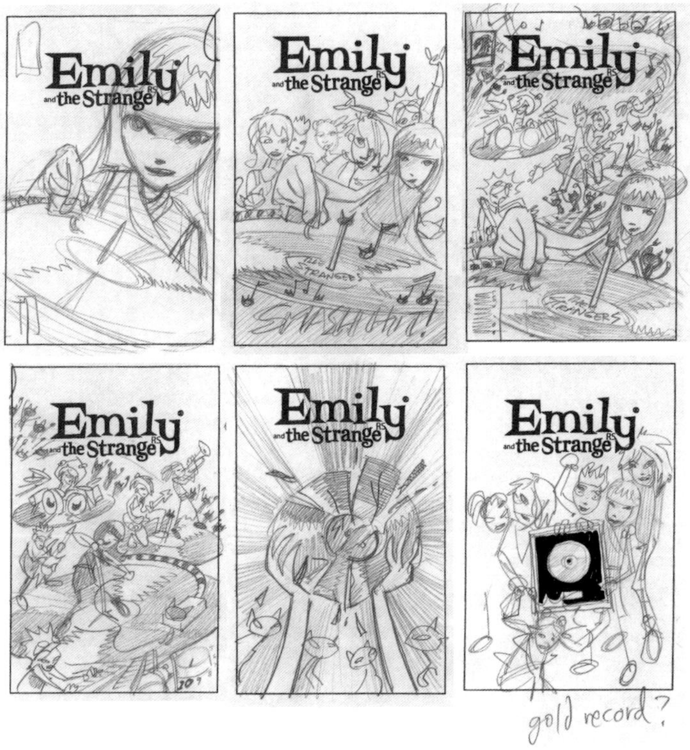
Emily and the Strange
Emily and the Strange
Emily and the Strange
Emily and the Strange
Emily and the Strange
Emily and the Strange
gold record?

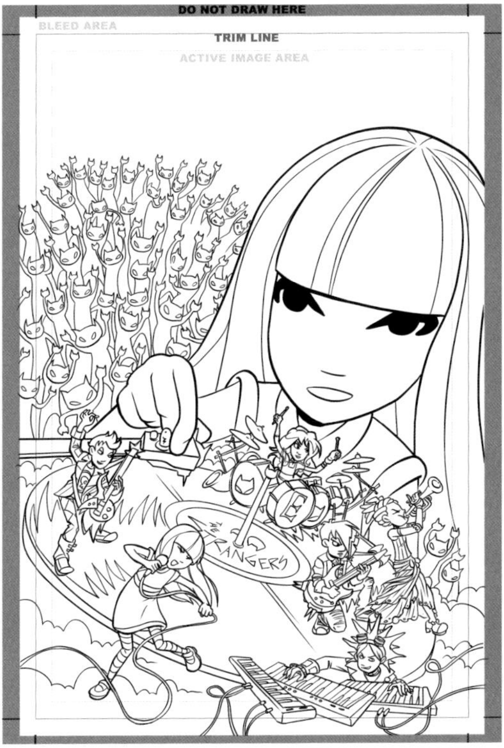
DO NOT DRAW HERE
BLEED AREA
TRIM LINE
ACTIVE IMAGE AREA

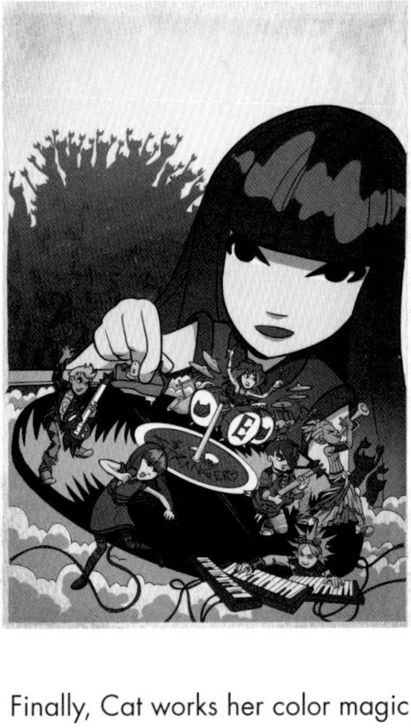

Finally, Cat works her color magic, and we've got our final cover!

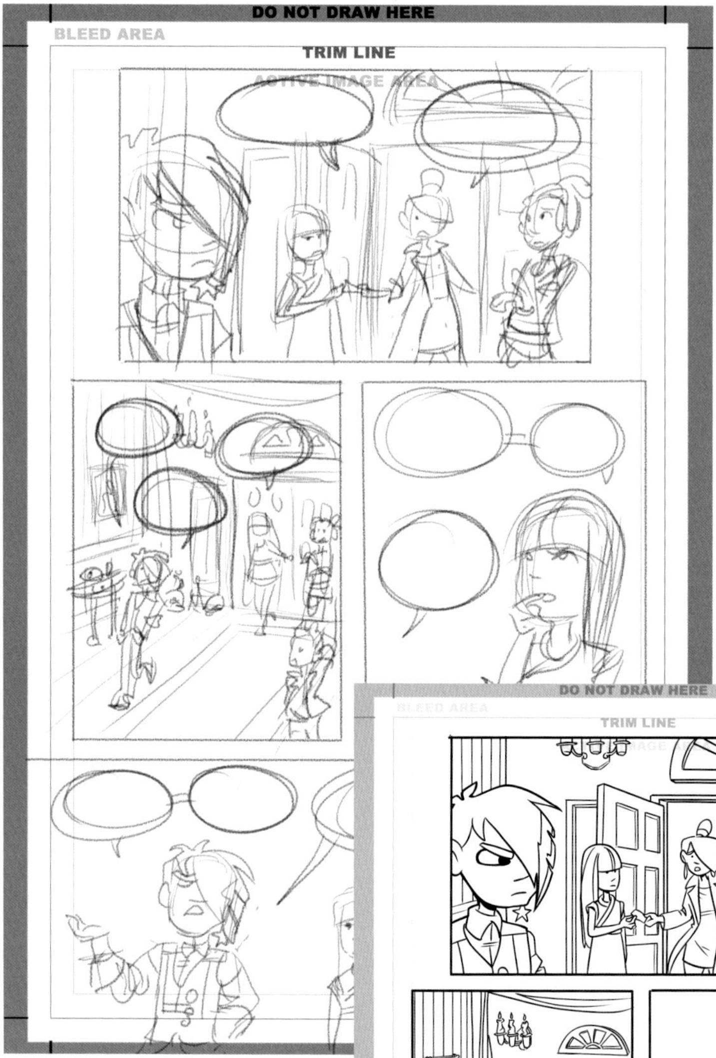
DO NOT DRAW HERE
BLEED AREA
TRIM LINE
ACTIVE IMAGE AREA

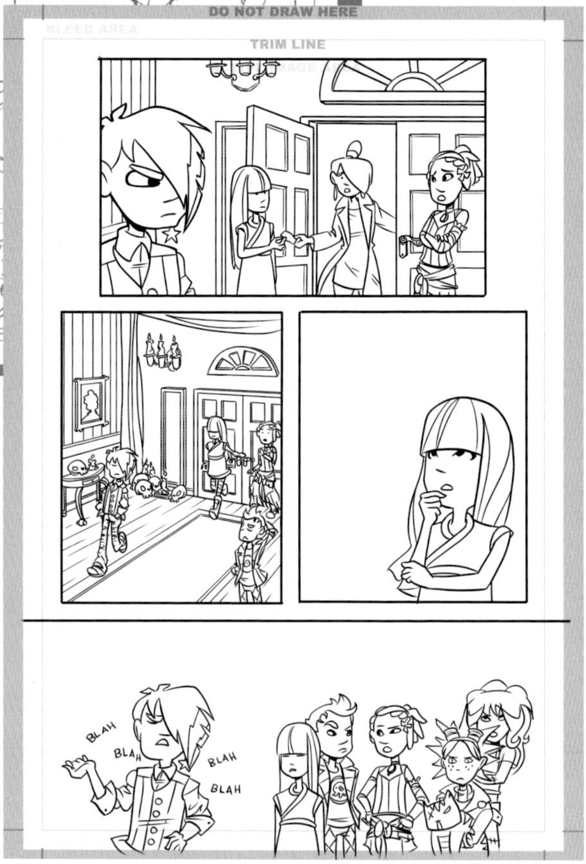
DO NOT DRAW HERE
BLEED AREA
TRIM LINE
BLAH
BLAH
BLAH
BLAH

Here's a comparative look at Cat Farris's rough layouts and pencils, compared to the final inks for a page from the book. See the completed version of this piece on page 36 of this collection!

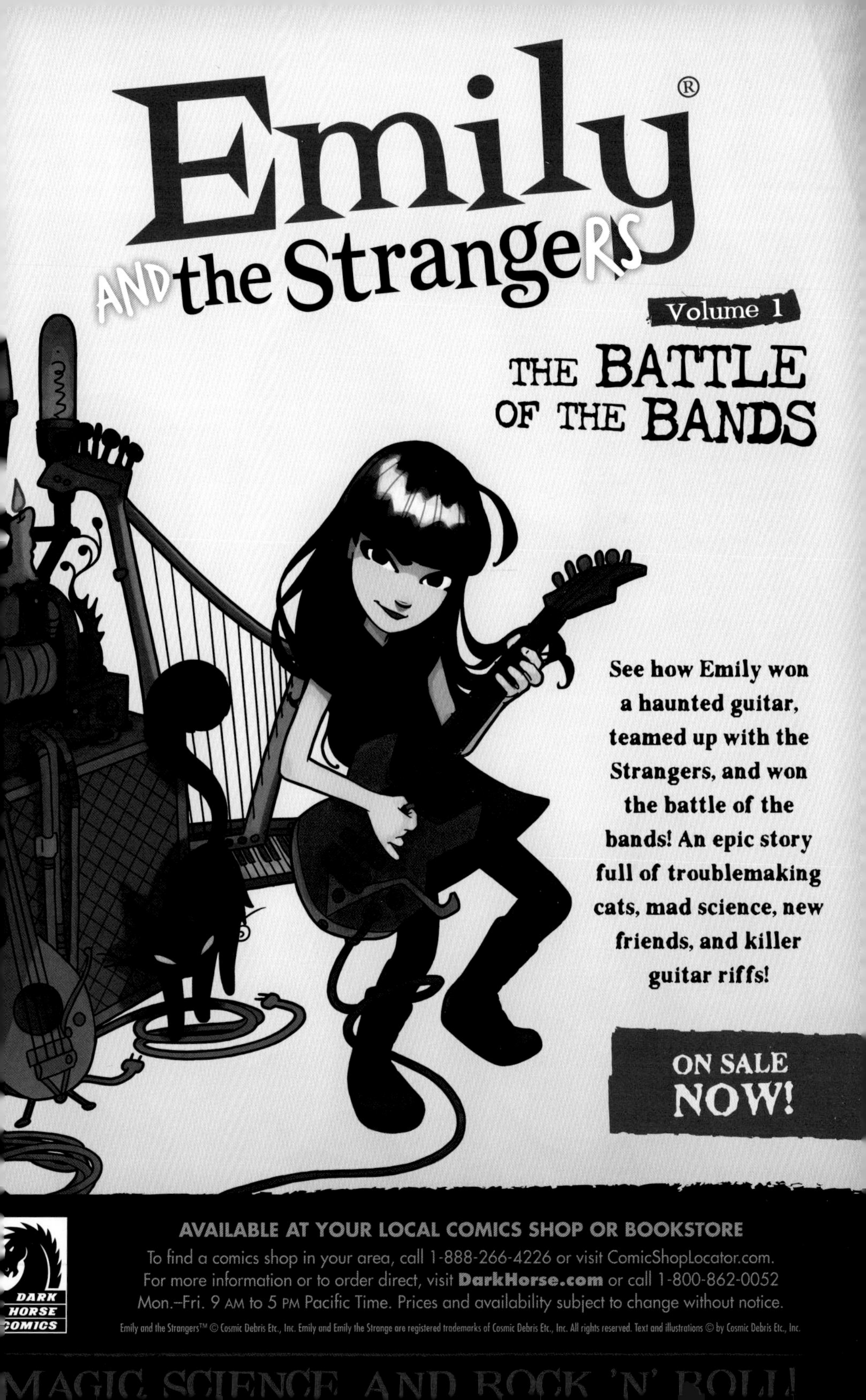
Emily®
AND the Strangers
Volume 1
THE BATTLE OF THE BANDS
See how Emily won a haunted guitar, teamed up with the Strangers, and won the battle of the bands! An epic story full of troublemaking cats, mad science, new friends, and killer guitar riffs!
ON SALE NOW!
AVAILABLE AT YOUR LOCAL COMICS SHOP OR BOOKSTORE
To find a comics shop in your area, call 1-888-266-4226 or visit ComicShopLocator.com.
For more information or to order direct, visit DarkHorse.com or call 1-800-862-0052
Mon.–Fri. 9 AM to 5 PM Pacific Time. Prices and availability subject to change without notice.
DARK HORSE COMICS
Emily and the Strangers™ © Cosmic Debris Etc., Inc. Emily and Emily the Strange are registered trademarks of Cosmic Debris Etc., Inc. All rights reserved. Text and illustrations © by Cosmic Debris Etc., Inc.
MAGIC, SCIENCE, AND ROCK 'N' ROLL!

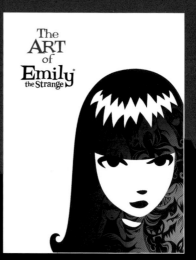